Reflecting Fires

Reflecting Fires

&

Thomas Claburn

To order additional copies of this book, contact:

Xlibris Corporation

1-888-7-XLIBRIS

www.Xlibris.com

Orders@Xlibris.com

Contents

Acknowledgement

In the beginning, there was a mess. Thanks to thoughtful comments and generous encouragement from Marg Gilks, Elaine Lovitt, Arleda Martinez, Cynthia Meier, Mark Nichol, and my wife Andrea—whose smile is everything—something better emerged.

LEXICON

Albedo:	Whiteness, reflective; a holy place.
Archaist:	Scholar of the archaic.
Artificer:	Technician, engineer.
Aver:	One who is true.
Caballine:	Of a horse, cavalier.
Cardinal:	Of the foremost rank, above Ordinal.
Cast:	The social hierarchy of the world.
Caval:	A genetically altered warhorse.
Celebrants:	Clergy.
Convalere:	Hospital; a place to grow strong.
Curia:	Religious court.
Curial:	Officials of the Curia.
Daub:	One who is false.
Decale:	Basic unit of Sarcosian currency.
Éclat:	A flash; aristocratic honorific.
Eclectic:	A human-machine hybrid.
Foundry:	A laboratory or machine shop.
Fulmin:	Energy weapon.
Helion:	Of the sun; celebrants of Halo.
Kame:	A low hill; masculine honorific.
Kyma:	A wave; feminine honorific.
Lancer:	A lightly armed cavalry soldier.
Limnal:	Of a lake; celebrant of Ekal.
Lucifal:	Luminous; celebrant of Halo.

Mere:	Shallow water; lesser celebrant.
Ordinal:	One of the numbered, of noble rank.
Pelage:	A holy place; of the deep sea.
Pelagines:	Followers of Ekal.
Picayune:	Lower Cast.
Pith:	The core of society, middle Cast.
Redan:	A fortress.
Screen:	The guards of the Council of Hierophants.
Thalass:	Oceanic; religious leader.

1

Like Tears in Rain

Who is the third who walks always beside you?
When I count, there are only you and I together
But when I look ahead up the white road
There is always another one walking beside you
                                   —What the Thunder Said

970, Year of the Cicada, Under Aquila
"What dream is that, father?"

The old man's gaze left his daughter's face, following her fragile hand to the stars above. "That is Hitch, Dahlia. I told you that tale but a week ago."

The little girl shook her head vigorously. "I remember. Notorious

Hitch is afraid of the heights he has ascended, and thus disguises himself among those of the lesser Cast. I know where Hitch lives."

"Do you, indeed?" Her father showed no surprise. "Soon you will be able to sail me home at night."

"Hitch is there." Dahlia pointed nearer the horizon. "But look above. There is one less bright. Perhaps Wild Brand offers us a new dream?"

The old man frowned. "I do not think I have ever heard such a thing. The night sky of Wild Brand contains all imaginings, the entire realm of possibility."

Dahlia remained silent for a moment. "Do dreams never die?"

"Most certainly they do."

"Then, like Halo's children, must they not also be born?" she asked. "Else soon the night sky should grow blacker than Telluria." Arching her slender neck back to look upon Stardome, she nearly lost her balance.

The old man bent slightly to steady his daughter. "You have inherited your mother's curiosity."

She smiled up at her father and grasped his rough hand. She missed her mother. "If all the sky were filled with dreams, would not night seem as bright as day?"

"That is a question for a celebrant, not for a man such as me."

"May I ask Limnal Anise?"

"Tomorrow. It is time to sleep, Dahlia. You have stayed up too late already."

***

The following morning Dahlia rose with the dawn, leaving the warmth of the bed she shared with her sisters for the brisk coastal air. She slipped past the cows waiting to be milked, and continued south toward the Pelage, where the dolorous song of celebrants lauded Deep Ekal for her strength in burying and bearing her two daughters–the sun and the moon–day after day.

Pale sunlight reflected off the surface of the great broadsword that loomed in the distance. Fully as tall as the mast of her father's frigate, the ancient marker, embedded point first into the ground, served as a lighthouse for land travelers. It pointed the way to the sacred places.

A short while later, she reached the mosaic path that led to the great stair and the Pelage below. Aware that her energetic gait had no place among the immaculate grounds, she tried to walk with the solemnity of a celebrant, but the child in her was not so easily cast aside.

The sacred broadsword loomed above her as she passed, casting a long shadow. She imagined the dark line a secret road, meant for her alone.

The hooded man with silver skin remained chained to the massive blade, as he had been for as long as she could remember. Within the circle described by the chain, he tended the close-cropped grass, plucking it with his fingers to the length of a hatchling's down. He scared her, though she knew well the length of the chain and always stayed beyond the eclectic's reach. Goosebumps rose on her flesh. She could feel his gaze. As she passed him, she broke into a run.

At the bottom of the stair stood the grand hall of the Pelage of Mecino, a domed marvel of black-and-red granite. Every inch of the stone floor displayed dreams from the Dim Age, carved in intricate relief and illuminated with gold.

Dahlia paused by one of the dreams of sacrifice. She remembered it because Limnal Anise had told her, "You must remember this." It was called *The House of White*. She observed her favorite scene in the iconography: two lovers separated by destiny, the woman departing into the sky with another man, leaving her true love behind in service of a greater purpose. It was a dream she used to understand the perplexing relationship of the gods Gard, Ekal, and Brand. One day, it would lead her to seek a higher position in the Cast.

A shadow fell across the fluid carvings and Dahlia looked up to see the curious face of Limnal Anise.

The slight Pelagine leaned sideways to better orient herself to Dahlia's perspective. "You should not spend your youth contemplating such dreams as these, my child. Why do you come hither to this woman's place?"

Dahlia ignored the tiny woman's mild reproach. "How many dreams can there be, Limnal? I wish to know and you are wise in such things."

"The same as there have always been," Anise replied patiently. "No one has counted them, but there are more than enough for you and me and the rest of the world."

"I saw a new dream last night." Dahlia beamed. "Just below Hitch."

Limnal Anise reached down toward the kneeling girl and hooked two fingers under her chin, bidding her to stand. She seized Dahlia's face as if she were trying to force-feed a squirming kitten, and stared without blinking into the child's eyes. "Do not lie in the house of Deep Ekal, for I will know it."

Trembling, Dahlia squeaked, "I tell you truly what I saw, Limnal."

Slowly, Limnal Anise released her grip. "Perhaps it is as you say, child. Though I do not serve Silent Gavo, I insist you look to her example and speak no more of it, lest the gift of wisdom Bright Halo has seen fit to bestow upon you bring ruin to us all."

Dahlia nodded. "I will do as you say, Limnal."

Anise turned her gently toward the staircase. "Now go tell your father that I intend you to be my aspirant. You will come to live here at the Pelage immediately after the harvest."

Dahlia smiled, delirious with joy. She hugged Anise and started to say something, then stopped. She took a deep breath and ran up the steps two at a time.

***

Limnal Anise waited outside as night fell, pacing on the damp grass. She wanted to be alone to verify Dahlia's tale. In the moments before dusk yielded to darkness, she prayed. The fog politely remained just beyond the coast, and she knew that Ekal had restrained it so that she might have a clear view of the sky and Brand's million dreams.

Each star was a different window onto the truelife, the divine narrative. To dream, to comprehend perfection, that was the greatest hope of a celebrant. It seemed such a vain hope. No one had dreamed for a millennium. Not since the Renunciation, when the gods abandoned the world.

She looked up into the blackness and saw that Dahlia had told the truth. A new fire burned in the heavens, a reveille that foretold the coming of the promised Aver.

2

Interrogation

Here alone I, in books form'd of metals,
Have written the secrets of wisdom,
The secrets of dark contemplation . . .

−The Book of Urizen

975, Year of the Ram, Under Serpens

Rose approached Gauss' house quietly, so as not to alert the dogs. She was not afraid of them. She simply disliked them, for they viewed their master's visitors with uniform suspicion. Hiding at the perimeter of the clearing, she waited until they bounded into the thick forest to the south, then she dashed for the door. Her subdued knocking drew no answer from Gauss, but finding the door open, she slipped inside.

Pinprick shafts of sunlight pierced the ill-fitted stone walls. Lingering tobacco smoke mingled with the scent of pine.

Rose stepped gently over upturned furniture and loose papers. The sound she made walking through the debris belied the cabin's offer of shelter, for it was the same as treading on the dry leaves outside. In the center of the room, a travel case lay open on a dirty rug.

A balding head popped up through a trapdoor in the floor, followed by a lit candle, shedding wax tears this way and that.

"Rose!" Gauss exclaimed. "What are you doing here?" The stooped man clambered awkwardly out of the trapdoor, which he shut upon regaining his balance. "By Bright Halo, you've become quite the young woman, though you still dress like a boy. The prettiest boy in the land."

Rose smiled awkwardly, uncomfortable with such cloying sentiment.

"To think you might have died as a baby. What a loss it would have been to the world." Gauss squatted and gathered up his papers. "I imagine you don't remember any of that. For the best, aye."

Rose gestured with her hands, making the sign of inquiry. Gauss did not notice and continued rooting about among his scattered possessions.

"I am in rather a hurry today, unfortunately. Time, time, time. So precious." Gauss paused in his musing and looked up to address Rose directly. "Use your time wisely, pretty Rose. The bloom is so swift, so very swift."

Rose felt sorry for her father's old friend. He seemed so alone, so like her.

"Bah, I become more mordant with each passing year," Gauss continued. "To what do I owe the pleasure of your company?"

From her vest, Rose withdrew the golden timepiece her father had given her and held it out to the old man.

"No, no, no. It is a gift. Tell your father he is a stubborn bull, and return the timepiece to him."

Rose shook her head, her long red hair swirling like a spun parasol about her delicate face, and extended the timepiece to Gauss once again. A ray of light fell upon the golden disk and danced about the room.

Gauss sighed. "Once these were as common as sand, Rose. It keeps time on land and sea, accurately enough to navigate by. It is my masterpiece, by which I mark the resurrection of the dark mechanics. Not that I deserve the credit. Others have worked to keep the art alive. When you are old enough, I will introduce you. Open the panel in back."

Rose complied, flipping the timepiece over and prying the cover off the back to reveal a machine that almost seemed alive. Spinning wheels of astonishing delicacy surged back and forth in perfect lockstep. It reminded her of a tiny beehive, buzzing with activity, at once chaotic and wholly singular in purpose.

"That little machine manufactures the present with seconds from the future and thought from the past," Gauss mused. "If your father will not take it—"

Outside, the dogs began barking. Gauss stopped talking and held up his hand to silence Rose. Amused by the futile gesture, Rose just shook her head.

Barking turned to furious snarling and voices could be heard. Seconds later, the dogs fell silent.

Rose, who found in sound a terrible intimacy, winced and looked to Gauss for some explanation.

The old artificer's shoulders sank. "Bright Halo protect us," he whispered. He scrambled back to the trapdoor and opened it. "Quickly Rose, hide yourself." He pointed down below.

Rose hesitated and gestured toward herself, as she often did, to request more information.

"There is no time to explain. You must not be found with me." Gauss gazed at Rose. The lines that gathered on his face spoke of sadness. "I have caused your father enough pain as it is. Do not be stubborn and injure him further."

Rose threw herself into the darkness. She landed on the soft dirt below, rolling to absorb the impact with the grace of an acrobat. The trapdoor swung closed, choking off the light from above. Enveloped in black, she tried to listen to what went on overhead, even as the dull scrape of the carpet being repositioned further isolated her.

"Kame Gauss," a stern voice said. "We are so pleased to find you at home."

"I know why you have come, éclat," Gauss replied, the fear in his voice audible through carpet and floor. "Do not mock me with insincere honorifics. To offer someone the respect due a mountain you must first revere Ekal and her land."

"Very well, Gauss," the stern voice answered. "Let us dispense with the pleasantries. Where is it?" The unseen man then addressed his companions. "Search the house. Tear it to the ground if necessary."

"By your command, Cardinal," responded another.

"You have no right," said Gauss. "I am a loyal citizen of Sarcos."

"We know about your work. We have seen those you defiled. Servants of Urizen have no rights."

Rose heard several men thrashing about up above, looking for something.

Gauss raised his voice above the din. "You did not find it before, nor will you this time."

The stern voice spoke again, unequivocal as a hammer. "We did not find you during our last visit. We feel certain your help will be invaluable."

"I will not help you."

"You will." The voice became softer, more insistent, more compelling. "You think you can measure time? You believe you can perform the work of the gods with some obscene lump of metal?"

"I can. I have." Gauss' voice quavered. "My methods are known to others. There will be more. The reveille has come."

"You lie," the voice hissed, colder than the mistral. "You are a deceiver of men, and when next you speak, it will be the truth."

"You are not...yet ready for...such elaborations, adept." Gauss' voice became strangely hoarse, his breathing more labored.

"You will tell me where you have hidden the timepiece."

A horrible sound poured forth from Gauss, as if words were literally being torn from his lungs.

Rose thought she heard her father's friend calling her name, then the howling ceased. All was quiet until the stern voice broke into a cacophony of expletives.

"We are done here," the voice barked. "Boreal, wait here until sunset and then burn the house. I want the fire to be visible in the village tonight and in the frightened faces of those who share this man's sympathies."

"Your will be done, Cardinal," a man answered.

With that, the other intruders left.

Rose lost track of time in the darkness while she waited for an opportunity to escape, though she could hear the seconds ticking by. Eventually, the sentry who remained went outside relieve himself. Rose emerged from the trapdoor and slipped out the back into the forest. The golden timepiece felt cold against her breast.

3

Trials

The adept alone has faith in the fecundity of pure knowledge; rational people know the act before the thought.
—Cardinal Wolf

990, Year of the Cicada, Under Cygnus

Empires do not collapse like buildings. There are no obvious signs,
no telltale fractures that reveal themselves like the blistered skin of paint
on an aging facade. There is only the paring of respect until idleness
and familiarity conceive contempt.

Cardinal Skye came to this realization while attending a trial at the
Curia of Sansiso. In the twenty years since Limnal Anise had reported
the new star in the sky, there had been no sign of the reveille, the long-

foretold awakening of the gods. Was this what the new star brought, a dream of slow decline?

For almost a thousand years, the Empire of Sarcos had ruled the Ocean of Peace and the long stretch of coast called Useland, from the forests of Urgun down to barren Aqal, where the shadowskins held sway, and east until the mountains flattened into the Testing Desert. Sarcos had endured by force of will, under the loving strangulation of a leadership fearful of change and the countless wars against practitioners of the dark mechanics. The architects of ignorance, however, could not dam the river forever. The old secrets flowed underground, by word and whisper. The eclectics, those who defiled their flesh with metal, hungered for the dreams of their banished god, Urizen, just as humankind yearned for the Aver. Despite a history of hatred and mutual suspicion, certain heretics now suggested that if man and machine shared such similar aspirations, perhaps their deities might likewise be the same. In such thoughts grew the seeds of ruin.

And yet they could not be denied—apologists for the dark mechanics had resurrected the economy and the luster of the ancient city even as they whored the sacred traditions. The tall row houses of the capital were being refaced; the muddy streets were hardening into a scab of cobblestones for the sake of the coach and the omnibus, as if the naked soil offended. Streetside braziers of charcoal were discarded for luxes—globes of effulgent chemicals that lent a strange new vitality to the night. The caballines patrolling the streets had become more tolerant of artificers, as religion yielded to commerce.

Beyond the buildings crowning the jaw of the horizon, out in the glistening blue bay, moored galleys, their sails slack as if in recognition of their numbered days, saw the return of steamships. Twenty years ago, the Council never would have allowed such technology.

Though he had recently celebrated his forty-second winter, Cardinal Skye seemed older. Tall and confident, he nonetheless moved with geriatric caution. The flecks of gray in his coal-black hair suggested strength tempered by wisdom, and so it was that his peers regarded him. His features were as sharp and angular as a cut gem, and he always dressed more formally than the occasion demanded. His eyes spoke of weariness, unfathomable to any but another adept.

From his box seat, Skye could observe every aspect of the trial. He cast a glance up at the lone box above his, empty, as it had been for ages. He hoped he would live to see a day when Sarcos again knelt before its Aver. To either side of him, other cardinals of renown leaned back in their stiff black coats and high-collared sarks, not particularly engaged by the heated arguments below. By their presence, they flew the flags of their families and if they were in the city when the Curia met, they had no excuse for absence. For most of the Cardinals, this was a night at the theater, full of good food, fine wine, merriment, and a death sentence if everything worked out.

Across from Skye, on the other side of the Curia, were the boxes reserved for the Cardinals' religious counterparts: the Limnals of Ekal and the Helions of Halo. These boxes were full, every seat occupied by a woman of distinction clad in formal habit of black or gold, as suited the respective god. The celebrants hung on every word of the tribunal, for the charge was, after all, heresy.

The level below offered slightly less plush box seating for the Ordinals and their relations. The Ordinals tended to view public trials with somewhat more seriousness. They frequently presided over civil disputes, being vested with civil and judicial responsibilities on behalf of the ruling Council of Hierophants. Likewise, the Meres and Lucifals, the celebrants of lower rank also seated in the second tier, regarded the trial with fascination.

The third tier, or gallery, held reserved seating for the lesser éclat, civil officials, eminent citizens, and families whose distinction exceeded their means, along with adepts and caballines of minor import. Occupants of the third tier split their attention between the proceedings on the floor and whichever seat in the tier above they happened to desire.

The vast floor of the Curia was partitioned into three areas. The benches in the center provided first-come seating to the pith, those members of the middle class who took the honorifics "Kame" or "Kyma" in lieu of a true title. They might someday look down upon their kin from the gallery, but none dared look back over their shoulder, for fear of offending. Behind them, the stalls reserved for the picayune had no seating, only rails to lean against. These common-born, uneducated citizens didn't particularly mind that they were fenced in like animals. They were out for blood. They attended such trials religiously, more so than they attended the sacred projections, though in truth the two events relied equally on the promise of violence. Many of the Meres who staged these poorly attended rituals complained that people were abandoning the gods, a not entirely baseless charge. But it was hunger for the divine that brought people to the Curia. The gods were never more present than when their worshippers sat in judgment on their behalf.

Separated from the onlookers by a raised stage, the members of the tribunal gazed out upon the assembly from beneath the proscenium arch, reposing on hand-carved stools with the legs and clawed feet of lions. They represented Gard, Brand, and Ekal, in whose names the Curia's decisions were made, even if their judgment served Sarcos more than the gods. A fourth stool always remained empty, reserved for Silent Gavo, whom no one would represent—or omit. The Thalass alone, as the supreme religious leader, had the right to sit in Gavo's seat, though she never did so, as her presence would undermine the authority of her subordinates.

Behind their featureless masks and tent-like gowns of swirling black silk, the Curials were still, unwilling to betray even the slightest emotion by movement or gesture. They were unmovable in their passions and in their decision, or so the tradition held. In the jittery light of a thousand torches, these three became the gods they claimed to represent.

The accused, an artist known as Scrim, sat downstage center, facing the audience. He was, by all accounts but his own, a dangerous heretic. Sitting at the edge of the stage, he posed the most danger to the pith seated on the front-row benches, for in his current state of malnutrition he might have collapsed and fallen into the audience. He was a slight man, coarse in his speech and bearing, but generous and kindhearted. The guards who had watched over him during his pretrial incarceration had testified so, as had his sole living relative, a sister who had traveled to Sansiso at great hardship. It was difficult to see how a blind man could be so dire a threat to the Empire, but the charges against him were made with the utmost seriousness.

The circumstances by which Scrim lost his vision were central to the defending advocate's arguments. Cardinal Skye had heard about the circuitous course of events that finally led to Scrim's arrest, and was himself torn as to the necessity of this trial.

Several months prior, Scrim had received a commission from Mere Jonquil to paint the Renunciation. As the painting was to be displayed in a small Pelage being constructed on the edge of Sarcos' northeastern border, near Urgun, Scrim insisted on seeing its future location to gauge how the light would play on his canvas.

Skye recalled that Mere Jonquil had been impressed by Scrim's dedication and that she had even offered to pay for a dray to transport him and his equipment so that he might receive inspiration beneath the great broadsword that marked the land as sacred.

Though Scrim survived the arduous journey, his obsession with authenticity led him to the use of certain opiates and hallucinogens favored by adepts and the more unconventional celebrants. Scrim's pharmacologically induced vision left him in a temporary paralysis while he gazed upon the face of Bright Halo. Staring wide-eyed into the sun left him blind, but rather than abandon the project, he continued working. According to the picayune laborers who had already testified, no one was really sure just what he painted because he worked at night, alone.

Though Skye had not attended the formal dedication when the Pelage was completed, he had heard the tale nearly a dozen times at various formal dinners. The unveiling of Scrim's painting was to be the highlight of the ceremony, and the assembled guests anxiously awaited the revelation of his work. Among them sat none other than the Thalass herself, whose unexpected presence made the evening an affair of solemn ritual rather than yet another northern land grab. The celebrants in attendance—particularly Mere Jonquil, who had hired Scrim in the first place—were understandably concerned that ceremony proceed without complication.

When the moment finally came, Scrim himself withdrew the shroud. Silence fell as the guests gazed slack-jawed upon Scrim's unspeakable rendition of the Renunciation. Finally, the Thalass said, "Burn it!" That night, the entire Pelage of Haugh, not a day old, went up in flames, and Mere Jonquil with it.

To further complicate the situation, the presence of the Thalass that evening prevented the éclat of the northern territories from settling the matter by having Scrim disappear. There would have to be a public trial to redress so grievous an insult.

The prosecuting advocate–masked like the Curials and the advocate for the defense–had the advantage of the many distinguished witnesses in attendance that evening, along with the implicit sympathy of the tribunal, but there was no evidence to present, for the canvas had been incinerated.

The picayune clearly preferred the defending advocate, whose cross-examinations frequently elicited howls of laughter from the stalls. Scrim was one of their own, a person of no import, and though the verdict was a foregone conclusion in their minds, the trial had become a forum to ridicule their betters.

When the defending advocate observed that the Curia was trying a blind man for his vision, Skye repressed a smile. He wondered about the faceless woman far below who was running circles around the factors of the Empire. Here was the real enemy, someone so skilled with words and ideas that she could shape truth. Someone not unlike himself. Rather than fall into the trap of defending Scrim's innocence, she argued that Scrim was guilty, but guilty of fraud rather than heresy.

According to tradition, it was heresy to depict the gods as people. Icons were used instead, the sun or a candle for Halo, a wave or a mountain for Ekal. By all accounts, Scrim's canvas had been layer upon layer of thick black paint. The charge of heresy arose because the Thalass considered the blackness a denial that the gods existed, which was clearly Scrim's intent. But the defending advocate argued masterfully that Scrim's work was merely a poor attempt to deny his blindness, to counterfeit the divine inspiration denied him by his inability to see.

Conviction for fraudulent representation meant the forfeiture of all real property, a sentence nearly as harsh as death for one of the éclat, but hardly a slap on the wrist for an artist with few assets. Skye appreciated the subtlety of the defense, knowing the Curia tended to rule in whatever fashion enriched the Empire the most—and death meant having to share Scrim's meager estate with any heirs. Given a face-saving way to punish Scrim, invalidate his work, and deny the querulous picayune a martyr, the tribunal found itself in sympathy with the defense very quickly. When the verdict was read, everyone seemed satisfied except for Scrim, whose bitterness toward the gods remained undimmed. No one heard his indignant protests as he was hauled away, not to some exalted end in flames, the decreed fate of heretics, but to rot with cutpurses and highwaymen in prison.

Skye made his way down the stairs from the first tier, through the perfumed throngs of the éclat bustling on their way to some fashionable soiree. He nodded politely to friends and acquaintances as he pushed through the shifting foliage of silk and velvet. Cardinal Azo, a fleshy obelisk of a man with a predatory smile, sported a newly granted red sash to mark his elevation to the Council of Hierophants. Skye stopped briefly to offer insincere congratulations, fully detesting the nepotism and maneuvering that had brought this backstabbing thug to power. Moving down the grand staircase, past four decadent Aqalese dignitaries in their silk robes, he wondered where he had stored his own Councilor's sash; perhaps in some trunk somewhere.

In the chambers where the advocates and Curials changed out of their judicial garb, Skye inquired after the woman who had saved Scrim from immolation. He followed the directions he received and came to a partly open door at the end of a dingy wood-paneled hall that smelled of pipe tobacco. Through the doorway, he could see the partially clothed figure of a woman, her bare back drifting in and out of shadow. He averted his eyes, which unfortunately led them to fall upon a series of devotional watercolors depicting bland rural landscapes, consigned to hang in these dark passages precisely for their lack of sightliness. Scrim's lost Renunciation would be an improvement, Skye thought as his gaze flirted with more promising vistas.

"I crave your pardon for intruding, éclat, but I had to express my admiration for your presentation."

The woman continued dressing, reaching around behind her back to cinch her corset. "You are my first admirer."

Skye dropped all pretense of decorum and stared at the woman, overcome by the beauty of her bare skin. She could not be more than thirty, though her posture conveyed a sense of authority that belied her youth. "I would believe that only if you lived among the blind."

The woman laughed and took up her advocate's mask again, holding it over her face as she turned to address Skye. She stood half-dressed in the doorway.

"In truth, Curial Dure offers me praise, but he is long in years."

"Give me as many with you and I would die a happy man."

"You flatter me fairly, éclat, especially for one who has not seen my face."

Skye smiled broadly, despite himself. "I would soon be cured of that ignorance, if it please you."

"You would please me, then?"

"Aye, in such ways as I could."

"Tell me your name."

"I am Skye."

"Sky? Are you then Endless Gard, or merely a mortal who aims high?"

"To gaze upon you, I can aim no higher, though you mock me."

"Men with famous names seldom get their just share of mockery."

"It would be soon forgotten, if I knew yours."

"There is a great house with your name. Skye Redan. Perhaps you have heard of it?"

"Perhaps I have." Skye felt as if he were the one who was naked.

"A Cardinal of renown lives there. I would very much like to meet him someday."

"That could be arranged if I were to tell him whom he was to meet."

"Tell him to wait at the north end of the Lake Dolce, at sunset three days hence."

"How will he know you?"

"There are signs. My smile will tell him as much as any man can know. But he will have to bring his own certainty, for I have none to offer." The woman paused for a moment, then added, "I will answer to the name Dahlia."

The door swung closed.

So it was that Cardinal Skye realized that lovers, like empires, collapse from the inside.

4

Dissembling

Silent Gavo, with no child of her own,
Stole the seed of Brand.
Cruel Urizen she made with hands alone,
Blackening all our dreams.
Who will redeem us, clean the ash?
Who will lead us home?
How many lives will the chimney break,
'Til a sweep takes the stone?

—Song of the Chimney Sweep

998, Year of the Wolf, Under Pavo
The first day under Pavo was the annual holiday for the lily-whites,
as the people of Sansiso called the children who swept their chimneys.

All the rest of the year they plied their trade during the night hours, when their soot-blacked skin read as camouflage instead of stigma. They existed out of sight and mind because no one wanted to think of the ugly lives the sweeps led, of the tiny hands rubbed raw in flues, of the rows of little coffins. Society was meant to be immaculate in its conception. No one wanted to see the deformed ash children, who themselves did not wish to be seen, except one day each spring that marked the world's renewal.

On that day, they rose from the gutters, flowers blooming from dirt. They assembled at the north gate come dawn, dressed in pristine white robes, to celebrate Ascension. They wore flour in their hair and white face paint. The girls donned garlands of honeysuckle, while the boys traded their brooms for sugarcane walking sticks, and together they paraded up Broad Way to the cheers of the éclat, pith, and pica-yune alike. For the people of Sansiso, from high Cast to low, Ascension was a time to venerate the shunned. Thus, it was also called Gavo's Day, being an opportunity to appease the dark goddess by recognizing her influence. Those who confessed their misdeeds to the lily-whites were made clean again for the price of a single decale.

When the throng of powdered children reached Hangman's Cir-cus and the outer wall of the Redan Inviolate, the fortress of the Coun-cil, the gleeful shouting subsided. The lily-whites waited in the shadow of the great Circus broadsword, eyes skyward.

The blade rose from the cobblestone plaza thick as a man and wider than extended arms. Unlike the neglected broadswords rising in the countryside, this frozen geyser of steel shone with the spit and polish of Sansiso's celebrants and righteous citizens. Such was their zeal that a low wooden barricade had recently been erected around the base of the blade to protect the metal from the wear of adoring hands.

The towering weapon's crossguard reached out like the arms of a titan above the five-story row houses that encircled the southern end of the Circus. Atop the giant pommel, an acrobat placed a stone the size of a grapefruit. Suspended upside down from a wooden crane that might once have been the mast of a ship, the lithe man made sure the stone was well balanced, then gave a wave to an observer atop the curtain wall of the Redan Inviolate. Slowly, the counterbalance ascended, lowering the acrobat down into the cheering crowd.

Each year Ascension was the same. One among the Council would appear with a baton to be tossed into the white sea of chimney sweeps. Whoever recovered the baton would then have a chance to take the stone from the sword by climbing the blade and returning to the ground, stone in hand.

The reward for accomplishing such a feat had been forgotten, since no one had ever succeeded. Some said the one who did was destined for greatness. Others saw it as a more general sign of deliverance, like the new dream that had appeared in the night sky almost thirty winters past. Most believed only the Aver, the sword made flesh, could make the climb. The éclat frowned on this interpretation because they did not want it believed that one might change his or her place in the Cast through mere agility.

There seemed little sense in considering any outcome other than the inevitable failure. Though most sweeps were skilled climbers, the blade of the city's broadsword offered no handholds. Climbing it compared to riding bareback up a cliff. By embracing the blade and sustaining inward pressure, a climber could ascend, as long as his knees held fast while his hands moved higher. On those rare occasions when it seemed possible some miraculously agile sweep might actually take the stone, gravity always won.

***

Her face dirtied, her teeth darkened, and disguised in rags like the picayune, Dahlia watched the rowdy celebration from the back of the crowd. She appreciated the power and prestige that came with being a celebrant, but the restrictions were onerous. Among the Lucifal, who toiled long hours in the heat of Bright Halo's gaze, devotion taxed both body and mind. But she was a Limnal of the Order of Pelagines, and spent so much time in darkness that she often feared for her sanity.

Certain zealots in her order went so far as to wear blindfolds in public, that they might be closer to their goddess and not suffer the distractions of modernity, the freak show of invention, the gears and wheels by which Cruel Urizen's followers hoped to seduce the devoted away from the other gods. The increasing popularity of this practice made Dahlia more determined than ever to live outside the dogma of her peers. She also liked being able to see where she was going.

Dahlia's deceit kept her on edge. Her eyes darted from shopkeeper to sweep to soldier, like a pair of dragonflies harried at every landing. She could not escape the feeling she was being watched, and a part of her enjoyed the tension. Being fair of face, she had grown used to the attention of others, and as an advocate and a celebrant, she often stood before an audience, disguised by distance, duty, and assumptions. So long as she had something to withhold, something inviolable, she felt comfortable in the company of her other selves.

There could be no dissembling when one went before the gods, she thought. Perhaps that was why her life outside the dark confines of the Pelage seemed so much more vital. Immediately, she reproved herself for such notions. She would permit herself a crisis of faith, but not outright heresy. Her duties in the dark still had some meaning. That, after all, was why she feared being recognized. Discovery might well mean excommunication. She had a position in the Cast, and failure to fully embrace her obligations put her on dangerous ground.

When Cardinal Ocher appeared to address the crowd, Dahlia was surprised and even a bit disappointed. She had expected to see her former lover, Cardinal Skye, delivering the oration. Like her, Skye shared a love of the theatrical and had the wit to turn his passion into compelling speech. That he had not been chosen to make the Ascension address suggested a change in the political winds.

Cardinal Ocher acquitted himself passably. Though the crowd cared little for his tepid speech, he was, in truth, distracted. Moments earlier, the sentinels had spotted a man with a metal hand, causing a great commotion. After knocking the man to the ground and piling on top of him in some semblance of a juvenile game, the embarrassed soldiers realized their quarry was not a crazed eclectic, but a retired Curial, wealthy enough to afford such an expensive prosthetic.

The sweeps at the base of the wall, churning like whitecaps, were watching the Cardinal's eyes, trying to guess where he would throw his ceremonial baton. There was an excited burst of applause and then silence.

Ocher held the ivory baton aloft for all to see.

"Action!" cried the lily-whites. "Action!"

Responding to the crowd, Ocher heaved the white rod skyward. It flew in a graceful arc, pulling the crowd as Silent Gavo drew the tides, descending in lazy rotation toward the base of the broadsword. To everyone's surprise, it hit the great blade and ricocheted backward, leaving the pursuing surge of sweeps moving in the wrong direction.

From where she stood, Dahlia saw the deflected baton tumble into the arms of a lone boy left behind by the swelling crowd of youths. No more than thirteen or fourteen, he appeared quite startled to find the baton in his hands, and fell backward, sinking beneath the bobbing heads of his peers.

The lily-whites cheered and raised the boy upon their shoulders. Though the hero's teeth seemed the color of caramel against his alabaster face, evidence of his poor health did not diminish the shared euphoria. The sweeps had more than enough worthless pity. Ascension was their moment in the sun and they put on the best face they could.

They carried the boy to the base of the towering sword, just beyond the barricade. Again, the crowd went silent.

A minute passed and Dahlia wondered why the boy had not started his climb. When those closest to the boy turned him and guided him through the wooden railing until he could touch the sword, she knew something was wrong.

A murmur spread through the crowd, and quickly reached Dahlia's ears.

"The boy cannot see," whispered a stooped man beside her, and there were nods as others repeated as much to their immediate neighbors.

The news did not surprise Dahlia. Many blind children without means or family became sweeps, since sight did not measurably affect job performance. Though the grueling work paid a pittance, most found it preferable to life in an orphanage.

Cardinal Ocher shouted, "You may begin at any time."

Finally, the boy put his hands up against the steel wall before him and all talking ceased. In the Dim Age, it was said, the swords spread the dreams of the gods like seed so that bits of Stardome might take root in the world. Though now it was celebrants who spread the word, reverence for the ancient monoliths remained.

Out in the harbor, a distant bell seemed to signal a start. With the aid of one of the nearby sweeps, the boy tore off his trouser legs, then placed one hand on each side of the blade. Straddling the facing edge, he slowly began to climb. His bare legs and hands provided sufficient grip, and one white-knuckled minute later he had risen above his second-story observers.

At this point, climbers tended to slip off. Physical effort and fear usually made the climber sweat before reaching the crossguard, and once the surface of the blade got wet, nothing could keep the climber from falling. But the boy's small size lessened the effort required, and his lack of sight kept the thousands watching him from his mind. Aided by the unusually cool breeze rolling off the bay, the painted sweep rose above his third-story observers, beyond the midpoint of the blade, and kept going.

Passing the fourth story with the speed of a sloth, the boy had already made his essay one of legend. The crowd trembled anxiously, many forgetting to breathe. One awestruck observer shouted, "Long live the Aver!" only to be silenced by the protective masses, afraid that any distraction might splatter their hopes on the cobblestones.

Up above, the boy continued, his body taut with determination. When he reached the crossguard, a tremendous cheer ripped through the air, followed by a repressive wave of hushing. Dahlia, her neck aching from looking up, let her hood fall back. No one looked twice at her.

***

Up on the curtain wall, the Hierophants grew worried. Cardinal Ocher called urgently for more troops. He had followed Auric's advice and dispersed his men in civilian dress among the crowd to watch for eclectic infiltrators. No one had really thought the youth might succeed, and if he did, men out of uniform would be useless in keeping the peace.

"This presents something of a problem," Ocher said to the other three members of the Council at his back. The boy inched his way up the hilt to the pommel and the stone resting on top.

Cardinal Skye nodded and adjusted his stiff collar. The suits of the day were uncomfortable affairs. "No one has been this close for as long as I can remember. But I doubt he will get much farther. The hand required to hold the stone will be sorely missed when he tries to descend."

Cardinal Auric chuckled and slapped Skye across the back. "You sound as if you have wagered a few decales on the outcome, Skye. Every little detail plotted out, eh?"

Skye smiled back contemptuously, stepping away to make it clear he did not appreciate the bigger man's habit of masking physical intimidation through social contact. "Wagering is for imbeciles."

Auric, who had a stake in the city's gambling houses, took Skye's meaning clearly. His fist drew tight, the black leather of his glove stretching across knuckles pregnant with hate, but he did not act. Without a weapon in hand, he knew enough not to strike a skilled adept. There were other ways.

The crowd roared.

Somehow, the boy had managed to reach around the curve of the pommel and grasp the stone before sliding down the hilt to a hard landing on the crossguard. The impact reverberated down to the sweeps. For a minute, he rested. Finally, he rose to his feet, standing on the narrow crossguard, full of fear. He looked straight ahead, listening intently to the voices below.

"He appears to be confused," Ocher said.

"He realizes his predicament," Skye added. "There's no way to make the descent with one hand."

"There is one way, Skye," said Curial Clove, who was trying to remain motionless, as if his movements might precipitate a fall.

The boy clutched the stone to his chest with both hands and slowly leaned back into the arms of the air.

He fell.

In the moment before impact, no one screamed. The boy disappeared in the chaos below and the lily-whites ran riot.

The Caballine Azure urged their frantic mounts through the tangle of men, women, and children, trying to restore the peace.

Then, still holding the stone, the boy reappeared, raised upon the hands of the crowd. Was he alive? Other sweeps remained prone, knocked senseless, perhaps dead.

"Aver! Aver! Aver!"

The cry of the sweeps resolved itself from many voices into one. They pressed forward, toward the gates of the Redan Inviolate, bearing their savior above them. They jabbed their sugarcane walking sticks skyward, a bristling forest on the march, and soon the rest of the crowd joined them.

Lancers from the Redan Inviolate met the mob at the gates and held them at bay with spears leveled.

From the relative safety of the curtain wall, Curial Clove rubbed his hands together. "Most unexpected, this."

"The Council must meet immediately," Ocher said to no one in particular.

Around him, Auric saw only paralyzed politicians. Passionless mediocrity assured a meteoric rise in Sarcos. In such people, no one ever saw a threat. But the likes of Clove and Ocher were worthless in a crisis.

Though he preferred to pull strings from the shadows, Auric immediately began barking orders to the watch commanders and messengers within earshot. "Skye, we must secure the boy!"

But to his dismay, Cardinal Skye had disappeared.

Auric spun, scanning the courtyard below, but there was no sign of the Cardinal, nor of the black-shirted adepts he had positioned near the west gate. Then he saw his detested peer, leading perhaps one hundred men on horseback through the crowd below. They poured into Hangman's Circus, unarmed but for their minds. Even from above, he could feel the knot of adepts working the bright mechanics, cowing those before them by will alone. The Sansiso militia would file a grievance against Skye, but that would change nothing.

"Ordinal Celadon!" Auric shrieked down at the commander of his fusileers. "Stop those adepts!"

Celadon threw up his hands. "What would you have me do? Fire into the crowd?"

Auric watched helplessly, furious that he had been outmaneuvered. How many years had Skye hidden his men about the Circus for just such an occasion? He realized how seriously he had underestimated Skye's ambitions. He would not do so again.

***

Below, Dahlia fought against the tide of flesh, finally managing to reach the safety of a doorway. It dismayed her that this sacred day had devolved into a brawl, but she knew there was nothing she could do.

Just outside the doorway, she observed a second group of adepts carrying away the sweeps who had broken the boy's fall and who had themselves been broken by the impact. Some hung limp as rag dolls, the only sign of movement being the passage of blood across their ivory faces, while others protested ineffectually, slung over the horses of their rescuers.

Almost an hour later, when the Circus was all but empty, Dahlia slipped from her hiding place, still wondering what had become of the boy.

5

Alignment

Brand cared little for his daughter Gavo and gave her nothing for her inheritance. When she came crying to him to ask why, her tears becoming oceans, he told her that only through privation are dreams begotten. Jealous of her sister Halo, Gavo went to her father in the guise of her mother, Ekal. While he slept, she castrated him, making impotent all our dreams, that he too might know privation. From Brand's flesh and blood, Gavo fashioned Urizen, and called him her son.

–The Book of Creation

998, Year of the Wolf, Under Serpens
Calx made his way through the crowded ballroom of Fin Redan and joined Ordinal Fin outside on the balcony. His new suit made him

sweat, despite the evening breeze. "I have changed as you asked, éclat. May I ask why?"

The flushed Ordinal looked him up and down and seemed satisfied. "I want you to search the rooms upstairs and if you went as one of my caballines, you would draw notice."

"Search the rooms for what?"

Fin shrugged, his simian features protesting his disinterest without conviction. "Sometimes guests get lost, find their way into places they should not be. It is best to be discreet about such concerns."

"I will see to it at once, éclat." Calx turned to go, surprised that his liege actually offered an explanation beyond "I wish it." Regardless, he had no choice but to humor the drunken man's whims.

"Calx?"

"Aye, éclat?"

"Do not assume that my guests are my friends." Fin's voice turned bitter. "They come because Auric comes. And as he goes, so goes the Caballine Azure."

"Cardinal Azo might not agree with you." Calx could tell the Ordinal was off on one of his wine-addled ramblings. He had never liked Ordinal Fin.

"The old guard do not see how little time is left, Calx," Fin muttered.

Calx ignored the Ordinal, his attention elsewhere.

Fin turned and followed Calx's gaze to his wife, Rose, as she gestured in her graceful language of signs. "You find her pleasing?"

"I find nothing in another man's wife." Calx suspected that Fin enjoyed seeing other men desire Rose.

Rose saw the men looking at her through the window and waved cheerfully before taking to the dance floor with a young caballine, her gown sparkling like a storm of emeralds.

"What she lacks in speech, she more than makes up for in passion," Fin said, as if to bait Calx further.

Calx nodded, and averted his eyes. "I had best organize my men before the guests return to their rooms."

"No, do it yourself. Tensions have been running high since Gavo's Day, and with many of the Hierophants here, I do not want to give the impression that we fear an infiltrator."

"I live only to set your mind at ease, éclat," Calx deadpanned before departing.

***

Ordinal Fin stood alone on the balcony, watching the water flowing past far below. Following the stream northwest, out to the sea, he saw a light in the summer fog, a galley bound for Sansiso. He cast a side-long glance back to the ballroom at his wife. He worried constantly that she would lose her temper. If only she were more like his calm river, more like him, he thought as he emptied another glass of wine, he would not have to take such drastic action.

His one act of impetuousness in a life of firstborn responsibility, marrying this woman for her fiery beauty, had been a mistake. His brother had told him not to marry lower in the Cast, and now he found himself between the crushing humiliation of his misjudgment and the unyielding truth of an ill-conceived union.

He closed his eyes and listened while his chamber orchestra rendered the coda of a particularly energetic piece.

With the song complete and the musicians resting their aching hands, Cardinal Auric arrived, his face glistening with sweat.

"Dance and drink will kill me yet," Auric said, breathing heavily. He was a large man, but quite athletic. The long golden hair that had earned him his birth name also became a badge of honor. Known as a straw man in his youth, on account of his empty boasts, he had spent his second twenty years making his enemies regret their words.

Ordinal Fin held out his wrist to offer his life, but Auric waved it away and laughed.

"Wean yourself of these musty rituals, Fin. If our families are to be joined, you had best get used to my way of doing things."

Fin grinned uncomfortably. Auric's imperiousness proved hard to bear, even softened by humor. The price he was paying for this alliance seemed to keep going up, even though it was Auric who owed him.

"Come now," Auric continued. "Looking upon such a clouded face, I might almost believe you are having doubts."

"Is it not natural?"

"Bah, you shall have a wife worthy of you, and your money back tenfold." Auric planted himself next to Fin on the edge of the balcony. "A new wife for new times."

"You are certain of the boy's demise?"

"Absolutely," Auric said. He looked around for eavesdroppers in a fit of uncharacteristic wariness. "I have it on good authority that he passed away three days ago. We can now move on Skye Redan with impunity."

"Surely it would be better to lure them into the field. Adepts are most dangerous when protected by a fortress."

"True, but they are not prepared for a siege and I have made certain arrangements with the eclectics to borrow some of their siege engines. Skye Redan's walls will be as paper before the fire trumpets."

Fin blanched. "If the Council hears of this . . ."

"But who would tell them? Not I, certainly. Nor, I imagine, would you, since your money paid the eclectics. And after it is done, who will care?" Auric smiled, revealing his gold-capped teeth.

Fin's heart sank. He had thought himself a silent partner and only now understood that his signature on the letters of credit would make him the natural scapegoat if Auric's plan failed.

"You should lay off the wine, my friend," Auric observed, peering over the edge of the balcony. "One misstep and my niece will have to look for a husband elsewhere."

Looking down at the water below, Fin felt as if he were drowning.

***

Calx went dutifully from room to room, checking every closet, wardrobe and antechamber for malingerers. It seemed such an arbitrary assignment. Fin Redan contained thirty guest suites, and with even the most cursory search, he would be busy for at least another hour.

Inside the great trunks brought by the éclat he discovered no spies, only treasures of silk and velvet, and jewelry worth ten years' pay. Finding in one a striking black cloak trimmed with gold brocade, he looked about to make sure no one was watching, and slipped the cloak over his suit. He imagined himself higher in the Cast, one of the éclat, revered, his cloak hanging majestically off his shoulders. Ordina Rose would smile upon him. Almost immediately he felt foolish and repacked the garment with care, resigning himself to the tedium of the task before him. The words of the Mere who had taught him as a child still chastened him. "Wishes are the thieves of happiness," she had said. The gods did not look kindly upon those ungrateful for their lot in life, and he resolved to steel his mind against vain desire.

After a thorough examination of the guest chambers, Calx had but one elderly Curial caught napping to show for his efforts. He regretted startling the old man, but he had to determine whether the Curial was still alive. Given the Curial's decrepitude, it proved a hard call to make even after there was some movement.

Calx walked to the edge of the landing and observed the celebration below. He spied Rose among the whirling gowns and long coats. Though she was small, her red hair and haunting eyes could not be missed. He stood motionless, leaning against the banister enraptured, until by chance she looked up at him. He stepped back quickly and turned away. He decided then and there to seek new employment. He knew he had no choice. His infatuation with the Ordinal's wife would only bring him trouble.

He was about to report to Ordinal Fin when he realized he had not checked the master suite.

At the end of the hall, great oak doors barred his way. He wondered what had become of Rance, the sentry, assigned to the Ordinal's chambers. He cursed himself for not noticing earlier, while he'd been passing back and forth across the hallway. He tested the doors, but to his relief they remained locked.

He tried his key but it would not fit properly. Kneeling down on the faded hall runner, he peered into the keyhole but saw nothing. There was a key jamming the lock from the other side. He could account for his own keys, and those that always remained on the person of the Ordinal. Rose had the only other set, and she was downstairs.

Reinserting his master key, he pressed his key against the one already in the lock. With a bit of work, he managed to push the obstructing key out of the keyhole. It fell to the floor with a dull thump and he carefully unlocked the door, well aware that someone had to be on the other side.

Inside, shadows hid the opulence of the Ordinal's private antechamber. A dead lux sat on a granite table in the middle of the room, its phosphorescence spent. There were no less than a dozen artifacts of the Dim Age, elevated in their obsolescence to the realm of art. Garments lay strewn over the couches, waiting patiently for servants to return them to the fold. Doors on the right and on the left led to separate bedchambers for the Ordinal and his wife.

Calx advanced cautiously, more fearful of knocking something over than encountering an intruder. It seemed absurd that anyone would trespass upon the Ordinal's property with hundreds of caballines patrolling the grounds. Still, the eclectics had grown bold of late. One of their incendiary devices could level the entire redan, so perhaps Fin's concern was justified.

Opening the door of Rose's bedchamber, Calx froze.

Atop the Ordina's bed lay the missing sentry, naked as the day he was born.

"Explain yourself, Rance," Calx demanded.

There was no reply.

Furious, he walked toward the canopied bed and examined the prone man. No pulse. No breath. Had Rance died from lovemaking? There were other possibilities, to be sure, but his jealousy chose the most damning explanation. Rose had not joined the other guests until a short time ago. Perhaps they'd been together. The scenario that formed in his mind made no sense, but passion needed no rationale.

There was one problem, however. His report would end Rose's life, for adultery among the éclat was punishable by death.

While he tried to think of some way out of his predicament, he heard a voice in the hallway. "Rance? There's been an accident. Quite the mess."

It was the Ordinal's valet. What to do? He moved to shut the bedroom door, just as Tule poked his head in.

Instead of retreating, the prim little man braced the door from closing. "Careful!" He looked up at Calx indignantly. "Auric spilled wine on the Ordina. She needs a new gown. I'm in a hurry." Then he saw the corpse.

Calx stepped back. It was too late.

***

It was one of those long summer days when the stain of the sun seemed indelible. Ordinal Fin observed his shadow stretching out to indistinction and wondered, if only for a moment, what would become of his great estate if he were to die.

The inhabitants of Fin Redan and environs stood nearby on the west lawn, anxiously awaiting the commencement of the duel. Most of them believed that Ordina Rose came to defend her honor against charges of adultery, and, in fact, the determination of Rose's guilt or innocence would be the end result of the engagement. But the circumstances that allowed Rose to meet her husband with sword rather than words remained unknown but to a few of the éclat.

Among those who knew the truth, none was more angry than Ordinal Fin himself. Women were not permitted to defend themselves on the field of honor. So it was written in the Civil Codex. Yet, with her twisted words, Limnal Dahlia had convinced the Curia that Rose had the right to champion the dead sentry Rance because, by implication, he too stood accused. It irked Fin that the very laws meant to reserve the martial sphere for men were being used to obviate the charges against his wife. By making Rance the focus of the trial, by transporting his family down from the north to challenge their son's dishonor, Dahlia had transformed the stigma of an adulteress into the aura of a righteous champion.

Behind Limnal Dahlia, Fin sensed the subtle hand of the Thalass reaching out from Vejas to chasten the Caballine Azure for marital profiteering. He watched the dark-robed Limnal conversing with Cardinal Auric and wondered whether his would-be ally had intended this outcome all along. If he fell, so did Auric's debts.

Fin's eyes alighted on each face in the crowd and everywhere saw contempt. He gripped his sword more tightly to stop his hands from shaking. He hoped she would not be stubborn. He hoped she would cry mercy once he had disarmed her.

***

Calx sat still on his caval, one of the hairless war-horses from the southern plains. Slower than a lancer's horse, cavals seldom tired, and their leathery hide eliminated the need for expensive barding.

He watched Rose in her brown riding slacks and emerald blouse, testing the weight of her sword, and prayed the fight would be called off, even if that meant he would be called to testify. The Ordinal was reputedly a fair duelist and no one believed Rose could defeat him outright. The rumor most often heard was that she intended to let herself be slain to raise the ire of the Pelagines and the other religious orders against the Ordinal. But she did not seem the type to seek martyrdom.

"You look worried, Calx," said the lancer to Calx's right. "There are other commissions to be had. I have a friend on the Council . . ."

"I am sure you do."

"Ah, I should have guessed," Elinvar said, a cocky grin on his face. "Your eyes never leave her. It's no wonder the Ordinal dislikes you."

"I do not believe she should die. Even if she is guilty."

Elinvar snorted derisively. Denied a commission in the Caballine Azure, he had turned bitter. The scar under his eye marked the wound festering within.

"You found Rance in her bedroom. If you cannot believe your eyes, why did you not champion her?"

Calx looked away in shame. "Would that I were blind."

***

With his horn, the Seneschal of Fin Redan called the two combatants to the field. Rose and Fin approached on the soft grass, each ignoring the other. From a scroll, the Seneschal read aloud, "By order of the Curia of Sansiso, Ordina Rose stands here today to defend the honor of Rance, a soldier accused of adultery by Ordinal Fin."

The Seneschal looked at Rose and Fin directly. "I remind you to fight with fairness and grace. At first blood, the injured party may cry mercy."

Rose looked questioningly at the Seneschal.

"You may also cast down your sword to yield," the Seneschal added in haste.

"Rose," Fin said, "I have no wish to harm you. Surely, you can see that–"

Rose shook her head and put her finger to his lips. In her pocket, she could feel the ticking of her timepiece. Its constancy reassured her. She nodded to the Seneschal and stepped back, testing the weight of her sword.

Ordinal Fin took his position with a sigh. "At your leisure," he said to the Seneschal while removing his coat and cravat.

***

Calx reined his caval back and prepared to ride off.

"They are about to begin," Elinvar said smugly. "Care to wager on your lass? Perhaps it will help her."

"I have no desire to watch this butchery," Calx replied, shaking his head.

Standing nearby, Limnal Dahlia heard and looked over her shoulder. "Caballine, did you know that the Ordina Rose studied under Kame Torrefy?"

Calx gazed incredulously at the brown-robed Pelagine below him. "Where did you hear this?"

"Who's Torrefy?" Elinvar asked. "Calx?"

"If you'd learned the blade from Torrefy," Calx replied, "you'd not have that dueling scar."

"Keep your eyes on the field, Caballine," Dahlia said, but it was too late.

There was an audible gasp, and when Calx looked up he saw Ordinal Fin transfixed on the end of Rose's blade. A small red sun had risen on Fin's white shirt, shining forth from his stilled heart.

6

Asylum

Feign sleep and you cannot be awakened.

–The Book of War

"You know the risks?" Peregrine squinted through the viewing slot at the hooded man standing outside his cell. He wished he could see his visitor's face.

"It must be done," said the hooded man.

"His parents consented?"

The hooded man chuckled. "Can you do it? It is said you are among the best."

Peregrine glanced about. The wet stone walls with their patchwork moss sickened him. Slowly, he nodded. Nuclear somatic transfer worked best, but he could tell from the hooded man's demeanor there was no time for that.

"If you are successful, I am authorized to grant you whatever you wish."

"My freedom?" Peregrine asked as he put his hands against the stout oak door between them.

"You are safer in here, if you ask me. But if you wish to leave the asylum, it can be arranged. I have a friend on the Council."

Peregrine could not conceal his surprise. "You must be desperate," he joked, to no effect.

"Will it take long?"

"Show me the portraits again?"

The hooded man held up two images.

Even in the dim light, Peregrine could see they were very fine. "These are platinum based, are they not?"

Shrugging, the hooded man returned the images to his travel case. "It is best to be ignorant of the dark mechanics."

"There is a substantial similarity already. It should not be too difficult, provided I have access to the necessary tools. It should take no more than one day." Peregrine knew it would take longer, but he had to get out, to feel the warmth of the sun once more.

"You will have whatever you require. How long will the recovery take?"

The artificer licked his dry lips. His patron had to be wealthy to afford platinum prints and well connected to have access to a dermalathe.

"A month or so. The young heal quickly."

"Excellent. We will come for you tomorrow."

"I will be here," the artificer remarked dryly.

"Not for much longer. Speak of this to anyone and I will hear of it."

"They took the others away. There is no one left to tell."

The hooded man ignored him, and departed in haste.

Peregrine watched his unknown benefactor gliding away like an apparition. He feared he would soon be dead.

7

Resemblance

I am beyond the minds that have no soul,
beyond what you're told, bought or sold.

—The Words of Urizen

998, Year of the Wolf, Under Lacerta

Summer raged against Skye Redan, drenching the somber fortress
with rain. The wind besieging the walls mimicked the wretched screams
that clawed their way up from the oubliettes. The complicity of nature
in its own perversion brought a faint smile to Cardinal Skye's thin lips:
an exquisitely cruel harmony, the prisoner and the railing wind. He ran
his fingers over the ancient stone of the antechamber where he took his
ease at the border of sleep. The warmth of the weathered granite made
pleasant report to his skin, but it was not the news for which he waited.

From his voluminous coat, he removed a vial of muscarine, a hallucinogen derived from mushrooms. Putting a pinch to his nose, he inhaled. Sleep came quickly, then the lights, the luminous shapes–if they were truly shapes at all. Muscarine opened a window into the sacred world clearer than the projections Pelagines coaxed from their gray glass.

***

In time, the wind died down to a tense silence, punctuated only by the pizzicato footsteps of a reticent messenger.

Skye awoke, still lethargic.

From the approaching sound, he knew what was to be said, but he wished to hear the news spoken to him. The knock on the door was barely audible.

"Enter."

Skye observed the boy who entered, as awkward as a puppy. A dirty blond shock of hair stood up above a wrap of white cloth that completely covered his face, except for his foggy gray eyes.

"Éclat," the boy stammered, standing in the doorway, "I am bade tell you that your prisoner has died."

"How?"

"In aiding Kame Slate, I applied the burning iron too vigorously. The pain was too much for the prisoner and his light fled."

Skye knew the fault was Slate's, yet this boy bore another's guilt without question. Such devotion was not easily come by.

The boy remained impassive, staring at the flecked wall without blinking.

Skye waited a moment.

"You are called Flux, are you not?"

"I am, éclat."

Skye took another pause, more because it was expected of him than because he was cruel; cruelty was not so versatile a servant as mercy. "See that such clumsiness does not hinder my inquiries again."

A smile creased Flux's bandages. He extended his right hand, palm open to the sky, offering his life.

Drawing a slender dagger from the recesses of his cloak, Skye turned the blade in his hand and brought the hilt down gently to meet the boy's palm.

"Your future flows through me." Skye used the old words, from a time when the ceremony was one of bonding rather than bloodless formality.

"Éclat," Flux ventured, "will I be scarred?"

"Are you afraid people will see a warped soul in a warped face?"

"Aye, éclat."

"Appearance is that important to you?"

"Perhaps it would be less so if I could see."

Skye thought of his old friend Handel and his hideous injuries. The boy's fears were not unfounded. "I was told your flesh would be unblemished. You must guard against disfigurement at the hands of your fears. Now off with you."

Flux bowed and excused himself.

"Flux?"

The boy turned, halfway out the door. "Aye, éclat?"

"How is it you do not fall?" Skye asked, wondering if the boy realized how his lack of sight had honed his mind.

"I can see a bit, éclat. Only light and dark. But I am told what is in between is less worthy of attention, so perhaps I am not so badly off."

Skye laughed. "Come closer."

Flux complied, his hands shaking.

"Remove your bandages."

The boy gingerly peeled away the strip of cloth encircling his head, revealing a handsome, youthful face, still somewhat swollen.

The Cardinal could not suppress his smile. Perhaps there was a use for artificers after all. "You should wear the bandages a bit longer."

Flux nodded. "By your command, éclat."

"Tell Kame Slate I wish to have a word with him."

"I will, éclat." Flux gently closed the door.

Skye offered thanks to Wild Brand for favor passing all expectation. It was a thoughtful gift for a man of fifty.

8

Steel Tongue

Laws of peace, of love, of unity,
Of pity, compassion, forgiveness;
Let each choose one habitation,
His ancient infinite mansion,
One command, one joy, one desire,
One curse, one weight, one measure,
One King, one God, one Law.

–The Book of Urizen

998, Year of the Wolf, Under Aquila

Mere Calico washed her raw hands in the ocean, working the soil from beneath her nails with the white sand. The sky above was untroubled and she was grateful. Recalling the storm that had nearly driven her and her party back to Sansiso, she thanked Ekal for her forbearance. The excavation would have been much more difficult had the island suffered the usual summer rains.

She returned barefoot to the embers of the campfire, her sleeves rolled up, long skirt shifting in the wind. Informality of dress was one of the principal pleasures of fieldwork, and she relished every minute of it.

As she brushed the sand from her knees, there came a cry from the site of the dig. She rushed toward her two companions, their heads barely visible above the rim of the pit they had dug.

"Have you found it?" Mere Calico asked, gasping for breath as she looked down upon the two women.

Two white smiles shone against the dark earth. The taller of the two women below, Mere Saffron, drummed her knuckles on the floor of the pit. A hollow sound.

"A wooden box?" Mere Calico held her hands together, so as not to appear anxious.

Mere Saffron nodded. "See the outline in the dirt?"

"It is exactly where you said it would be, Saffron," said Mere Teal, her eagerness masked by the mud on her face. "What a marvelous brain you have."

"Indeed. Though let us open the box, to be sure." Calico tried to be polite to her odd colleague, but it never came easily. There was something hard about Mere Teal, something that seemed out of place, even in the wild.

Teal immediately set to work clearing the dirt from the top of the box, brushing rapidly but not without care. Saffron took the opportunity to stretch her cramped limbs.

"To think that a vision led you here, Mere Saffron," said Calico from above, beside the pile of upturned dirt. "Truly, you are blessed."

Saffron blushed, hearing the envy in Calico's praise. "Had my vision been a dream, had it come while I slept, I would agree. I saw this place during an evening walk. Gavo's face shone in the sky and I am wary of her influence."

"Halo's dark sister has her merits," Teal said without looking up. "She is nearer Deep Ekal in disposition, and more beloved of her mother for that reason."

Calico saw the surprise on Saffron's face but said nothing so as not to distract from the task at hand. She too had noticed how often Teal defended Silent Gavo. An inquisitive look from Saffron brought a shake of the head. Now was not the time to argue.

When the dirt had been cleared from around the box, Teal looked up plaintively. "I am having trouble pulling the box loose."

Saffron knelt to help Teal.

Calico hesitated. "Perhaps I can be of assistance up here?"

Teal rolled her eyes. "There is no shortage of soap, sister."

Sighing, Calico joined the two other celebrants, though the presence of a third made the pit rather cramped. The scent of the damp soil reminded her of the Pelage of Mecino, constantly beset by the northern rains.

While Calico stood by helplessly, Teal worked her fingers between the earth and the box, which was roughly half her height, and Saffron took the other end. The rotting wood crumbled as they pulled the box free. Beneath the debris, something caught the sun.

With a giddy laugh, Teal removed a slender sword from the debris. She stood and wiped the blade on her filthy tunic. It looked like a replica of the great broadswords on the mainland, recast for human hands.

"Behold the Aver's Tongue," Teal said, turning the sword in the light.

Mere Saffron grinned. "It's beautiful."

"In the Aver's hands, it will be more so," Calico added softly. "Truly, the time of reveille is upon us." She fell to her knees and closed her eyes. In darkness, she could better thank Deep Ekal.

Then Mere Saffron screamed.

There was Teal, pulling the sword from the neck of the wide-eyed Saffron, beneath an arterial spray. There too were motes of Saffron's memories, described for all to see by the Aver's Tongue. Borne on the celebrant's dying breath, the phantom images rose like a dream pageant of fireflies, vanishing almost as soon as they appeared.

Calico gave them only passing thought as she reached in desperation for something, anything.

"The reveille that comes is for the one god, the one on the other side," Teal declared as she turned. "For Urizen."

With her groping hand, Calico found the handle of a wooden trowel and swung it with all her might. Her slash caught Teal in the neck and tore a gash in her skin that exposed a shiny silver jawbone.

Teal winced but held her ground.

"That hurt, sister." She tried to replace the flap of skin that hung off her face like a third ear, without success. "I regret that I will have to hurt you back, but only pain provides entrance. Pray to your gods while you can."

Mere Calico did.

9

Lessons

With the children of Bright Halo dead upon the field
Urizen appealed to Cardinal Gray
"Your kin lie slain, why then not yield?"
And silence reigned, ears strained to hear
Amid wave on wave of spear and shield
Gray's words rang out true and clear
"I alone here shall survive the day"
And thus Urizen learned of fear

                    —The Song of Cardinal Gray

The first day of the month of Aquila, Flux's situation changed suddenly and irrevocably. He was going about his chores in one of the many underground storerooms where tables and chairs in need of repair grappled with each other, their wooden legs intertwined like stiff fingers clasped in prayer. Nearby, crates of wine waited to be inventoried, beside sealed jars of assorted conserves, drawers with faded labels, full of herbs and spices. While scrubbing the tile floor, he heard the Cardinal approach. He recognized the metronomic stride, then heard the fear in the voice of the servant directing the Cardinal toward him. Never before had the Cardinal sought him out.

Flux had grown used to being forgotten. To pay for his mother's board while she rotted in prison for adultery, he had gone to work at the age of ten in Telluria, the great foundry outside of Sansiso. It was a city unto itself, a cairn of bleak structures resembling the petrified bones of titans. He would walk for hours amid the fires, finding his way by the hiss of steel ingots melted and reforged until the last profane taint of Urizen was removed. Within the fuliginous clouds of smoke and steam, he went unnoticed. He carried a water skin that resembled the udder of a cow, by which he saved the sweating smiths from dehydration. Rarely was he thanked.

There was one man, with rounded features and bulging blue eyes, who used to look after him. He didn't know his protector's real name, but everyone called him Morphine on account of the narcotics he would get from adepts to ease the pain of his burns. As Flux knew well, everyone who braved Telluria's storms of ash and ember required medical attention sooner or later.

Flux had heard that Morphine had a young son very much like himself somewhere. He had never felt particularly worthy of attention, and when it came he invariably felt guilty, as if his near blindness was an act of thievery, stealing concern from the more genuinely deserving, like Morphine's real son.

When he heard the Cardinal asking after his well-being, Flux marveled at how similar the Cardinal's and Morphine's voices were, not so much in tone but in the quality of their concern.

His real father had been something between madman and performer, eking out a marginal living on the streets between trips to the asylum. The dirt-faced boys from Flux's old neighborhood called his father Cuckold on account of his mother's crime. The name followed him thereafter.

In running from the shame of his lineage, Flux had found himself first under Morphine's wing, and now under Skye's. Though he felt indebted to his surrogate fathers, both seemed to feel it was they who owed him.

The Cardinal entered the room where Flux was working and observed in silence.

Flux ceased working and offered his wrist with deference. "How may I serve, éclat?" Though Flux could not read the Cardinal's expression, he felt the adept's questioning gaze upon him.

"Do you know the truth?" asked Skye.

Flux thought for a moment. "Sometimes, éclat."

"At such times, how do you know it?"

"By having lived, I suppose. A thing is true or it is not."

"But for one so young, having so little experience of the world, truth must be quite elusive. Especially if you cannot see."

"It is not so hard to find, even with your eyes closed, éclat."

Skye chuckled. He began ambling aimlessly along the narrow straits between the islands of huddled furnishings, touching the various sundries as a cat marks its territory. "You have a certainty I envy, Flux. But it is time to open your eyes, if you will forgive the expression. You will die before day's end. True or false?"

Flux stiffened. "I do not know, éclat."

"What do you believe?"

"I believe you are a kind man and you would not see harm done to me."

"Some think me a cruel man."

"I do not believe you are cruel. You saved my life once before." The burns he received in Telluria still stung in his memory.

"So you believe I will again?"

"I suppose I do," Flux replied.

"From belief comes truth. There is perhaps no more awesome, no more horrible fact in the world."

"I believe you, éclat, but I do not understand."

"Understanding is the bridge you build to a point of view, from you to your beliefs. The bright mechanics allow you to build a bridge strong enough to carry both yourself and others. That is no small feat, to bring others to your understanding, with only words and thoughts. Do you think you could do such a thing?"

Skye seemed drawn to something near the back wall, where mortar squeezed from the surrounding stones remained forever frozen in the midst of its escape.

Though Flux could not tell what had caught the Cardinal's attention, he realized he was being offered a chance to become an adept, to study the bright mechanics. Stumbling over his words, he responded, "With your help, I think I could do anything."

Skye smiled almost imperceptibly. "Then let this be your first lesson. Listen: 'Flux killed the spider,' 'Flux caused the spider to die.' Which is the stronger phrase?"

Flux thought for a moment. "The first one?"

Skye nodded and reached down to pick something up. "But why?"

"I do not know."

The Cardinal placed a spider on Flux's hand. Flux shivered and tried not to squirm.

Skye continued, "The idea, the content of the thought, is shaped by the form of its expression. The thought expressed in each case is the same, but the first form, the phrase itself, is shorter. By confining the energy of the thought in a smaller space, you focus the force on a smaller area, just as a blow from your fist will hurt more than a blow from the flat of your hand."

Flux gazed quizzically at the Cardinal, barely able to divine the outline of his form. "I am not sure if I follow." He could feel the spider on his forearm, and it seemed the far less nervous of the two. The arachnid traversed his gooseflesh at a leisurely pace.

"It takes time. The bright mechanics is the language of possibility, and with further study you will be able to shape the possible into the actual. Consider the spider on your arm. When you know the mysteries of the spider, when you know the space between you and it, you will be able to describe its death perfectly. With but a word or a gesture, all the possibilities will yield to the one you have described, and it will be so."

Without a perceptible action from the Cardinal, the tickling spider footfalls on Flux's wrist stopped abruptly. The spider was dead.

"Think upon what I have said, Flux. It is a great honor to be an adept, but it is also a great burden. You will be hated and feared for your power, and enlightenment can blind you as easily as show you the way."

"As I am nearly blind already, perhaps that is not such a problem," Flux said, smiling.

"That is my hope. Kame Slate will arrange for your new quarters shortly, and your lessons will begin when your face has healed." With that, Skye turned to leave.

"Éclat, why me?"

"Because sight preys on faith."

Flux listened to the diminishing footfall of the Cardinal as he walked away, and wondered if he would ever have a less cryptic answer.

***

To Skye's apprentices, Flux was an interloper. Fear of the Cardinal saved Flux from direct harm, but the resentment of these would-be adepts seethed out in other ways. They devised a series of errands, practical jokes, and mean-spirited chores to put Flux in his place.

Eager to please, Flux accepted the abuse stoically. He even provided blood transfusions to help the apprentices recover from their elaborations, as the taxing evocations of the bright mechanics were known. Eventually, he gave so much of himself that he collapsed and remained bedridden for days.

Upon learning of the abuse of his protégé, Cardinal Skye flew into a rage. Nettle, the senior apprentice, was summoned to the Cardinal's chambers and was never heard from again. No one dared say anything openly about the matter, but given the rumors concerning the generous amount of gold Nettle's parents were said to have received from an anonymous benefactor, speculation about Nettle's fate was not sweetened with optimism. Two other apprentices were dismissed from Skye Redan in disgrace, and each soon developed an inexplicable stutter, making elaboration of the mechanics impossible. (Ironically, many years later, one of the two became a celebrated mime, much in demand for his caustic characterizations of the éclat.)

After that, life at Skye Redan returned to normal, though the dozens of servants who took care of the daily chores benefited from the newfound humility and politeness of the remaining apprentices.

***

The day his bandages finally came off, Flux received a remote room in the upper west wing of the redan, away from the apprentices, away from everything he had ever known.

Introductions to a variety of tutors followed. They became his constant companions and their desperate eagerness to see him learn made the lessons tolerable. But the attentions of such a formidable assortment of archaists and adepts furthered his sense of isolation. They were men and women of great knowledge and achievement. Who was he?

Despite their formidable urbanity, Flux sensed they were terrified of the Cardinal, and whenever he had difficulty understanding a given lesson, he felt compelled to study harder for the sake of his teachers. Only fear could explain the humiliation these learned men and women endured teaching him, for the Cardinal insisted that they instruct while blindfolded. When he inquired about this odd restriction, the Cardinal replied, "They will have greater sympathy for the condition of your eyes and they will not be distracted from the tasks I have set to them, for time is short."

After his duties were assigned to others, Flux discovered that his friends and fellow servants had been forbidden to speak to him, even to look upon him, unless absolutely necessary. It seemed to him a punishment of insidious cruelty, stemming from nothing he could understand and flowering into an intangible barrier between him and everything he found familiar in life.

But soon he stopped blaming himself for the change in attitude among his former peers. He imagined he would feel the same as Wren and Ouzel and the rest of the staff had someone else been elevated in the Cast. Fear and jealousy were a delicious mix and he knew he would do better to not develop a taste for it.

Still, he realized something deeper was happening. The Seneschal placed various sections of the redan off-limits at odd hours. The level of supplies stored underground would change drastically, and it seemed as if someone were always loading or unloading something or other. He could only guess that the Cardinal's soldiers were preparing for an engagement.

Because his eyesight was so poor, Flux remained ignorant of the curious goings-on, and no one was willing to enlighten him. Though he had no reason to know the business of the éclat, his curiosity had been awakened by his tutors and now extended to other matters. Having been in the dark all his life, he realized how much he hated it.

10

Ink and Blood

> History is the fermentation of blood into ink.
>
> —Nausil of Nevta

998, Year of the Wolf, Under Cygnus

Tweed held the crumpled decale up to the dull light of day. The portrait of Cardinal Skye had melted away in the rain, replaced by what looked like the smudged map of a river delta, where the thin ink tributaries came together in a muddy brown swill and drained off the southern edge.

"A red-haired lad passed me this fake note, sentinel." The grizzled merchant struggled to catch his breath.

Kaolin could not but agree with Tweed's assessment, despite his inclination to the contrary. He had patrolled the Fig Street market for three years with the same cautious stride and knew Tweed was an unreliable witness. Almost every month the old merchant would pry himself from behind the stall where he sharpened knives and trot over to report some phantom thief or some more exotic apparition. Kaolin, however, would not put his dislike of the old man above his duty, and he listened with the attentiveness of a man enamored of details.

"He wanted his sword sharpened," Tweed panted, "likely having heard my reputation for being able to bring a keen edge to the dullest of blades. He kept quiet about it, of course, but he was a wily one, that boy, hoping to get a better price by refusing to haggle. But I was on to him. He was small-framed, and fair of face, too young to have a beard, with short hair the color of . . . red. I was going to say wine, but wine is much darker than his hair was. Anyway, his sword did need sharpening. It had more notches than my belt! To get a rise out of him, I asked if he had been slashing at rocks and he just nodded. He wanted no words with me, that's for sure."

Kaolin nodded, though his sympathies were with the boy, for he knew how trying a conversation with Tweed could be. He glanced about to keep an eye on the beggars. The picayune frequently rushed food vendors en masse, knowing that only a few of them could be detained. "Was there anything else distinctive about the boy?"

"Well, Kame, most men would have missed it, but I noticed he had a good deal more clothing than usual, like he was going somewhere. He had a traveling sack and a bedroll, too. No doubt in my mind he's a vagrant, in and out of trouble wherever he goes. Probably a tax dodger."

"A counterfeiter would pay his taxes, don't you think?" Kaolin immediately regretted his observation. Tweed's orations were like fires that needed to burn themselves out without being fueled by more questions.

"This boy is too clever for that. By posing as an impoverished wanderer, he has the perfect cover to pass forged notes. And being on the move, he's always one step ahead of the collectors. Now, mind you, you didn't hear this from me. I don't want a visit from the Certain Ministry. It would cut into my sharpening business."

Kaolin knew Tweed made his real money from the black market, as did many citizens. "How much better for everyone that you can still afford integrity."

"I wonder sometimes how you, my friend, can live on a sentinel's pay. I imagine you could get your hands on several ingots of good metal if you were really to put your mind to it."

"You imagine too much, Tweed."

Tweed smiled sardonically, the wrinkles of his face twisting together like a mass of tangled hair. "Not that you would. I'm told, though on dubious authority, that the magistrates care deeply, deeper than their own pockets, about the integrity of their men and give them liberal raises to keep up with this dismal inflation. You can probably afford all the essentials . . . "

"If a caballine ever heard you speak that way you would not be such a cheerful man," Kaolin said without conviction.

Tweed slapped Kaolin on the back and grinned. "You do have an imagination, even if you keep it on a tight leash."

"You know I will have to file a report about this."

"Must I be mentioned by name?"

"They will want to know the merchant who received this decale." Kaolin stepped beneath the awning of Tweed's stall as the rain fell faster. He glanced back over his shoulder, looking south down Fig Street toward the center of the mostly empty market. The weather kept people at home today. Behind him, a pair of horses drew an omnibus over the slick, gray cobblestone, heading down toward the docks.

"Perhaps if you saw this lad drop the note, I would not have to be involved."

"They would ask why I failed to arrest the lad on the spot."

"Because you wanted to see if he would lead you to the printer."

"If you could tell me where I could find him, I would truly be in your debt."

"Sadly, even I do not know everything, but I can tell you where he was lodging. I happened to note the shape of the key in his money belt, a shape I recognized."

Kaolin knew that Tweed wanted him to beg for the information, but he had his dignity. It would not be long before Tweed told him anyway.

***

Amid upturned refuse barrels meant to delay travelers long enough for thieves to strike, Kaolin waited in the light rain for reinforcements. He kept watch on The Jovial Inn, a newly painted row house in the middle of Dove Alley, a street barely wide enough for a coach. Because it was midweek, the time of reversals, he worried that his good fortune would not continue. He tried to be as inconspicuous as possible, but, standing alone in the middle of the alley, he looked every bit a sentinel. The picayune who lived in this transitional neighborhood watched their territory carefully.

The Jovial Inn was aptly named. It had been refurbished three years earlier by an enterprising young couple who realized there was a need for affordable rooms for travelers. The very notion of traveling was alien to anyone except those with the most substantial means. On those rare occasions when one did travel, a hard floor was all the comfort that could be expected. With the continuing advances in navigation, foreign merchants were becoming much more common in port cities like Sansiso, and the innkeepers made a decent living catering to the needs of these men and women. Though the inn paled in comparison to the plush grandeur of the hotels on High Street with their liveried doormen and obsequious attendants, it offered privacy. Guests at The Jovial avoided becoming the fodder of the public criers and private surveillers who infested the hotels of the éclat, and for many this was a strong selling point.

Four men approached from the south, walking brazenly down the middle of the alley. One seemed to be a woodsman, fit and energetic, clad in a brown tunic and heavy cotton fatigues. Two were clearly adepts, having the glazed stare common to their kind, dressed in formal long coats, vests, cravats, and black trousers. The last wore the field uniform of an Ordinal of the Caballine Azure, buttoned up to the neck. He looked as mirthful as a corpse.

"Kame Kaolin?" inquired the Ordinal as he combed his damp, thinning hair back with his fingers.

"At your service, éclat." Kaolin offered his wrist.

"I am Ordinal Verdet. With me is a brother of my order, Calx, and two adepts, Scull and Niter. We come as factors of the Certain Ministry. Is this the place?"

Kaolin nodded. "I received an anonymous tip that the boy who passed this decale had taken lodging here." He handed over the counterfeit note.

Verdet donned a teak-framed pince-nez. He held the counterfeit decale up, examining it against the stone sky before crumpling it into the inner pocket of his coat. "Poor work. The counterfeiter did not bother to fix the ink. But well done nonetheless, Kame."

After a brief consultation with the two adepts, Verdet announced, "I will enter through the service door, along with Niter, to prevent our quarry from escaping. The rest of you shall enter through the front door on my signal. It will be like flushing a grouse from the bush." The Ordinal drew his falchion, wheeled about, and headed toward the alley that accessed the rear of the row houses, with Niter close behind.

Kaolin waited patiently with Calx and Scull. None of the three men were particularly talkative. They eyed each other like actors who had lost their lines.

Suddenly, Scull flinched. The laughter of boys pealed from nearby.

"Wretched children," Scull muttered, rubbing the back of his neck where a sling stone had struck him.

Kaolin caught a glimpse of Calx smiling and almost broke into laughter himself. "What brings factors of the Verifex into this insignificant case?" he asked, struggling to keep a straight face.

"An edict came down from the Certain Ministry last week," Scull replied, still scanning the street for his tormentors. "There are no insignificant instances of counterfeiting."

"Information corrupts," Calx recited. "The body has natural defenses. In time it develops resistance to alien notions, making it difficult for a single person sick with some strange idea to infect others. But put an idea on the page and there is no stopping it. There is no biological frailty to mitigate its virulence. Thought becomes chronic in print, ever ready to flare up in the acts of some lunatic. Printing currency is the worst form of this plague, for it empowers rebellion even as it undermines authority."

Kaolin sighed. "As usual, the civil authorities are the last to be informed."

Scull chuckled at Calx. "The renewed interest has political motivations. Ink suppliers have had their inventories seized. No doubt one of the Ministry's patrons on the Council intends to sell the confiscated ink back to its owners to ease his debts."

"Spoken like a true adept," Kaolin teased. "Presses are licensed through your order. It sounds to me like your crusade comes from your purse."

Having given up on finding the urchins who had assaulted him, Scull sneered, "And it sounds to me as if you object to our methods, sentinel. It can be dangerous to harbor such eclectic views."

"At least I do not counterfeit decency," Kaolin muttered.

Scull took the insult exactly as intended and glared back at the impertinent sentinel. His narrowed eyes relaxed and, mouthing a silent word, he closed his hand.

Kaolin felt his throat constrict under the will of the adept. He gasped for breath and his face turned red. His knees buckled beneath him.

Calx smacked Scull with a backhand to the face, knocking him to the ground. "Try that again, adept, and I'll kill you."

The adept's hold broken, Kaolin coughed and gulped down great drafts of air. He nodded to Calx in thanks, knowing a mere sentinel could not have struck an adept and gotten away with it.

Scull stood up slowly, fuming. "I will remember this, caballine."

"In case all that mental training fails," Calx replied, "you will still have a fat lip to remind you."

A gurgling scream echoed through the streets, followed by clatter of metal on stone, and then silence. Kaolin glanced at Calx. That was not the signal they had been expecting.

***

Kaolin reached the inn first, bounding up the rain-slick stairs and throwing the door open. Calx and Scull came close behind.

The foyer ran the length of the house, with a steep staircase leading up on the right. The living room, now converted into the proprietor's office, could be seen through a door on the left.

The foyer was all confusion. The colorful wool runner that normally stretched from front door to back lay bunched up as if it had been wrestling with the fallen coat rack. The proprietress peered out warily from the living room, while a similarly cautious guest observed from the top of the stairs.

At the far end of the foyer, Niter sat propped up against the frame of the open back door, clutching a gruesome gash to the neck. Kaolin and Scull rushed immediately to his aid, while Calx stepped over the bleeding adept, looking for Verdet.

The Ordinal lay beneath a canopy of clothes hung out to dry, just beyond the knee-high stone wall that marked the end of the lot and the beginning of the rear alley. He still clutched his pristine falchion. His head had escaped him, though it remained nearby amid refuse bins.

Spitting a stream of curses to the accompaniment of barking dogs, Calx scanned the alley in both directions but saw no one. He stared down at the corpse of Ordinal Verdet and could only marvel at the precision of the decapitation. Lying nearby in a patch of dandelions that had long since given their seeds over to the wind was a fine sword, its blade streaked with blood.

Upon closer examination, he recognized the mark of the blade. It bore the sanctification mark of the Pelage of Lee, the source of Ordinal Fin's arms. He thought upon the description of the boy Kaolin had reported and silently scolded himself for not voicing his suspicions.

Kaolin called out, "How fares the Ordinal?"

"He's dead," Calx replied. "He didn't even land a blow."

"A fair swordsman, this lad." Kaolin descended the back steps quickly and hurried over.

"Short red hair. I'll wager your swordsman is a woman, Rose of Fin Redan. She's no counterfeiter, but there is a price on her head."

Kaolin seemed unmoved. "I'll wager that price just went up."

"Aye, but not enough to make it worth the risk," Calx said, as he toyed with the idea of pursuing the woman who had always been beyond his reach.

11

Flux

Memory is the bitterest reproach.

–unknown

With the coming of winter, Flux felt as if he had reached a new world in the nightscape of his mind. While his virtual blindness made him illiterate, the constant discussions and readings with his hooded tutors transformed him, from his posture and diction to his understanding of reality. Many of his lessons concerned the Aver and his previous incarnations during the Dim Age and the Roaming Empire. He endured heavy doses of theology and etiquette without complaint, though he wondered why Skye wanted him so thoroughly steeped in such esoteric lore. To keep from falling asleep during longwinded lectures about the protocols of the ether, he frequently meditated on the bright mechanics, a subject of endless fascination. He exhibited frightening acumen as an adept, showing more promise—and in some cases more ability—than the Cardinal's most experienced apprentices.

Flux accepted his demanding schedule, and during the few moments he was not being tutored in some arcane elaboration or courtly ritual, he walked carefully along the windy battlements of the redan, trying to come to terms with this unexpected change in his life. His insecurity was tempered with satisfaction at his achievements in the bright mechanics. Most children of high birth received some instruction in the mechanics even if they would never accomplish any feat greater than extinguishing a candle. The éclat considered the study obligatory to maintain the distinction between themselves and the picayune, who could never afford the expense of tutelage in the art. Like many of the children who only saw the world of the elite from the outside, Flux had assumed the mechanics were something magical, beyond comprehension or aspiration. But once he began to grasp the art, he realized that master mechanics—adepts as they called themselves— merely understood the grammar of reality and could thus, to varying degrees, manifest their thoughts physically.

***

Staring blankly across the gray-green hills beyond Skye Redan, Flux breathed deep the scent of winter. The smoke in the air reminded him of his days in Telluria. Without sight to enforce a sense of place, his memory too often whisked him elsewhere.

Below him, he could hear Wren and Ouzel laughing as they cleared the brush just beyond the great curtain wall surrounding Skye Redan. Before he had been quarantined, they were his only friends. He waved in their direction, but heard no response.

From behind, he heard the Cardinal's voice. "Kame Sirocco tells me you are making excellent progress. I am pleased to return home to such news."

Skye emerged from the door of the south tower and approached.

"I endeavor to earn the favor you have bestowed upon me, éclat," Flux answered.

"I am sure you will."

"Éclat, may I ask you a question?"

"You may always ask."

"Can you see the future?"

"No, nor would I, had I the choice."

"You would not want to know?"

"Not knowing defines us. It is that which is most essential. It is that which separates us from the gods."

"But among the picayune there are men claiming to be adepts who will tell your fortune, by stars and entrails."

The Cardinal laughed. "There are pretenders everywhere."

"But that is wrong, to lie to people."

"Aye, but it is wrong to be gullible, too. Each of us wishes for certainty, and so we are willing to believe, but certainty is even more pernicious than doubt. Certainty is death. It is another word for the end. Those blind to the bright mechanics fear us because we embrace possibilities and are stronger for it."

The Cardinal fell silent for a moment, then continued.

"When I was your age, there was a beggar who claimed to be an adept. He lived on the streets, and I saw him frequently on my way to and from my lessons. He performed a variety of tricks for those who passed by, earning a marginal living thus. He was young and full of energy then, always waving his arms and gesturing wildly. As an accomplished student of the mechanics, I resented this fake. It seemed obvious to me that he used sleight of hand and misdirection to perform his tricks, but the others who gathered to see him perform seemed genuinely astonished. One day, I decided to expose him as a fraud. Each time he would make a coin disappear, or produce a piece of candy from midair, I pointed out how he did it. 'It's in his other hand,' I would shout, or 'Look in the fold of his sleeve!' Eventually—and it did not happen overnight—his audience stopped coming. People who used to stop and find amusement in his act would pass him by. 'How pathetic,' they would say, and soon he became thus. A few months later, as I passed by him, he beckoned me toward him. He gestured for me to come closer still. Though I was afraid, I leaned over to hear him speak, and he whispered in my ear, 'You are a thief, and while no law will convict you, you will pay for what you have done.'"

Skye paused for a moment, then added, "After that day I never saw the beggar again, but I hear him still, in silent moments."

Flux felt a strange empathy toward the Cardinal, indentured by shame to this beggar. The embarrassment he felt toward his vagrant father had left him with a similar debt.

12

Arm's Length

A true sword must be straight, as stands a man. In measure
its crossguard shall be to the blade length as the height of a
man is to the width of his shoulders, for blade and man are
one and each is incomplete without the other. As a man
draws a line to his past, so shall a sword draw a line to his
future, in blood conceived and in blood destroyed, in flesh
giver of life and death.

–The Book of the True Sword

999, Year of the Chameleon, Under Draco
Winter was beginning to turn bitter. Rose could feel the temperature
dropping as Bright Halo hid her warmth behind the Sere Mountains.
She would reach Tajo an hour or two after dark, and it would be none

too soon, though she dearly loved the majesty of the jagged peaks, their silence and strength.

Though she was a small woman, she possessed fierce determination and endurance. Being without the faculty of speech, she articulated herself physically, athletically. Since fleeing her life with Ordinal Fin, she had come to believe that traveling was a means of self-improvement as much as an outlet for frustration or the occupation of high Cast fugitives. In the end, the life of a wanderer agreed with her because she had nothing else.

While trudging along the crest of a forested ridge, parallel to the Tajo road and discreetly out of sight, Rose began to feel dizzy. She recognized the sensation as the symptom of a chronic heart irregularity that had been with her as long as she could remember. She knew it was not life threatening—a minor biological protest, as Gauss had once reassured her—but she stopped and waited for the feeling to pass.

To her right, on the side of the ridge that descended away from the road, Rose noticed the prone figure of a traveler at the edge of a frozen pond. The body was partially covered by snow. She glanced about warily. Seeing nothing but trees, snow, and brush, she opted to investigate further once her heartbeat returned to its typical rhythm.

Once she descended the precarious slope to the edge of the pond, she saw the corpse more clearly. The woman's clothes were unremarkable and gave no indication of her identity, beyond suggesting, by way of her thin raiment, that she was someone with a high tolerance for cold. The body lay face down, encased in ice up to the waist, splayed legs protruding onto shore like the antennae of some giant crustacean exploring the land for the first time.

The absence of any predator's tracks led Rose to believe that the woman had died naturally at the water's edge and then had become frozen in the ice. Then she noticed a ragged gash in the dead woman's neck. Since the corpse had not been looted, she guessed the woman had escaped her assailants, only to succumb to her injury later. As Rose turned to go, a sparkle of green from beneath the ice caught her eye.

Brushing the irregular patches of snow from the hard surface of the pond just beyond the dead woman's head, Rose discovered a sword frozen in the ice. It appeared to be a long sword, with an emerald the size of a human eye set in the pommel.

Though Rose lacked the piety of a celebrant, she offered thanks to Wild Brand for such unexpected fortune. Having abandoned her sword in Sarcos over a week ago after a melee with the factors of the Verifex, she desperately needed a new blade. Her reputation precluded purchasing a replacement in the city. She knew she would not find a licensed metalworker until she reached a town with a military presence, like Tajo.

After twenty minutes of chipping at the ice with her skinning knife, Rose exposed the frozen sword. She withdrew it tenderly from its glassy cradle, a slender weapon at once silver and black, with a simple leather-wrapped hilt and crossguard. It reminded her of the great broadswords that stood throughout the land. She slid it into her scabbard, which had been empty since the incident at The Jovial Inn. The sword was thinner than her previous blade, but it fit well enough.

The shadows deepened about her, spilling nighttime ink over the trees. In darkness, she continued onward.

***

High in the hills guarding one of the three northern passes between Sarcos and neighboring Nevta, the desolate town of Tajo saw few visitors and fewer diversions. Escape from the harsh winter wind could be found only in the confines of a tavern.

Rose shivered. Despite her long cloak, her fitted cuirass, and several other layers of clothing, the cold air insinuated itself into her skin. She made her way to the nearest tavern, the thought of a crackling fire driving her on. The packed snow on the street muffled her brisk footfall, leaving the rhythmic clicking of her scabbard against her leg unaccompanied except for the occasional roof groaning under its burden of snow.

With her newfound sword at her side and her short hair tucked into her hood, she seemed but another man seeking shelter. She received no more than a passing glance from the red-faced soldiers in The Night's Rest.

Through the smoke-filled air, weapons and shields adorning the tavern walls glowed orange in reflected fire. The low ceiling proved a constant hazard for the taller patrons, and the oak columns supporting the uneven roof provided an additional obstacle for the unwary.

Rose welcomed the sweaty heat of the tavern. She settled into a chair vacated only moments before, beside a gaping fireplace where a boar was blackening on a spit.

Weaving through teetering soldiers, a cherubic boy made his way toward Rose, who gestured at a mug of steaming hard cider being nursed by a slouching man at the next table. The boy nodded and turned toward another patron tugging at his apron.

A tall, conspicuously presentable man had been staring at Rose since she entered. The obviousness of his glance seemed calculated to invite a response, but Rose was in no mood to socialize. Unfortunately, her efforts to remain oblivious to his gaze ensured she would not notice the heavyset soldier stumbling toward the bar and her interposing feet. She did, however, notice him fall.

The firelight and shadow flickering across the soldier's flushed face did not hide his displeasure. Rose offered her hand to help him up, though she doubted she could lift him upright.

"Fool!" the heavy man bellowed. He struggled to his feet, refusing Rose's hand. Grabbing an empty tankard from a wobbly, ale-soaked table, he hurled it toward her. She watched the ill-aimed missile strike a bystander's head, sending the unfortunate man sprawling on the floor, unconscious.

Rose saw the bystander's many friends reach for their weapons, as did the companions of the soldier she'd tripped. A predictable response, at least, she thought.

Undeterred by the threatened escalation of hostilities, Rose's persecutor lunged at her, only to find her much quicker than his inebriated assessment had suggested.

Ducking and rolling to the side among a tangle of bodies and chairs, Rose convulsed in silent amusement as her adversary slammed into the wall where she had just stood. She stifled her smile as best she could, fearful of drawing attention to herself. Then someone grabbed her from behind, pinioning her arms and crushing the wind from her lungs.

"Salt, I have him," a man shouted in her ear.

Dazed from his encounter with the wall, Salt took a moment too long to strike. Snapping her neck backward, Rose slammed her head into her captor's face, breaking his nose and dislodging her helm. Free again, she wasted no time in delivering a vicious kick to Salt's groin while deftly catching her tumbling helm.

Rose's well-placed boot elicited a howl, and Salt fell to the ground once again.

Replacing her helm, Rose looked for a way out of the melee raging throughout the tavern.

Salt, whose one arguable virtue was persistence, stood unsteadily and drew his sword, his fleshy face aquiver with rage.

Seeing the flash of steel, Rose turned her attention back to Salt. She pointed at him, then drew her finger across her throat. Unsure whether Salt understood her, she repeated the gesture.

Salt burst into laughter and roared, "A mute wench!"

Silence returned to the tavern and the storm of clashing blades dispersed. Throughout the room, men in the midst of hacking, punching, and kicking each other suddenly found time to turn and gape, as if they had never seen a woman.

Rose reached for her sword.

Salt was almost upon her. His iron-shod boots crushed the already bruised bodies of prone brawlers, whose bellows heralded his advance. Those onlookers still standing stumbled over themselves in their haste to give the two combatants room.

Rose adjusted her grip on the hilt. Her new sword felt strangely warm. She would have to word her warnings more sharply to get through to this idiot. She held her blade low to mollify her adversary—or, if that did not work, to strike underneath his guard.

As if to be certain his attack was anticipated, Salt grunted as he lashed out at Rose's neck. His blow was high, as she had expected. In a lightning-fast parry, Rose whipped her sword up from her side, striking her opponent's blade and sending it whistling harmlessly overhead.

With a sudden downward sweep, she caught Salt overextended, severing his hand at the wrist.

Everything went white for a moment. A torrent of visions inundated her mind, as if she were drowning in Salt's memories. Countless scenes of battling soldiers crowded her thoughts, gore punctuated by odd moments of serenity. Vignettes of smiles and subjugation came in waves, breaking down her identity as they crashed in her head. The tide of Salt's life had been ebbing constantly from the moment of his troubled birth, out past the flotsam of his aspirations into the present, where a pool of blood collected upon the floor.

Through his clouded eyes, Rose saw herself and recognized the likenesses of fears and angers that pointed the way to her own past. You were warned, she thought, and for a moment understanding passed between them. This strange empathy faded as her mercurial sword attempted to reorient itself in her hand as might a dowser's rod.

Overwhelmed, Rose felt as if she'd grabbed a serpent by the tail. She thought to hurl the blade away, but her arm would not obey her wishes. Her hand tightened around the handle instead.

Salt stood there in shock, his blood draining away, unable to find quite the right words for the moment.

Rose knew Salt's comrades would be upon her as soon as they gathered their wits about them. She slipped into the kitchen, past a startled cook whose grease-stained clothes and dirt-caked nails matched the curious odor of his food, and out the back door into the snow.

Threading the back alleys of Tajo, away from The Night's Rest, Rose missed the cloak she'd left behind. It wouldn't take long for the cold to kill. Behind her, she could hear the dull footfall of someone in pursuit. The weather made running all but absurd. She turned, still breathing heavily. This would be as good a place as any. The narrowness of the street would prevent encirclement. She slipped into the shadows, hoping her chattering teeth wouldn't give her away before she could strike. Her sword shifted in her hand of its own accord, as if it were testing her. It reminded her of the gyro Gauss had given her in her youth, the way it resisted her movements.

"Éclat?" The sound of the voice died quickly, muted by the snow.

Rose cocked her head to one side. Someone had recognized her. Her mind raced, trying to recall the faces in the tavern. No one could have tracked her to Tajo in the storm. A chance encounter with a bounty hunter?

"Éclat?" The man had a rusty sort of voice. "I can see your breath hanging in the air. Hear me out. My sword is sheathed."

Around the corner of the alley stepped the tall man Rose had noted earlier in the tavern. He moved into the light spilling from a half-shuttered window, his hands visibly empty. His stern, weathered face marked him as a woodsman, or at least not a member of the timorous garrison so grateful for the walls surrounding this forsaken town. His drab olive and brown clothes had a studied plainness, though his pale blue eyes and round face had a certain boyish innocence.

Rose advanced, her sword leaping like the tongue of a snake to rest just inches from the neck of the startled man. Her aggressiveness surprised her, for she had made a successful habit of allowing her opponents to move first. She tried to retreat but instead slipped and fell, indignant.

Her sword stirred, as if slowly waking from a long slumber. She felt for a moment more endangered by her own hand than by the man standing before her in the alley.

"Éclat," the man ventured with some delicacy. "I mean you no harm. I know you to be Ordina Rose of Fin Redan. I served your late husband briefly. Perhaps you do not remember me. My name is Calx."

He smiled slightly and bowed, offering his wrist.

Rose regarded Calx coldly. He did look familiar. She beckoned, that he might explain further.

"Your reputation precedes you, éclat," Calx said as he glanced over his shoulder. "I am not looking to carve out a name by dueling you. In fact, I believe you were poorly used by Ordinal Fin. But what care you for my thoughts? I am no one."

Rose looked about impatiently.

"There are six or seven men coming after you. I would be honored if you would accept my help."

Rose smiled wryly and shook her head, unwilling to take up with a stranger despite their tenuous association.

Calx held a hand up and listened. The sound of voices. "This is hardly the time to argue, éclat. I know of a cave no more than two hours' march from here. Though I have little to offer you besides the cloak you left behind and my companionship, I think I offer better than you would find at the hands of Ordinal Amber's men."

Rose knew well that Amber had been a friend of her late husband. He would be no friend to her. For Calx's benefit, she counted out seven on her fingers. Too many for the two of them. Full of weariness, she nodded to Calx, though she remained uncomfortable with the idea of following this man, of whom she knew so little. True, she had seen him before, and perhaps that tipped the scales in his favor. The gratitude engendered by his retrieval of her cloak went a long way toward allaying her suspicions.

***

Well after midnight, Rose's doubts were wide awake. Struggling through the snow, hurrying after a man she could barely claim to know, she couldn't help thinking that she went willingly to her doom. The flickering light from luxes atop the perimeter towers of Tajo had long since been devoured by the swarm of snowflakes that filled the icy night sky and bit mercilessly at her exposed skin. With little chance of finding her way back alone, and considerable ambivalence about returning, she turned her thoughts toward keeping her footing.

A few feet ahead and almost out of sight, Calx kicked through the knee-deep snow, glancing back on occasion to reassure both himself and Rose, though without much success so far as either of them was concerned.

In the red flare of his magnesium torch that sputtered and hissed defiantly against the blizzard, Calx's face looked flushed and waxy, like the work of a drunken embalmer. It was a grim vision of their mutual future if shelter could not be found.

Again and again, Rose's thoughts returned to her sword, hanging impatiently at her side. It reminded her of the dogs Gauss always had around, willful and infectiously exuberant. Though she could not recall their names, she remembered that she did not get along well with them.

Rose drew her sword without realizing what she was doing.

Calx glanced back, but said nothing.

Even in the dim light of the flare, Rose could tell her sword was a thing of great beauty, in a deceptive sort of way. The simple design of the blade belied the weapon's power. It grew warm in her gloved hand, its weight shifting slightly, as it attuned itself to her mind.

Lights danced around her head, and she remembered things she had never experienced. The memories came so fast, as if she were falling through them. Some were Salt's, and many belonged to others, though it seemed not to matter, as they all became hers, fighting, screaming, laughing, loving. Adrenaline drunk, she felt as if she was losing her sense of self, and that made her afraid. Having always been separated from others by her inability to speak, the erosion of the borders of her individuality was an act of war.

She fought as she never had before. She fought upstream against the torrent of images, trying to get to the source. The water was so cold, like the snowstorm around her. Just before she blacked out, she saw a boy, dirty blonde, the million dreams of the night sky imprisoned within his eyes. His death would set them free.

***

Rose awoke to the pungent odor of burning pine, confused as to her whereabouts. She lay on Calx's cloak beside a small fire that sighed and popped, protesting the dampness of its tinder. Above her, thin streamers of smoke drifted leisurely up toward the ceiling of a cave. The last thing she recalled was tramping through the snow with Calx. She smiled thinly, pleased that her skepticism about their chances of finding shelter had been unwarranted. But her goodwill faded when she realized she'd been stripped to her undergarments.

On the opposite side of the fire, her emerald green tunic, her cuirass, and the remainder of her wardrobe were hung to dry on a large tree branch that evidently had donated several limbs for kindling.

A glance around the cave confirmed Calx was nowhere to be found. The presence of his backpack and his own patched cuirass, though hardly suitable proxies on which to vent her anger, at least suggested he planned to return.

Rose dressed quickly. The comfortable warmth of her raiment's proved a potent advocate for Calx's actions, though not quite enough to thaw the icy reprimand forming in her mind.

Cinching her goatskin belt around her slender waist, she noticed how lightly her scabbard hung. Her sword was gone, and she remembered casting it into the snow. Perhaps she had gone mad. She bit her lower lip, as she tended to do when nervous. She felt profoundly alone.

Rose retrieved one of the few remaining torches from Calx's pack and pulled the ignition cord, flooding the mouth of the cave with diffuse ruby light. She made her way around the corner that sheltered the interior chamber from the wind and up the small incline to the mouth of the cave.

The snow had not let up. Knowing it was foolish to look for her sword, Rose marched calmly into the blizzard, all the while feeling her actions had already happened and therefore could not be changed.

Rose's short red hair gathered ice as she struggled through the unrelenting storm. Though the snow had hidden her tracks, she knew where she was going. She could hear her sword calling out in her mind.

After several minutes of excruciating exposure, she saw it. The sword stood upright in the snow. Faint wisps of electricity played over its surface, giving the blade an otherworldly halo against the bleak horizon. It looked almost human, its vaguely plaintive crossguard stretched out—as arms might be—for an embrace, under the watchful eye of its emerald-inset pommel.

Rose wasted no time retrieving the blade, which seemed strangely pleased. She sheathed the weapon and retraced her footsteps even as they vanished under new snow.

**

Some minutes later, Calx returned with a dead snow hare to find his companion gone. Thoroughly annoyed and, though he wouldn't admit it, even a bit disappointed that his timely, well-provisioned return would bring no grateful embrace, he swore off the company of women henceforward. He recanted his oath a while later, when the aroma of roasting meat had lifted his spirits. He recalled how many times he had foresworn himself where women were concerned.

The fire had burned low, too long untended, and the hare was slow to cook. Calx occupied himself with a more thorough examination of the cave. He noted wax drippings amid the slush just inside the mouth of the cave, where one might choose to observe the exterior hillside from concealment.

The splattered wax confused him. Candles were common in civilized areas but impractical for travelers. Calx glanced once more out into the storm, not wanting to accept his overly pessimistic assessment of Rose's chances. He then turned his attention toward the dark recesses of the cave.

The possibility that someone might dwell here proved unsettling enough to warrant donning his armor again. Calx had learned of the cave some ten winters past when, as a new recruit, he was assigned to the garrison at Tajo, lacking sufficient funds or family influence at the time to secure a more comfortable posting. Back then, border skirmishes with the eclectics were more frequent. During one particularly savage raid, he and nine others on his patrol had been caught outside the walls, and had managed to escape capture only through the providential discovery of this cave.

Following the retreat of the eclectic raiders, one member of Calx's patrol had inexplicably vanished. Given the siege mentality of the soldiers at the time, prosaic explanations were abandoned in favor of some mysterious, lurid demise.

One particular suggestion, put forth by a beardless youth whom Calx distrusted for his uncanny luck, proved quite worrisome: the eclectics had kidnapped the lost soldier for their perverted rites. Though the worship of Urizen was punishable by death in Sarcos, rumors persisted that the eclectics operated in the northlands, where metal could still be found and where the mountains offered a place to hide.

Weighing his chances at the hands of the eclectics against Rose's in the storm and finding little hope in either, he sighed, drew his sword, and advanced cautiously down the slick incline that led deeper underground. True to his memory of the place, the glistening, water-worn passage seemed uncomfortably reminiscent of some great beast's throat.

After several hundred feet, the tunnel narrowed to end abruptly at a ledge overlooking a seemingly bottomless abyss. The chasm was terrifying in its magnitude. Among the Pelagines, such a place would be revered as one of Ekal's many wounds. Calx held a more circumspect view of theology, which explained why he had not risen quickly in the Caballine Azure, among whom independent thinking was regarded as something chronic but treatable.

Peering down into the blackness, Calx postulated that his lost comrade from many winters past probably took one step too many. The hissing flame of his torch leaned toward the same conclusion, caught in the insistent caress of wind rushing down into the deep. He kicked a pebble and watched it drop silently into the darkness. After several seconds, he remained unsure whether he had heard it hit bottom. Peering down, he saw what seemed to be a series of metal bars protruding from the chasm wall, possibly a crude ladder of some sort.

There was a rusted iron ring hanging from the roof of the cave, just beyond the ledge. He concluded that the ring had served to affix a cord or pulley, and promptly returned to the mouth of the cave to retrieve the rope with which he always traveled.

13

Skye Redan

In her ninth year of service, any Mere of Ekal aspiring to the
rank of Limnal must complete the Goddess' Labor. To
honor the nine months in which Ekal created the world,
the aspirant must weave a tapestry three times her height by
three times her height using silk dyed with her blood.

—The Doctrine Epistle

While the snow-dimmed twilight peered in through splendid stained-
glass windows, Cardinal Skye approached from the far end of the Great
Hall to greet Limnal Dahlia, summoned six days past on the first day of
the penultimate year of the millennium. He walked slowly, as was his
habit. He was in all things deliberate, and those who had known him
for any length of time came to expect his obsessive nature. A long robe

of blue and black swirled around him, leaving only his sharp, pale face visible atop his high-collared sark.

At the foot of the grand staircase, the woman he once loved waited.

"Take your time, Skye," Dahlia teased. "I have been conversing with the ghosts of the stonemasons who built your home. They are wondering why you mock them by submerging their work in darkness."

"The shadows conjure such flattery as honesty forbids," Skye answered. "And I, for one, would see you well flattered."

Dahlia caressed the silk tapestry hanging on the wall. Pursing her lips in disapproval, she traced the intricate design with the tip of her finger.

"The shadows are poor fakirs when it comes to lovers, or artifacts of such renown. This is the Labor of Limnal Myx. It has been missing from the Pelage at Vejas for many months."

"Has it indeed? Three men died that it might hang again where it belongs. I will perhaps make it a gift to you."

"A gift, or an inducement?" Dahlia spoke softly, but her voice had an edge, as if she feared that the arduous recovery of the artifact would require a similar feat in return.

Reaching the foot of the stairway, Skye paused to appraise the woman standing by his tapestry. Beneath the cascade of darkness, Dahlia's coal-black hair seemed to bleed into infinity. She was still as stunning as ever, porcelain skin and defiant eyes.

Skye walked slowly to greet his guest. She extended her right hand, palm open to the sky.

"I hope the storm did not inconvenience you?" inquired Skye, resentful of Dahlia's defensive formality.

"It is not for me to find a manifestation of Endless Gard inconvenient. He and Ekal weathered a great tempest once without complaint, on the island of Largo. The sacred dreams depict houses in the air, and cows flying. I had only snow with which to contend."

"If you traveled all this way only for me, I would die a happy man. But you want news of the Aver."

Dahlia smiled. "I have waited nine moons to hear how he fares. Though the Thalass grows impatient, I can wait a few minutes more for the sake of civility."

Skye nodded. "Indeed, there is a proper way to do things." She stamped her boots to shake off the remaining snow and let the damp hood of her cloak slip to her shoulders.

Skye helped Dahlia with her cloak, his hands resting on her shoulders a moment longer than necessary. "Nine moons? Has it been so long?"

"A child might be conceived and born in that span."

"What do you mean by that?"

Dahlia laughed. "My dear Cardinal, you look ashen. I merely muse at what might have been."

Skye smiled. A chance comment, nothing more. "Have some wine with me before you retire," he said. "The Seneschal will see to your belongings."

***

Since Skye seldom danced, he had converted the ballroom into a library. It was a splendid, massive wood-paneled room with vaulted ceilings, elaborate frescoes, and more books than any other private library in Sarcos, some worth more than the entire redan. The room smelled of books. They were everywhere—piled on tables, locked in cabinets, wedged onto shelves—unbound manuscripts, sheaves of crumbling parchment, and scrolls curled like dry leaves.

As if an army of fishermen dangled lures overhead, hundreds of silver disks, so beloved during the Dim Age, served as ceiling reflectors for an array of luxes. These globes of phosphorescent liquid made the room seem as if it were underwater. Their primary virtue, however, was that they would not start a fire. As Dahlia knew well, Skye feared outliving his books more than anything.

"Little has changed," Dahlia remarked. Only in Skye Redan did time stand still. It was part of the charm of the place. She settled into a leather chair, cracked and worn to such an extent that a palmist might read its future.

"You are kind to say so." Skye sat too, though he did not look relaxed. "My motives for inviting you to our celebration of the New Year are not entirely selfless."

"So I guessed. Celebrants are not so scarce in these parts that you need to bring one all the way from Sansiso. But I am pleased you wish me to bear news of the Aver to the Thalass."

"It is the least I could do for you, Dahlia. It was you who first saw the reveille all those years ago. Tell Her Eminence that the boy is out of danger and will shortly be well enough to appear before the Council."

Dahlia beamed. "That is wonderful news, Skye. The word among the éclat is that he died."

"You know I would not allow that. He was near death for many months. But he is out of danger."

"Perhaps Ekal heard our prayers after all," Dahlia said, as if to convince herself.

"There is other news I would discuss of perhaps more immediate importance. As we speak, Cardinal Auric is approaching my lands with a thousand fusileers."

"Auric intends to besiege you?"

"He believes the boy dead." Skye reached over to a silver tray and decanted wine for the two of them. "Reliable spies are so hard to come by."

Dahlia savored the tannic bouquet. The grapes from Scoria were among the best. "I suppose he is in for a surprise when he arrives, if the boy truly is the Aver."

Skye leaned forward in his creaking chair. "Do you have doubts after seeing him make the Ascension?"

Dahlia looked down into her glass at her shifting reflection. "I have more doubts than I know what to do with."

"That was why I asked the Thalass to send you. The approval of a skeptic will advance our cause."

"Even if he is the Aver, many will resist his elevation. The people find comfort in their lack of dreams."

"Why not judge for yourself?"

***

The halls of Skye Redan grew increasingly narrow toward the top of the west wing. The Cardinal explained that the recently built upper floors had been designed with thicker walls to withstand bombardment from black-powder weapons. The lower floors relied on curtain walls and the height of surrounding trees for protection.

Dahlia had heard it all before, years ago, and knew that his thoughts were elsewhere. Small talk was a sign of some preoccupation.

"You are repeating yourself, Skye." She enjoyed impugning his mental acuity. It always provoked him. "You told me that story before."

Breathing heavily, Skye stopped just before the landing and grinned. "Did I? Well, there's nothing wrong with a little repetition."

"You and I, we make the same mistakes again and again," she said ruefully. She read desire in his smile.

He continued the last few steps. "We are creatures of habit. You with your endless iterations of prayer, me with my elaborations."

Such things his look promised. Yet, she remained uncertain. Better that she should lock her door tonight than leave it open to regret. She turned away and surveyed the corridor, full of closed doors.

At the end of the passage, a lone sentry stood bathed in red chemical light. He was an adept, with short sword, long coat, and loose clothes. A talented apprentice, no doubt, to be so trusted. He stood at attention at Skye's approach. With a nod from the Cardinal, he unlocked the door.

Within the modest chamber slept a boy. His mouth was open, his wool blanket pulled up to his chin. Beside him, the glow of a spherical lux leaked out from under the black dampening cloth.

"He is dreaming," Skye whispered. "See how his eyes move?"

Dahlia crept closer, fascinated. "What do you suppose he sees?"

"We will know soon enough. He dreams our future."

Skye led Dahlia out and the sentry locked the door behind them. As they retraced their steps, the Cardinal remarked, "Do you worry that we will be changed by his dreams?"

"I am certain we will be changed. I hope for the better."

14

Visitation

The distinction between reality and experience and vision and dream cannot truly exist, for many speak with undisputed authority on subjects known only through a glance or a word. A mother seeing her child suffer may herself suffer as much. The revelation of a god to a celebrant may be tangible or illusion or dream, yet of immeasurable power regardless. Indeed, falsehood weaves as strong a tapestry as truth and is often more compelling.

—The Madness of Mere Fiona

Dahlia dreamed she awoke that night to the sound of someone in her room. She sat up beneath the sagging velvet canopy and looked around. Though she was alone, something felt wrong. She removed the black cloth covering the lux on her night table. The flood of warm light did not reveal anything unexpected.

Holding one of the bedposts as she stood, she walked across the faded geometry woven into the prayer rug that covered the floor. She sat at the vanity and stared into the mirror at her blank face. She thought it strange that she would have no features, for surely she had a nose and eyes and a mouth. Fumbling for her makeup, she drew her absent features on with her fingers. She had trouble remembering just how she looked, so she glanced back over her shoulder at the bed, where she slept still. But she was not sleeping, even if she knew she was. Instead, she saw herself sitting on the bed. It seemed that she had two reflections, one in the mirror and one behind her on the bed. Yet the woman sitting behind her wasn't a reflection, for when Dahlia faced forward, toward the mirror, that was her reflection, and no one appeared behind her. Facing the opposite direction had to be something else, the genuine Dahlia—except that, being that person herself, the woman on the bed could not also be her. She dared not admit to the existence of a second Dahlia. She felt her own legitimacy too tenuous already.

Try as she might, she could not draw her own features accurately without looking over her shoulder. In so doing, she caught the second Dahlia looking back at her for a similar reference. How will I ever be complete, she thought, if each of us copies the other? Then, for a moment, she saw that her fingers had become little swords, and she found that she could carve her features properly, though in so doing she bled.

Dahlia awoke with a start, terrified and wishing she was not alone in bed. Having never dreamed before, she remained uncertain she had truly dreamed at all. Only the Aver dreamed. He was the only living star. By gray glass and by muscarine, she had seen the moving pictures of Stardome, but that was her vocation—to screen, to interpret the dreams handed down from the Dim Age. Not to have dreams of her own.

After a few minutes, knowing she would be unable to go back to sleep, she rose from her bed. She wrapped her silk blanket around her shoulders and slipped out of her room. Descending the stairs where she had waited for the Cardinal only a few hours earlier, she returned to the library. To her exasperation, she found the door locked. Desperate for something to occupy her, she headed for the kitchen.

Though it was a massive room intended for the preparation of feasts, Dahlia found the kitchen had a certain coziness lacking in the Cardinal's more formal chambers. The solicitous smell of food, the sacks of grain in disarray, the casks of wine, and the variety of pots and pans together conveyed such a sense of chaos that she felt welcome in a way that had escaped her while she was in more ordered areas of the redan.

Dahlia heated a pan of milk in the embers of the main fireplace, which was large enough to hold a bear standing on its hind paws. When a thin skin formed on the milk, she added powdered chocolate, then stirred the mixture until it resembled brown liquid velvet, twice adding a pinch of nutmeg. It took some searching to find a suitable flagon from which to drink her concoction. Even alone, in the dead of night, she would not sip from the pan.

Reclining on a large sack of rice, Dahlia was enjoying her hot chocolate when she heard someone enter. She turned to see Handel, aiming at her with his fusil.

"Who goes there?" Handel demanded.

"It's me, Dahlia. We've met before. Put that thing away before you hurt someone." Dahlia spoke slowly because Handel was slow. It was no fault of his own. He had taken the fire from a fulmin when an assassin ambushed Cardinal Skye on the road to Sansiso seven years past. Though he survived the encounter, his wounds were quite serious, beyond even the power of the Pelagines. Skye, however, would not allow Handel to die. At great risk to his own reputation, he secretly arranged to have Handel repaired by an eclectic who owed him a favor. Though the alterations made to Handel were illegal, no one who knew ever spoke of the matter. Skye's servants repaid the Cardinal's fierce loyalty with silence.

The hideous scarring of Handel's face deterred most questions about the incident anyway. Dahlia remembered asking Skye why he jeopardized his position by breaking the laws he was empowered to defend. "Laws are but the shadows of our principles and, as such, are frequently ill shaped. Besides, it is better to choose where I am vulnerable that I may know where to defend myself." It had been an answer that impressed her, and that led them both soon after to the same bed.

Handel regarded Dahlia with a mixture of curiosity and suspicion. Though neither his mind nor his bulky frame were particularly limber, his dark eyes filtered truth and lie with instinctive facility. "You are not an intruder."

"No, I am a guest of Cardinal Skye."

"You are a guest. I think so."

"You may stop pointing your fusil at me now."

"Yes, I think so." Handel gently slid the fusil's hammer forward to rest on the contact plate and lowered his weapon. He moved uncomfortably close, staring.

"Hot chocolate." Dahlia observed a flicker of childish delight on Handel's marred face, but a moment later it was gone, as if happiness could be recognized but not experienced.

"You are the wife of Cardinal Skye," Handel pronounced as he stood. "I did wonder where you were all this time."

Dahlia laughed and shook her head. "I think you do remember me. But I was never his wife. Merely a close friend."

"Close like us?" Handel leaned toward Dahlia. "Or closer?"

"Closer." Dahlia could see her reflection in Handel's scar-smoothed skin. His proximity made her very uncomfortable.

"Then you are the Cardinal's wife."

"No, Handel. The women of my order do not marry."

"But you married Skye. I remember."

"No, we were merely friends."

"You say I remember wrong?"

"Aye."

"I remember the great miracle that comes and that is not wrong."

"The great miracle?"

"Soon I will remember it."

"What are you talking about?"

"I am not talking. It is a secret."

"I can keep a secret. Will you tell me?"

Handel shook his head.

Dahlia stared at him, hoping to unnerve him and shake loose some clarity. "Are you talking about the reveille? Has the Aver made his dreams known to you?"

"I think I remember wrong. I think I am wrong about you. I think I do not know you. I think you are an intruder."

"Handel, go ask the Seneschal whether I am a guest."

Handel backed away, his steps as stiff as his starched uniform. "Yes, I will do that. Seneschal stays behind like me." He stared at her as if examining a painting of dubious provenance, then turned and left, bumping into a crate of melons on the way out.

Dahlia wondered whether Handel remembered himself as he was before his disfiguration. He had been a handsome young caballine from a prominent family, with a future full of promise. A worthless promise, as it turned out, redeemed far below face value; one of many such notes issued by the gods. His family and friends thought him dead, as was the Handel they remembered. No one really wanted to know how he passed his days in a strange half-life, confined to Skye Redan, for both his own and the Cardinal's protection. He would no doubt die wandering the endless corridors by night like a revenant, as if searching for his lost identity. Dahlia preferred to see it thus, since the possibility that he had achieved a state of bliss through his incapacitation reflected poorly on her own frustrated search for enlightenment.

***

Dahlia arose at dawn, having slept a fitful night, and offered her obeisance to Ekal. A steaming bath had been drawn for her in the adjoining chamber by an attentive servant and she embraced the rapture of warm water. She lay there until the water cooled, her long black hair hanging just above the mosaic floor. She thought about the many things she had planned to say to Skye that, once said in her mind, seemed less important. She could not live here now any more than she could have a decade ago.

The air was still cold despite the hot water pumped beneath the floor, and she dried herself quickly. She donned a casual dress rather than her robes of office, welcoming the brief moments when she could shed her skin and simply be a woman, without expectation or responsibility. Often, she wondered whether the enjoyment she derived from being anonymous reflected discomfort with herself or such confidence in her identity that she could casually disassemble it. No one else she knew masqueraded as one of the picayune, dressing in tatters and mingling with the lower Cast. Perhaps, she mused wryly, each and every one of the picayune was actually a man or woman of great power and influence beneath false rags, wanting to know the meaning of want. It was said among the Pelagines, albeit with as much irony as sincerity, that every beggar ought to be treated well, in case the glorious visage of a god should be revealed behind a dirty, toothless grin.

She passed silently through corridors clogged with paintings and sculptures, toward the east wing where Skye always worked at first light. Nervous servants were visible through doorways for moments at a time as they rushed to bring the redan back to life. The clangor of rattling pans heralded the imminent approach of breakfast. Outside, the stripe of sluggish gray clouds visible through the ground-floor lancet windows seemed ready to move on.

In the east wing, the conservatory door was closed. Dahlia knocked on it insistently until Skye finally emerged, releasing the pungent odor of chemicals. His pupils receded into specks in the ashen morning like stones dropped down a well. Behind him in the darkened room, a tangle of tubes, beakers, and valves lay on a worktable as if someone had allowed a madman to conduct an autopsy. Several white mushrooms with cream-colored gills lay on a tray beside a stained tome.

"Your research appears more and more eclectic," Dahlia teased.

Skye smiled. "The hallucinogens favored by my order can be easily mistaken for more harmful varieties." He stepped outside and closed the door. "Have the villagers begun to gather already?"

"Aye, on the south lawn." Dahlia regarded Skye as he shifted about on his feet uncomfortably, unusually inscrutable this morning. "Does it seem to you that your brothers have come to rely too much on chemicals? At the Redan Inviolate last week, you could not turn around without stumbling over some sprawled, glaze-eyed adept in the midst of augury."

"I cannot say I have noticed any change. Is this what you wanted to speak about?"

"Not really. I was merely curious." Dahlia shrugged, noting a certain defensiveness in his tone.

"You do not believe me."

"I cannot tell anymore, not in the way I used to. You were much easier to read then."

Skye smiled enigmatically. "Did you see Curial Dure while you were there?"

"Only briefly. He is as well as can be expected. He sends his regards."

Plucking a brown-edged leaf from a potted fern perched on the narrow ledge of a lancet window, Skye mused, "He will be gone soon, and in a strange way I envy him. When he climbs to Stardome, he will leave behind the world and its diminishing possibilities."

Dahlia sensed a great sadness in her old friend, and for the first time in many years felt that she had made the right decision in leaving him. Or was she the cause of his melancholy? "Has life become so unbearable?"

"On the contrary, it has become too precious. We hoard it like opium addicts. Life is so weighty that it deforms us, it bends our backs, it gnarls our fingers, until we resemble the beasts we have spent our lives trying to escape."

"We tend the sacred fire Bright Halo set within us—some with more fervor than others, but that is the way of things."

"Fervor and fever are reflecting fires, one of health and one of sickness. Who can tell which burns within?"

Skye reached out to touch Dahlia's face. She pulled back a bit, but not out of reach. His hands felt rough against her face. The tips of his fingers passed over her lips, light as a zephyr of breath.

He whispered, "There is nothing more precious to me than you, and I hate you for permitting me that weakness."

For a moment, Dahlia again believed they could be happy together, but something so hungered for could not but be disappointing in the end. She had chosen to serve the gods instead of a mortal, and would not drown in regret to hold Skye's head above the waterline of their tears. But her doubts followed her like vultures. They would devour her if she stopped running.

"Why do I feel as if I would cuckold the gods to lie with you?" Dahlia asked, hoping Skye would save her from herself. It would be so easy to give in.

Skye backed away, perhaps recognizing Dahlia's reticence. He turned and gazed out the window.

Dahlia followed and put her arm around him.

To the north the great pines receded down the hill, thinning when they reached Dry Creek, frozen as it usually was at this time of year. Beyond lay fallow fields, deeded to Skye when the Council granted him the rank of Cardinal. Midway to the horizon, the land grew wild again, the domain of tall grass and migratory fowl that would return when the ponds thawed. Farther into the distance stood the rough hills and vineyards of the district of Scoria, and farther still rose the Supine, named for the resemblance of the mountains to the silhouette of a woman lying on her side.

"Do you see that bird out there?" asked Skye.

After a moment, Dahlia spotted it, small and gray, hopping along one of the battlements visible from the window.

"It is a cuckoo. It survives by deception. When the female lays an egg, she seeks out the nest of some other bird. She waits until the nest is unattended, then replaces one of the absent bird's eggs with one of her own. When the other bird returns, it is none the wiser and raises the young cuckoo as its own."

"Deception is as old a stratagem as strength," Dahlia said, unable to sift any meaning from Skye's tale. He frequently used the presence of others as a pretense to speak to himself.

Skye nodded. "Older, else Ekal might never have stilled the hatred between Gard and Brand. Let us join the celebration."

15

Celebration

The First War raged long ago between Gard, the god of the sky, and Brand, the god of dreams. Until the birth of memory, the two gods battled ceaselessly, their blood filling the void around them. From this blood, Ekal, the mother of the world, formed herself and came between the warring gods. Ekal offered herself to each god in turn. She lay first with Gard, and thus begot Halo, who shines platinum bright. Then she lay with Brand, and so begot Gavo, who knows only silence and darkness.

–The Book of Creation

The pith and picayune of Downskye turned out in their best clothes. On those rare occasions when the villagers did receive an invitation to

Skye Redan, they spared no effort in mimicking the conceits of those higher in the Cast.

Yapping dogs in tow, Kyma Tessera, wife of the mayor, hid beneath her parasol, lest anyone mistake a bit of winter sun as time spent in the fields. Chuff, shaved driftwood-smooth this once, brought his prize sow on a leash and a rusted iron collar to show that he too could afford metal. Thindle, the toothless veteran, had walked all the way up from the village without aid to display his familial riches: a dozen children and several similar wives, past and present. Brazen Chalia proudly wore her gown of serpent skin and fur, along with the eyes of young men who could not believe something so well fitted could keep her warm enough.

In all, they numbered nearly fifteen hundred, perhaps a third of which were the Cardinal's lancers and general staff. They came to express their appreciation for the Cardinal's protection and to get something back for the tribute they paid.

Red-and-white striped tents, square and conical, had sprung up on the south lawn overnight, as if the process of sweeping the snow away had allowed them to bloom.

A great wooden broadsword, resembling the steel ones as much as two perpendicular logs could, stood aflame near the inner perimeter wall. Among those who knew the lore of the great swords, and perhaps unconsciously among those huddled nearby for warmth, the heat served as a reminder of the sacred emanations that had once carried dreams to the people of the Dim Age.

The day's grand entertainment was to be the ascension of a balloon and a man up into the sky as far as Endless Gard would permit.

The artificer behind the proposed stunt, Kame Mustard, had been petitioning Cardinal Skye for three years in the hope that he might demonstrate his contraption. He remained unwilling to believe that his would-be patron despised the dark mechanics, despite warnings to the contrary. When the invitation arrived a month ago, he was unprepared but energized by what he perceived to be his vindication. He had no idea he was being used.

With but an hour left to prepare, he urged on his team of seam-stresses and laborers with vocal whippings. The balloon would be ready. It had to be.

***

Into this carnival, into the smoke of pine-grilled meat and the joyous noise of flutes, rode Cardinal Auric and two dozen of his fusileers, stiff as the frozen ground.

Walking in the company of Dahlia, through the smiles of well-wishers, Cardinal Skye observed Auric and his men as they dismounted. They lingered at the perimeter of the festivities, aware how vulnerable they were while the bulk of their army waited politely at the bottom of the hill.

"Shall we go to greet Auric?" Dahlia asked.

Skye shook his head. "Let him come to us."

By noon, when everyone had eaten past contentment and the for-tune-tellers had made their predictions for the coming year, thoughts turned toward entertainment. The balloon was swelling with fired air, and many took the opportunity to compare the contraption to a puffed-up acquaintance or pompous magistrate. The villagers gathered in a loose ring around Kame Mustard in his ridiculous flight suit, eager to see whether the road to Stardome was open to those other than the dead. Many believed that the coming of the Aver heralded an exodus to the stars.

With the balloon almost fully inflated, Auric and his men approached the raised platform where Skye and Dahlia and assorted hangers-on sat. The two Cardinals exchanged rote pleasantries, neither willing to let their rivalry poison the day. Dahlia too was all smiles, though she reminded herself that her first duty was to Pelage and Thalass.

Auric looked up at the flawless sky. "You have outdone yourself with the weather, Cardinal. The storm has abated and all is well at Skye Redan."

"Adepts do not meddle with the weather," Skye explained as if speaking to a simpleton. "That is the domain of Endless Gard."

Dahlia knew how easily Auric could nettle Skye, but she also understood Skye's tactics. He would let himself be abused, insulted–whatever it took to draw his adversary out into the open. Then he would crush him.

"Perhaps I am thinking of a different reign." Auric took a seat hastily vacated by a young adept and gazed upon the revelers. "But no, no. You do protect these people. You are, more than you will admit it, a parasol for them."

"A parasol?" Skye laughed. "My dear Cardinal Auric, you are too kind. Dahlia, have you ever heard so fine a compliment? A parasol! Your imagination must be boundless, my friend, boundless." Skye sounded Auric's insecurities all too well, but then what good was an adept who could wound with thoughts but not words?

"Is it my imagination, or are there clouds forming on the horizon?" Auric had come to fight with swords, not words. But if Skye began the engagement thus, he would not yield. After all, he still had his army.

The balloon stood ready, straining at the ropes that held it down. With a few waves from Kame Mustard, the Seneschal nodded to Cardinal Skye and said, "The contraption is ready."

"Let them begin," Skye said before turning back toward Auric.

"Cardinal Auric," Dahlia interrupted. "I believe you mistake your caballines for clouds. I see only soldiers on the horizon. If you come to besiege Skye Redan, you jeopardize the Cabal's relationship with the Pelagines."

Auric laughed. "And you jeopardize your profits. The Cabal will modernize with or without the Pelagines. There are other sources of metal."

"Not sanctified metal."

"Perhaps tainted metal works just as well." Auric grinned smugly.

Dahlia glanced at Skye, appalled that Auric would suggest something so profane, but found her friend unmoved, staring instead at the balloon.

"This fellow, Kame Mustard, seems quite a capable artificer," Skye observed. "I heard you offered him a commission recently, and I thought who better to demonstrate the dark mechanics than a factor of the most modern man in Sarcos."

Auric went white. "Stop the balloon!" he shouted, but his words drowned in applause.

The balloon rose. The pilot detached the tethers anchoring it to the ground and adjusted the inboard furnace, a costly bit of machinery. The hiss of the blue flame heating the air grew louder and the treated silk balloon stretched and groaned in answer. Up it went as jaws dropped.

Having spent many years in the company of an adept, Dahlia could tell when someone essayed the bright mechanics. Most adepts were easy to spot, like amateur thieves. But the good ones could conceal their elaborations, and Skye was among the best. Still, he seemed more focused than the casual observer.

Their heads craned back like newly hatched birds awaiting food, the villagers saw what Dahlia had guessed. The balloon had caught fire. Far above, the pilot's screams could be heard. The balloon descended slowly at first, a teardrop from the eye of the sun. Then the flames engulfed the balloon and it fell more quickly. The fireball roared down and struck the ground near the edge of the forest in a splash of cinders.

Auric's face burned likewise with anger. "This is your doing."

"Come now, Cardinal," Skye protested, "If you knew anything about the bright mechanics, you would realize it would be nigh impossible to elaborate over such a great distance. We were all aware of the dangers of this experiment. Sadly, my pessimism concerning the dark mechanics has once again been realized. I can only hope the weapons your soldiers wield prove more reliable, lest some catastrophe befall your men in battle."

"Your library will soon be burning, and you with it!" Auric bellowed as his bodyguards moved to interpose themselves between the two Cardinals.

Furious though Auric was, Dahlia could tell Skye's threat gave him pause. Few knew Skye's limits, and fear came to roost in the absence of understanding. If Skye could ignite the black powder in the weapons of Auric's fusileers, the siege would turn into a rout. Such a thing ought to be impossible, but the handful of great adepts could not be judged by the spoiled dilettantes who demeaned the bright mechanics.

Skye raised an eyebrow. "Take your pleasures where you may. But take my lands, and you steal from the Aver."

"Come now, Skye," Auric hissed. "The charade is over. Your Gavo's Day stunt bought you nine months, but you cannot delay the inevitable. The boy is dead, and even the Thalass cannot save you now."

"But the boy lives."

"Bah, you lie."

Dahlia shook her head. "I have seen him."

"Very well, take me to see him," Auric demanded.

"Oh, but you are too late." Skye smiled gleefully. "The Aver departed for Sansiso this very morning. He was eager to see the site of his Ascension again."

Staring coldly at Skye, Auric said nothing.

"If you wish to make war upon me, Cardinal Auric, I suggest you ask the Aver for permission. Unless you wish to forfeit your lands."

Auric scowled. "Twice now you have abused me, Skye."

"See how your Cardinal's hand is shaking?" Dahlia said to Auric's bodyguards. "You should take him somewhere warm."

Auric's men seemed to appreciate the suggestion, but looked to Auric for approval.

Auric turned without a word and stomped off, his men close behind.

"Thank you," Skye said. "You saved one of us from dying just then."

Dahlia watched Auric go, then turned to Skye for an explanation, recalling betrayals that had driven her away long ago. "Why was I not told of the Aver's departure?"

"It was a necessary deception. You will have to accept my word in this."

"I would sooner accept one of the decales with your face on it."

Skye glowered for a moment and waved to the Seneschal to indicate that he would attend to the accident momentarily. "So you have seen them too?"

"They are rather ubiquitous these days."

"Another one of Auric's ploys to discredit me," Skye muttered. "The sooner they are destroyed, the better."

"I doubt that will happen. The notes were distributed among the picayune—quite widely, from what I hear." Dahlia tried not to take too much pleasure in her old friend's dilemma and added, "To void what little the picayune have would surely cause unrest."

Skye watched his nemesis ride away. "I have a favor to ask of you, Dahlia."

"When have I ever denied you my favors?" Dahlia grinned. Though loath to admit it, she was pleased that he needed her still, after all these years. "Let us attend to the injured and speak of it after."

16

Parting

In coming together and parting, we weave the future past
that will dull the chill when Cold Gavo comes.
—The Testament of Mere Phaeo

Dahlia walked through new snow under a weary evening sun gone
shy behind the clouds. Through the ancient pines, Skye Redan stood
defiantly, at once a monument to power and a reminder of the fear that
erects such walls. To Dahlia, its five towers evinced the folly of men.
True power came from the roots and the soil, from the world, the
tangible personification of Deep Ekal. Even such a structure as this,
almost impervious to siege, splendid in construction, was as a speck of
dust in the grand design of the goddess, of forest and river, mountain
and ocean.

The fresh dusting of snow imposed an eerie silence on the wooded hill where the Cardinal made his home. Dahlia wandered along the path that snaked around the central keep and heard nothing from the usually active stables. She surmised the lancers would be out keeping an eye on Auric's men. Crossing the south lawn, only a few picayune remained, clearing the trash from the morning's celebration.

She passed a lone lancer sitting outside the shuttered barracks. He was making repairs to his saddle. He nodded politely, his fingers blue from stitching leather in the cold. She walked unchallenged through the formidable gate at the edge of the perimeter wall, and came upon a clearing with a view of the village of Downskye.

She sat for a moment on a fallen tree and looked out across the valley unfolding to the south, toward Sansiso and the sea. White smoke leaked from the freckling of homesteads, falling up into the arms of Endless Gard. It reminded her of the village in which she had been raised. She recalled awakening winter mornings on a bed of straw, wrapped in the wool blanket that had been her sister's, to the report of her father's axe splitting wood. She had always been ashamed of her mundane child-hood. She could not scrub it away, even when steeped in spirituality.

Her eyes turned toward her shadow, growing indistinct with the setting of the sun. Light shone through the weave of pine needles and not through her. She cast only an outline, a vague notion of within. She imagined it was her spiritual confusion showing through. Then a second shadow came into view beside her own.

She turned to see Cardinal Auric, clad in anonymous traveling clothes. Dull and worn like his wit, she thought, even as she scolded herself for her hardness. That was Skye's voice she heard in her head.

"I would speak with you, Limnal, before I depart," Auric said, casting a glance back at his mount, barely visible through the trees.

"You do not wear your colors? I had thought the Caballine Azure did not dissemble," Dahlia replied, sharp claws flexing in her words.

"I do not come to war. Ordinal Amber's men are on their way back to Tajo and mine are in retreat as well."

How easily the suggestion of cowardice baited him, even to the point of revealing his troop movements. "Of course, though I daresay traveling without your colors keeps you safe from ambush."

"Were I to wear my allegiance, I would no doubt be called upon by the picayune, and I have no time for their troubles at present."

Dahlia retreated into a deferential smile. "Of course. It matters not to me. Come sit and speak."

Auric complied, taking a moment to adjust his long coat.

"I understand you travel toward Vejas," he began.

"How did you come by such a notion?" Dahlia asked, astonished that he knew her plans.

Auric fidgeted with the piping on his coat, as if embarrassed by his drab costume. "Limnal, I do not possess so deft a tongue as your host, perforce I must be direct." He paused, weighing his words as carefully as if each were a newborn.

Dahlia found Auric's trepidation as calculated as his dress. "Speak your mind, éclat. A woman in my position knows well the need for discretion."

"Will the Pelagines support a war against the eclectics?"

Direct, indeed, she thought, like an untutored lover. "I do not know. The eclectics will not bear the persecution of the adepts and the Curia for much longer. There may not be an alternative."

"No, nor would many in the Cabal look for one. Even those who prefer the eclectics to the adepts see the profit of war."

Dahlia nodded, knowing too well that Auric and his allies were eager for a pretext to demonstrate the power of the dark mechanics. At least he is honest, she thought. "The Pelagines stand to gain from a conflict as well. In such times, people remember how much they need the favor of the gods."

"In such times, people remember how much they need metal from Pelagine mines."

Dahlia smiled despite herself. Skye and Auric, she thought, were more alike than they would admit. "I seem to recall you disapprove of our cartel."

Auric rose and paced awkwardly over the icy ground before replying. "How much does it cost to purify one steel ingot?"

"I am not certain."

"A considerable amount? Nine times melted and reforged? A blessing for each new moon over nine months? The expenses of portage, of storage?"

"The taint of Urizen runs deep," Dahlia said indignantly. "You have seen the sickness spread by unclean metal, what it does to the skin."

Auric clenched his jaw. "There are other ways, known by the eclectics."

Dahlia drew back her black hair, that Auric might better see the anger in her eyes. "You look but do not see. When Urizen returns to the world, he will come through eyes like yours, eyes that see all things as equal." Though she spoke with authority, she feared her words sounded hollow.

Auric held up his hands to calm Dahlia. "I am no friend of the eclectics, but one need not abandon one's humanity to appreciate the work of artificers. They are doing things in their hidden foundries that put adepts to shame. Did you know that the output of the Albion mill has risen tenfold since the Council of Hierophants permitted the installation of a steam engine? Six thousand bushels of flour a week."

Dahlia restrained her temper, knowing that she would benefit more from hearing Auric out. "I had heard something to that effect. In opposing it, the adepts stand to lose a great deal of support among the éclat."

"Think of the wealth that would come to Sarcos if we took a more enlightened view of the dark mechanics. We could end the ceaseless toiling of the picayune in Pelagine mines. We could bring something of Stardome to the world."

The passion in Auric's voice was clear, but Dahlia doubted his sincerity. Populism was his newest costume, worn more to distract from naked ambition underneath. Worst of all, there was an appeal of sorts to it. She had seen the young men dead from black lung, the hardscrabble shanties of tenant farmers.

"What is it you would ask of me?"

Auric grinned. "Nothing that would betray your beliefs, Limnal. Seek out the Aver and ask him of his dreams before he is confirmed. You have access that I do not. I fear Cardinal Skye has poisoned the boy against me and my allies."

Auric removed a miniature silver sword, half the length of his index finger, from his doublet. Holding it up by the delicate chain attached to the pommel, he offered it to Dahlia. "I would also ask that you give this to him. I hope it will remind him from whence he came."

From the sky, thought Dahlia, remembering his fall from the great broadsword of Sansiso. "A considerate gesture."

"A prudent one," Auric said. "So that you understand my apprecia-tion, I will have my factors draw up a contract for the purchase of some metal from your Pelage."

Dahlia nodded. Selling her influence made her uncomfortable, but refusing Auric would have put her too clearly in Skye's camp. Yet, wasn't this exactly the sort of vacillation that she mocked in Auric? Perhaps the blindfolded celebrants had the right idea.

"Tomorrow morning I make for Vejas," she said. "I will sound the Thalass concerning the Aver's disposition, and I will inform you of her thoughts when next we meet."

"I shall look for you at the Redan Inviolate when Gavo again waxes full, Limnal." Auric offered his wrist, bowed, and walked back toward his waiting mount.

Dahlia wondered whether she had become a pawn in Auric's game, or in Skye's. Perhaps it was time to pursue her own interests for a change. If only she knew what they were.

17

Flight

The blade is the universal tongue, spoken by all and well understood but with little power to sway belief. More complex forms of language allow for more delicate expression, less understood but more forceful in sculpting the mind. There must then exist a language expressing infinite possibilities, understood by none, and of infinite power. It is this language we would divine through the bright mechanics.

—The Way of the Adept

Across the white foothills, Rose heard Calx calling out, somewhere nearby. The snow muffled his voice. She followed the sound, ready for a much postponed rest and wishing for the mug of hot cider she had abandoned in the tavern. She imagined herself as the weather vane atop Fin Redan, blown this way and that by capricious winds.

She could think of no way to explain the sword or her recent actions. She would not try. The blade reminded her somehow of her father, at turns beneficent, angry, and infuriatingly enigmatic. But she did not think of it as sentient. Rather, it made her of two minds. That she should feel some emotional attachment to it seemed only natural. Perhaps there was something of Gauss in her that turned tools into totems.

She soon saw Calx standing in the mouth of the cave. He looked smaller there, as if he were the lone tooth in the maw of some wyrm from the Dim Age. She expected a reproach, even felt she deserved one, but he seemed genuinely happy to see her again.

"The two of you seem to be inseparable," Calx observed. "I have been wondering about that blade since you dismembered that man in Tajo. While I watched you take him apart, it felt as if I knew his thoughts. It was a strange experience."

Rose began to describe where she had found the sword in her language of signs.

"I do not understand your legerdemain, I'm afraid."

She shook her head in frustration. Here was the wall that had always surrounded her, through which only anger could be heard.

"May I see the blade?" he asked tentatively.

Rose pushed his outstretched hand away, but her lack of trust raked enough of a wound across his face to have her reconsider. She cautiously withdrew her sword from its scabbard and felt her pulse quicken as the blade attempted to reorient itself like a compass needle. Her eyes widened and a vision came.

She hid amid books. She saw men clearing a road six floors below, heard the cheering, saw the Aver passing in a carriage. And she was taking aim, taking seconds to take a life.

It was the memory of death in the Dim Age. It was a hint of her own. Future pain seized her muscles and she dropped to the ground, pulling Calx down with her and rolling.

A gout of fiery hatred streamed from the fulmin lance of an unseen assassin. The blast vaporized the packed snow, leaving a black scar where they had been standing.

Rose understood then the price exacted by her strange blade for carving her future into the present, into her mind and flesh. The blade translated the language of time into pain. In its strange temporal grammar, prescience came from suffering. It was the price the gods paid for their knowledge, and they did not sell at a loss.

Calx grabbed Rose's arm and dragged her to her feet and into the cave as another stream of fire struck nearby.

Struggling to her feet, she sheathed her sword, though the blade seemed displeased. She pointed outside and indicated she had seen perhaps ten enemies.

"Thank you." Calx tried to calm Rose, who slapped his hand away, unwilling to be handled like some frightened animal. "Ten of them you saw? I don't understand how we were followed."

Rose signed that they had not been followed, that their attackers were not the men who had pursued them from Tajo, but she could see she was not being understood very well. She pantomimed the figure firing at them from the ridge, weary of this childhood game that had no end.

"The garrison at Tajo would not have a fulmin lance," Calx said. He looked to Rose for an answer.

Rose knelt and wrote the word "eclectics" in the muddy cavern floor.

"If you are right, we are in great danger."

Rose pointed back toward the mouth of the cave. She studied the area, looking for the narrowest section of the passage to defend.

Calx shook his head. "It would be foolish to stand against ten, more so if they come armed with fulmins."

He headed deeper into the cavern. "If memory serves, there is another way out."

The pair moved as rapidly as the treacherous floor allowed. Snatching the hare from the spit, Calx wrapped it in a greasy cloth and stuffed it into his backpack. He grabbed his cuirass and, juggling his torch, they arrived at the ledge where Calx had stood not long before. The rope he had affixed to the ring trailed down from the ceiling to a coil at the edge of the chasm.

She rolled her eyes, doubtful of her guide's sanity.

"There is a ladder below, or part of one at least. It will be only a short climb. There is a river at the bottom that emerges on the south side of the hills. If we can reach it, we should be able to make our escape." Calx gestured at the rope.

Rose bit at her lower lip and wondered how she had let herself get trapped like this. Trust had too high a price.

"We appear to have few choices." Calx adjusted his leather gloves, wary of losing his grip.

Rose inched toward the edge of the chasm and peered into the abyss. She shook her head.

"Of course you can." Calx glanced back up the tunnel. "They will find us shortly, and they seem in no mood to parley."

He grabbed a large stone, fastened it to the free end of the rope, and threw it into the chasm. The rope snaked from its tight coil and gyrated into the darkness below, to the hiss of rope against glove.

The rock reached the limits of its tether without striking ground or water.

Rose looked at her companion and sighed.

Then came the rattle of soldiers and their equipment.

"Bright Halo protect us," said Calx.

Rose waved Calx out of the way, but he did not understand. She drew her sword, which emerged glowing a dull green in counterpoint to the red cast of the torch.

"I would feel better if you let me cover our retreat."

Minds were wasted on men, Rose thought. She shook her head and mimicked shouting for a moment.

"Ah, true. You would be unable to communicate." The footfalls of the eclectics announced their approach. "You are certain you can hold them off?"

Rose nodded confidently and again waved him away.

"We cannot both fight in a space so tight, regardless. I will call to you when I know what lies below."

Calx lay the torch on the lip of the shelf where they stood and used his sword to guide the dangling rope closer. With a brief tug to test the ring's commitment to the ceiling, he swung out over the abyss and slid down in stops and starts.

Rose stood motionless, waiting at the narrowest point in the tunnel, a few paces from the ledge.

A silver-faced man brandishing a saber rounded the bend in the tunnel. He wore a haik of layered white cloth, like the raiders from the Testing Desert, to better hide in a snow-covered landscape. He advanced warily, a few feet ahead of a second similarly attired man armed with a hand fulmin.

Rose immediately recognized the two figures as eclectics. They wore the sharp metallic visages of the Recast, a sign that they had almost completely shed their biological heritage. Though their impassive faces bore the dents and scars of many battles, she felt somewhat heartened by their lack of stature.

Memories of other battles, of strategy and tactics, invaded her mind. Though these thoughts were not hers, she had come to tolerate such violations. Her sword would have it no other way. She sifted out her own experiences, desperate to assert her identity.

The walls were too close for Rose to use her blade as a slashing weapon, but she had excelled in fencing under the tutelage of Kame Torrefy, and the astonishing lightness of her sword meant her thrusts would be viper quick.

Torrefy had never treated her as if she were weak or stupid. He always demanded her best. He had refused to fight below his ability so that his pupil might someday surpass him. She missed the tight-lipped nods that betrayed his poorly concealed approval.

The Pelagines believed a physical or mental hindrance meant extraordinary ability in some other area. She remembered being taken aside as a sullen girl of thirteen and told that muteness was a blessing she should cherish, that silence revealed things otherwise buried under wagging tongues. She hated it when people tried to dress up her inadequacies.

Yet Torrefy had proven the Pelagine bromides true. In the course of his lessons, he discovered that Rose had the spatial equivalent of perfect pitch. She could be standing on a horse, somersault off backward and catch a ball thrown at her in midair, then land on her feet without being the least bit disoriented. It was a gift that made her almost unbeatable with a blade, much to the relief of Torrefy, who had feared premature decrepitude when he had begun to lose to his pupil on a regular basis.

Torrefy's only daughter had died of the red fever, and from her death Rose reaped both benefit and guilt. During the hours he spent with her, she was never quite sure whether she played the role of his daughter or a woman desired but out of reach. She had come to believe the two roles shared many of the same speeches.

***

Some fifteen feet below the ledge the glow of the torch was already beginning to fall off. As Calx hung in the air, swinging in and out of the timid illumination from above, he laughed. He would certainly remember this vertical expedition, if only for his brief fall, as one of the most poorly conceived ventures of its kind. Already his arms grew tired.

He heard the enemy above and silently cursed himself for not being at Rose's side. He expected to see Rose driven back to the edge of the chasm, fighting for her life. Instead, he saw reason to hope.

In the shadow of the overhanging ledge, only a few feet above his current position, a series of pitons had been hammered into the wet stone, leading down. These spikes, which he had seen earlier, had evidently once reached the ledge.

A cry of agony rode the wind rushing over the precipice. It couldn't be Rose. Regardless, he was in no position to contemplate heroics. He had to be sure, before summoning her, that a means of escape existed.

Sliding a bit farther down the rope, he swung nearer the wall. When he was close enough, he grabbed one of the rusted pitons, but it proved too slippery. A second attempt met with success.

He tied the rope off on the piton below him and began climbing down, careful to grip the slick handholds securely. Another ten feet and he was beside an opening in the rock wall. Though it was almost pitch black inside, he stepped in, elated to feel stone underfoot again.

***

Rose lunged forward, her silver-black blade darting from the shadows toward her adversary's chest.

The eclectic stepped back into his companion to avoid the thrust, leaving no room for further retreat. Hoping to catch Rose off balance, he slashed as best he could in the narrow tunnel, but his saber met only with air and stone. Behind him, his companion took aim.

The first eclectic's poorly conceived riposte had left his weapon useless as a means of defense. He stumbled backward to avoid Rose's harassing thrusts, thus denying his rearguard companion an opportunity to fire.

Even as he tried to interpose his saber, Rose stepped in and feinted low. The eclectic desperately tried to parry a low thrust that wasn't there.

No longer leading this dance, Rose followed her blade, piercing the ceramic brigandine beneath the eclectic's haik and tearing into his heart as a dessert fork might skewer a ripe pear.

Still scrambling in retreat, the blood-soaked figure slumped to the ground in astonishment and death. The fall dislodged his silver mask, revealing a young man of flesh and blood. Not an eclectic, but a fully human soldier.

Rose rushed the second man, knowing that fear had muddied the clarity of mind he needed to discharge his weapon, and he turned and fled. She wanted to give chase, but the taste of the vanquished man's thoughts disoriented her, his thoughts and hers in delirious union. The pleasure of it horrified her.

She saw herself presenting a dead hare to her barely remembered father. His back was turned, and she waited as patiently as a child can wait, but he did not turn around and she had no voice to call to him.

Then it was too late. The flesh of the hare had rotted away, leaving a gleaming metal skeleton no one wanted. She ran to the lake, afraid her bones too were metal, and in the water she saw the reflection of the man she would kill as a young woman in a cavern outside Tajo. She recognized in him her fears, as he saw his in her. Somehow, that made it all right. The union of metal and flesh was not something to fear. It was something to be desired. Something Urizen wanted more than anything.

Rose had forgotten to breathe. Her head was spinning. Then the vision dwindled back to reality.

For a moment, she wanted to cast her sword away, but she could not, no more than she could cut off her own hand. The sword needed her. She could feel it, the lust of the god within.

She was alone again and turned to look for Calx, who had been calling out to her.

"Rose?" Calx cried from below. "Are you all right?"

She returned to the edge of the chasm and looked down into the darkness.

"There are spikes in the wall, leading to a passage. Slide down the rope before they come in force."

Easy for him to say. A glance behind. All clear. Heart racing, she sat on the ledge, dangling her legs over the lip of the chasm, the way she used to linger at the water's edge while her brothers tussled in Black Vine Lake. The clarity of the memory was disturbing. Behind her, she heard them again, coming fast, to push her in.

"Hurry!"

No time to think. Grab the rope and pray, and hope the gods hear the voiceless. Cruel Urizen was listening, at least.

Overcoming her instinct for self-preservation, she took the rope in her gloved hands and pushed off from the ledge, swinging out and around as a fulmin ignited a stream of fire in the air where she had just been.

The rope held. She slid down quickly. Up above, another fulmin discharge turned the rope to ash.

Rose fell silently into the abyss, clutching the severed rope tighter, as if it would somehow slow her fall. A second later, the rope snapped taut, the other end still anchored where Calx had tied it off. The shock whipped her around, redirecting her in toward the rock face, where a piton impaled her just below her shoulder blade. The rope slipped from her hands, while she remained suspended from the spike, a carelessly hung coat of skin.

18

Hospitality

As you slake your thirst in the tears of Deep Ekal, so let your tears slake the thirst of others. As you share the sheltering sky of Endless Gard, so share the roof of your house. As you are warmed in the sight of Bright Halo, so warm those you see. With each door Wild Brand opens, let others pass through. Then when Silent Gavo takes one such as you, tears will birth you anew.

–The Creed of the Pelagines

The narrow road descending from Skye Redan to the valley proved difficult to navigate in the snow. Dahlia glanced back at her two companions, expecting to see that at least one of them had tumbled from the saddle. Elinvar, the lancer Dahlia had met at the trial of Ordina Rose

Fin, had resigned from Skye's service to accept a commission in the Screen—the esteemed bodyguards of the Council. He seemed suspicious of his new mount, which repaid its rider in kind. Neither took orders very well. Cassia, a naïve aspirant traveling as Dahlia's attendant, had exaggerated her competence on horseback in order to secure her current position, which could hardly be considered secure, given the desperation with which she clung to her steed. Dahlia faced forward, quite amused, shifting skillfully with the tentative steps of her mare.

The frozen road twisted away southward from Skye Redan, through modest farms shuttered against the cold, past withered cornstalks. The few picayune they encountered bowed respectfully, careful not to make eye contact. The inhabitants of Downskye were cautious to a fault, finding it better to keep a safe distance from the Cardinal's many strange visitors.

They passed from the farmlands into the gentle hills farther south, with a brisk wind at their backs. Elinvar had taken an obvious liking to young Cassia, who seemed pleased by the lancer's attention.

Dahlia welcomed exclusion from the conversation and rode well ahead. Passing through a wooded area of leafless elms, she noted a vertical line of crimson painted on one of the trees. She recognized the symbol immediately: the sword dismembered. Without the crossguard, the sword no longer symbolized the three greater gods. This was the sign of the one god, of Urizen. It surprised her that the eclectics had grown so bold in their provocations.

The remainder of the day passed without incident. Dahlia allowed only a brief pause to eat, and tried to maintain a reasonably swift pace that afternoon. She sang softly to herself to pass the hours, having no shortage of liturgical chants to choose from. While most worshippers found such hymns ominous and imponderable, the haunting quality of Pelagine dirges set her mind at ease. Her mount, Gray Apple, seemed to enjoy them too, for her ears pricked up.

With dusk approaching, Dahlia led the others off the main road toward a small homestead barely visible through the brush. Traveling alone, she might have reached Lake Caelum before nightfall, but it was not to be.

Beyond the foliage, a one-room house could be seen in full, nestled among crab apple trees. Half consumed by ivy, it seemed a part of the land in the same way a sunken ship joins with sea.

Out in the fields, an elderly man poked and prodded the soil, as if anxious for a thaw. The large white dog accompanying him–half wolf, from the look of it–bounded toward the riders, barking a challenge.

Dahlia dismounted and crouched down, extending her hand. The snarling animal went silent and bounded to greet her, full of affection. The old man made his way up from the field.

"A daughter of Ekal, are you?" the old man inquired. He brushed the dirt from his ruddy hands.

"Aye, Kame, a Limnal of the Pelagines. My name is Dahlia."

"Mouse here would have chewed your arm off otherwise. Seeking shelter?"

"If it is offered." Dahlia smiled, already taking a liking to the old man's brusque manner.

"Who are the shy ones?"

"Elinvar and Cassia. They are not so shy as you might think."

Cassia giggled.

"Well met, Kame," Elinvar said, his eyes drifting back toward Cassia.

Glancing briefly at each of them, the old man waved his unexpected guests toward the house and returned to the field. "My boy is out back. He will stable your mounts. Dinner is at sunset."

"Might we know whose hospitality is offered?" Elinvar asked as he dismounted.

"Chesil. Been a Chesil on this land since the days of airships."

From the lines on his face, Dahlia could almost believe he'd been the only one. Curled about her legs, the white dog looked up questioningly. Dahlia nodded, and Mouse leapt up to chase after his master, sending bits of dirt and snow flying.

Brushing her hair from her eyes, Dahlia handed the reins of Gray Apple to Elinvar, bade him look after the rolled tapestry behind the saddle, and marched toward the house, leaving Cassia to hurry after her.

"You aren't angry with me, are you, Limnal?" Cassia said, panting as she reached Dahlia.

"No. Envious, if you must know."

"You fancy Elinvar?" Cassia gasped.

Dahlia laughed riotously, regaining her composure barely in time to avoid hurting Cassia's feelings.

"Envious of your happiness."

Chesil prepared a modest dinner of curried potatoes and salted lamb, excusing the luxury of the meal by the presence of guests. He refused Cassia's help, adding, "I do not allow others to work in my wife's kitchen. That is my remembrance."

Dahlia felt she understood Chesil immediately. She observed the ritualistic quality of his preparations, his complete absorption in something as mundane as peeling potatoes, and she felt honored to share a meal prepared with such devotion. It reaffirmed her faith to see such sorrow and dignity woven together in the tapestry of this man's life.

"How did your wife die?" Dahlia inquired.

"Gavo sent her the chills."

"Recently?"

The old man nodded. Even with his back turned, his sadness was apparent in the tired slump of his shoulders.

"Has she been commended?"

"Aye, by a Mere who passed this way."

Chesil's boy, Cork, seemed anxious to change the subject, so Dahlia let the matter drop. He was far more interested in Elinvar's hyperbolic tales of adventure, in part because he didn't know how to react to Cassia, who had taken an immediate liking to the awkward boy. He appeared intrigued but clearly lacked experience with young women, being all of thirteen. He took her constant attempts to clean him up as a challenge, and the two of them ended up chasing each other about the cluttered house.

Observing the two of them while Elinvar and Chesil discussed farming, Dahlia could not help but be happy for her attendant. She would never be elevated from aspirant to Mere, but she would make a fine mother and wife, perhaps for Elinvar.

After the meal, Chesil poured apple brandy of his own making. His evident pride in the drink proved justified. The smooth alcohol evaporated on the tongue, leaving the subtle flavor of apples and oak. Elinvar offered to buy any remaining bottles, but Chesil refused with a rare smile.

When the conversation and the fire burned low, Elinvar and Cassia excused themselves, retiring to opposite corners of the room, far enough apart to satisfy the demands of propriety. Cork had been banished to his straw mattress, though he showed no interest in sleeping, with such curious visitors about.

For a few minutes, neither Dahlia nor Chesil spoke. Mouse lay curled up at the old man's feet. Though she sensed the old man's loneliness, she knew it would not be alleviated by conversation.

"I noticed the sign of the dismembered sword upon a tree today," Dahlia said finally. "Do eclectics operate in these parts?"

"Mmmn, the augmen. A strange fellow called on me yesterday. Told me of the reveille, told me I would soon awaken. Asked me to join him among the servants of the one true god. Of course I laughed and told him even Cruel Urizen had a mother. That she was a god too, and though she asked to be left alone, she does not want to be forgotten."

The old man grinned, baring his brown teeth. "So he starts threatening me. Waving his arms and muttering about when the sword becomes flesh. Mouse decides dinner is early and sets on him. Might have killed poor Mouse, but I had my fusil nearby. Put a hole in his head, and he finally decides to leave. Staggers away like a drunk. I follow him and send Cork to get aid. Couple of caballines happen to pass on the road and they join in the hunt. Caught up to him about an hour's ride west. Strung him up by the neck at Stonesword. He's still there, most likely, feeding the crows."

"Might he still be alive?"

Chesil nodded emphatically. "Tough fellows, the augmen are. Even with a hole in the head, he kept talking."

Dahlia stood, her fingers fidgeting in anticipation. It was a rare opportunity. "Will you take me to him?"

***

It was a cold night and the fall of hooves on the hard ground was the only sound. Gray Apple was sluggish at first, but soon moved into an easy canter behind Chesil and his mount.

"We're lucky Silent Gavo shows her face tonight," Chesil remarked, hunched in his saddle.

Though the moonlight made the fields easier to traverse, Dahlia wasn't so sure. Gavo looked after the interests of her dark son, and he after his own.

Vague trees, looking skeletal without leaves, floated past in the darkness. This was how Dahlia imagined entrance, the eclectic state of bliss in which all minds are one. She had been taught entrance was but a void, a night without stars, but she wanted to see for herself. She had to be sure her bliss was better.

They arrived at Stonesword, faces stinging from the cold. The crude granite sword for which the clearing was named stood as it had for hundreds of years, a tribute to the larger swords of steel.

The naked eclectic lashed to the monument was a recent addition. He was one of the more unsettling of his kind, converted not too long ago. The living metal had only partially integrated with his skin, leaving him marbled pink and silver. His left arm was missing, while his right was a crude jointed pulley topped by a two-pronged pincer. His face resembled a steel helm that had seen many battles, but for his all-too-human eyes. In his forehead was a third eye of sorts, a blood-black hole where a ball from Chesil's fusil had entered.

"He lives still," Chesil said, noting the eclectic's breath in the cold air. "If you have something to say to him, say it. I am too old for this."

Dahlia hardly knew where to begin. "Can you hear me?"

The eclectic's gaze wandered, unfocused.

Chesil dismounted to pick up a stone and threw it at the bound man. The eclectic flinched and looked down at his two visitors.

"Pardon us if we do not offer our ... our ... " The eclectic seemed unable to remember the word that would complete his sentence.

"Your hand?" Dahlia offered.

"Yes, that's what we meant." The eclectic stared first at Chesil, then at Dahlia. "We recognize the old man, but the woman is new."

"I am Dahlia, a Limnal of the Pelagines. Do you have a name?"

"We do. We did, rather. It is gone out the hole in our head. We have only the memories of some of the others. They suffice. You may call us Daub. That is your epithet for our kind, no?"

"It means those who are false. Does that include you?"

The eclectic smiled as if he had just learned the expression and still needed improvement. "You are the first softskin to ask that of us, and since you ask, we will tell."

"I am curious to hear."

"Most are not." He glanced at Chesil.

"Do you deny the Trinity?"

"We do."

"Then you are false, and I cannot commend you to Stardome," Dahlia said calmly, though she meant it as a challenge.

"Cruel Urizen began life as a man," Daub said, "and he saw that the sacred fire within was our own. He understood that humans made the gods in their own image. You made Gard, Brand, and Ekal. You made their children. You set them in altars of gray glass and elevated them to Stardome. You set your gods apart in the sky because you are afraid of the whole. Your dreams did not desert you. You simply deny them. We dream still, of Urizen, of his return, of the time of reveille when we will awaken as one mind, eternal."

"You lie. You are a deceiver. You will die and be forgotten." Dahlia could not escape the futility of condemning so willing a heretic. How she had wanted him to break down and beg for forgiveness. How she had wanted to see her fear in his face. But she saw only serenity. She wished she had not come.

"We do not die, as you do. Our thoughts live on in each other. From the Aver's Tongue will come our lost memories, and we will be whole again. You, you will always be in doubt."

"What do you know of the Aver's Tongue?" Dahlia asked.

"It is lost no longer." Daub grinned.

It was more than Dahlia could bear. She seized the fusil strapped to Chesil's horse and pulled the hammer back.

"I am in no mood to play games, Daub." She wished she could compel him to speak, but it was futile.

The eclectic lifted his head slightly. "We are willing to die for what we believe. Are you?"

Dahlia released the hammer and the fusil fired. The kickback knocked the weapon from her hand, and a new hole replaced Daub's right eye.

The eclectic howled in pain. Violent spasms shook his body, but the ropes held him tight. By the time he died, Dahlia and Chesil were halfway home.

After Chesil lay down to sleep, Dahlia stepped outside into the cold night air to make her obeisance to Gavo and Brand. Though she served Ekal, she, like her sisters, honored all the gods. She offered thanks for the rest the night afforded both mortal and god alike. Drawing her cloak close, she stared up at the heavens to watch the tiny fires of Brand's million dreams struggle to survive the coming dawn.

19

Convalescence

Blood is the one true currency.

—a saying among the Caballine Azure

Rose awoke coughing blood. Soaked in perspiration, her face glistened as if she had emerged from a lake. She tried to sit up but fell back, anchored by her pain.

"Hello, Rose," Calx said softly. "Be still. Cold Gavo has been searching for you." He wiped the blood trickling down Rose's chin with a remnant torn from his spare tunic and felt her forehead. Worried that she would become feverish, he gently wrapped her in his fur-lined cloak. "We are in a cavern outside Tajo. Do you remember?"

Licking the blood from her lips, Rose nodded.

Calx poured a few drops from his water skin into his hand and let them fall upon Rose's open mouth. From a small wooden box that he had tucked away in his cloak, he removed a white lozenge of anodyne which he placed on her tongue.

"This will ease your pain," he said. He wished he had a few more lozenges and silently berated himself for refusing to pay the price demanded by the adept supplying the narcotic.

Rose nodded and lay still, exhausted. Her hand fell onto the hilt of her sword, stretched out beside her in its scabbard. The anodyne put her swiftly to sleep.

For over an hour Calx kept watch. Her shallow breathing reminded him of the sea, the ebb and flow of air so like small waves charging some gravel beach, then relenting, to the applause of smooth rocks and shells moved by the water's caress. He had confused her silence with absence and only now understood how much he missed the sound of her walking with him, the sound of her quiet defiance.

Like the tight-lipped disappointment of the dour Mere who had tutored him in his youth, the woman who lay bleeding before him weighed on his conscience. He lifted the cloak he had draped over her and her blood-smeared tunic, inspecting the stitches with which he had sewn shut the hole in her shoulder. Beneath the dressing, the angry wound stared back at him like the bloodshot gaze of a drunk.

Calx drummed his fingers on his knee, trying to think of something more he could do. Just as Rose looked over her shoulder for bounty hunters, he fled from feelings of uselessness, craving some imposed order for direction and purpose. Such fears made him responsible and reliable but all too frequently resulted in situations where he ended up laboring under orders contrary to his nature. Such was the case with Rose. How could he turn her over to the Verifex after saving her life? Better to let her die with honor. He decided to explore the caverns further, hoping to avoid the issue entirely.

The cul-de-sac where he had laid Rose seemed safe enough. From the look of it, the torch on the ground had another two hours of light. He whispered to her that he would return within that time. He did not want her to wake alone in darkness.

The right-hand path led back to the abyss, so Calx took the tunnel to the left. Apparently, this level had once seen considerable traffic. Where the cave above contained only natural formations, this passage had been artificed with wooden supports placed at irregular intervals. A thin coating of gravel provided better traction on the damp floor. Melon-sized luxes, like the ones that lit the ancient transit veins beneath Sansiso, lined the walls but gave off no light. The sealed leather tubes between the luxes sagged, suggesting the lumen pumps were inactive or broken. At periodic intervals along the length of the passage, small fixtures protruded from the gravel floor like stone flowers, likely used to anchor a rail coach or some similar cargo conveyance.

The purpose of the tunnel puzzled Calx. A refuge for outlaws or smugglers–belligerents, perhaps. Yet the mechanics required to light, support, and resurface these tunnels seemed to indicate a well-financed organization. An illegal mining operation was another possibility, but most mines were designed to bring ore to the surface, and this tunnel showed no such intent.

The passage continued at more or less the same level for twenty minutes, judging by the diminution of his torch. He passed a number of openings, but kept to the main tunnel.

Finally, he reached a lacquered wooden door. The red chemical fire of his torch shone in its surface. Where he expected to find a handle, there was a rough circular hole instead, ringed by black scorch marks. From the room beyond came the sound of movement. He entered cautiously.

Before him lay the smoking corpses of five men, each with a hole in the head, sprawled in a grotesque calligraphy of death. A sixth, blackened to a blistering crisp, sat upright against the wall of the massive chamber, his taut face frozen in an expression of surprise.

Amid damaged work beds, bellows, and dermalathes, the blackened man struggled to push himself away on scorched hands, his still legs dragging a swath through the debris of alembics and beakers. An orchestra of massive chemical drums gave rise to a few lingering pillars of acrid smoke, ascending with sated leisure toward the lattice of ceramic pipes near the ceiling. The stink of ammonia masked more carnal smells.

In the dim light, Calx gaped at the conflagrated tableau. He had seen skin foundries before, but never anything approaching this degree of sophistication. Most of the raids in which he had participated had been against basement artificers. The equipment here was an entirely different sort. He turned to regard the blackened man.

"How is it you live?"

The blackened man's jaw quivered for a moment, but only a few hissing sounds emerged. He became very still and stared back at Calx with lidless eyes set like stars in a charred firmament.

"Are you in pain?"

The blackened man seemed amused by this and convulsed briefly. He tried to stand but his knees folded, sending him sprawling face down on the floor, where he lay in turtled immobility.

Approaching to help, Calx saw a silver spine peeking through crisped flesh and recoiled. He drew his sword and cautiously helped the man return to a sitting position.

"You are an eclectic."

The man nodded and twitched as he better propped himself against the wall. The intermittent hum of damaged machinery whirred in the background.

"My name is Calx."

The man opened his palm to the sky that loomed somewhere far above and offered his wrist, revealing dull chrome tendons running up through his arm.

Holding his throat to restrict the flow of air exiting from holes other than his mouth, the man croaked, "I am Irae. My comrades will ransom me, caballine."

Calx could not conceal his astonishment. How could this eclectic know he served the cabal? "Have we met?"

"Your face is within." Irae gestured at his charred head. "That is Urizen's gift to us. And ours to him, for what is he but our connection?"

It was said the eclectics shared memories among themselves, as siblings might share clothes. Calx had never given the notion much credence, thinking it but another exaggeration to whip fear into children and soldiers.

"This is a skin foundry, is it not?"

"It was until three hours ago. The adepts found us."

"Adepts?"

"In disguise." Irae tested his facial muscles, and his expression turned lunatic.

"My companion and I were attacked a short time ago—"

"Silver face masks."

"How is it you survived?" Calx scanned the wreckage of the foundry.

"I am a coward. My companions were not." Irae's chuckle devolved into a fit of coughing.

"It's a shame you did not perish honorably with your companions. It would have saved me the trouble of finishing you."

"Ah yes, I'm an abomination and must be killed," said Irae, his frog voice dripping with sarcasm. "I apologize if it's any trouble for you."

"I am not troubled by it."

"You caballines are so tedious." Irae tried to rise on his damaged arms but failed. "You are troubled only when you see yourself in the face of your victim. At least we cowards are more constant than those of brave conscience."

"Mind your tongue, lest you lose it."

"Spare me your blustering. I endured quite enough hot air when the adepts set the foundry alight."

"And why should I spare you?" Calx growled in disgust, his blade drifting inches from Irae's neck.

"My appreciation of your rapier-like wit aside, I'd say you could use my help as much as I could use yours. You likely did not kill all the adepts, unless I am seriously overestimating your mediocrity. I also know my way around down here."

Calx wondered if Irae's grating voice would prove a more trying guide than dumb luck. "I take it you know something of medicine?"

Irae nodded awkwardly.

"Then perhaps there is a use for you after all."

20

Premonition

A sign is a box by the side of the road containing a set of directions. Some cannot see the box, some cannot open the box, some cannot read the directions, some get lost despite the directions. Lead by the hand instead of pointing the way.

–The Madness of Mere Fiona

When dawn came, Dahlia and her two companions departed Chesil's house and rode into the cold mist that covered the sleeping countryside. Dahlia rode ahead again, leaving Elinvar and Cassia to flirt in private, but she set a brisk pace so as to reach Lake Caelum before the coming darkness. A storm approached from the north.

Just before noon, the trio passed a fork in the road that led southwest toward Sansiso. A splintered wooden signpost loitered at the intersection, mourning its lost headpiece. They were well out of the Cardinal's territory and the land seemed more unruly.

From the road ahead, the clatter of shod hooves announced the first sign of life in the area. For a moment Dahlia considered waving her companions to the side so the approaching riders, in their audible haste, could pass unhindered. Instead, she decided to hold her ground, ready to exchange passage for information.

Thundering over the rise came two black horses with a black coach in tow. Fear shone in their eyes and steam rose from their sweat-slick bodies, rubbed raw where harness met skin. Atop the driver's platform, the coachman sat at an odd angle. The reins, severed somehow, had become entangled with the wheels. With every revolution, the leather strips whipped around, driving the horses forever onward. At the prompting of the rough road, the coachman slumped over the side but remained aboard, upside down, his leg wedged beneath the seat. The coach careened past, its side honeycombed with holes the size of a fusil ball.

"There is someone inside," Elinvar said.

Dahlia tapped Gray Apple with her heels and took off in pursuit. Elinvar followed close behind. Within a minute, they were on either side of the coach.

Elinvar made ready to jump on one of the frightened horses, but Dahlia's presence seemed to calm them. They slowed as she spoke to them and the lashings from their loose reins ceased.

Dahlia dismounted and approached the harnessed horses. The great, sweat-drenched beasts glistened as if they were made of obsidian. The nearest one leaned toward her.

"Is the passenger alive?"

Already looking inside, Elinvar said nothing.

"Elinvar?"

"I do not believe he ever was, Limnal."

Dahlia peered into the coach. A boy of wax, now gouged and disfigured, sat upright on a seat of crimson velvet, his posture as rigid as his starched suit. About the floor were bits of wool and wax torn from the artfully painted figure.

"Who would do such a thing?" Elinvar touched one of the holes in the side of the coach.

"Someone very angry at being deceived."

"Do you know who the waxwork is meant to resemble?"

Dahlia nodded. "Aye, but best not to speak of it. Detach the horses and set the coach alight."

Cassia, just arriving, looked questioningly at her mistress. "You will not commend the coachman to the ground?"

Dahlia shook her heard. "The fire will be his commendation. Let him burn as if he were one of the éclat. That should be honor enough."

***

Even at midday, the barren moors were bitter old parents, resentful of visitors disturbing their rest. The stooped hills and eroding shoulders of rock had done their nurturing long ago and now wanted only respite from wayward children seeking shelter. Time had taken most of what they had to offer, so naturally they were sparing in their gifts.

Thoughts of the tired land led Dahlia back to a memory of her father hauling his bright red skiff onto the shore and then presenting her with the angler fish he had caught. He showed her how it used its worm-like tongue to bait other fish into its mouth, a lure like the wax-work boy that had melted away before her eyes. How finely tailored a fate Ekal wove for the fish that fished, the seducer itself seduced by a fisherman. She wondered at her own fate. Would the sum of her existence be some fittingly tailored embellishment, or a tangle of loose threads?

Having thoroughly chewed over his tales of bravado with Cassia, Elinvar spurred his horse up alongside Dahlia in search of new conversational pasture. He struggled with the introductory pleasantries for a while, without much help from Dahlia. Though they had ridden together for two days, neither had ventured into anything but the most impersonal territory.

Dahlia politely provided the abridged version of her life. She touched on her childhood by the sea, which took on an increasingly mythical quality with the accretion of years. She told him how her infatuation with a young adept, whom she did not name, nearly led her to abandon the Pelagines and how she had come to respect the gods at a time when so many turned away from them. She felt an unexpected sympathy for Elinvar when she came to understand that in his queries of her past he sought a map to his own future, a path that did not traverse the unexpected. She had tried to follow a similar path but found no guide who knew the terrain half so well as claimed. She found herself pointing him toward a peaceful life with Cassia, and wondered if that direction really offered any more contentment than the one in which she traveled. She moved to another subject just in time to avoid a collision with her own ignorance.

"Do you think we have lost our way, Limnal?" Elinvar ventured.

"To Lake Caelum? It's straight up this road."

Elinvar chuckled. "I mean us, in Sarcos. Cardinal Skye said we had."

"The Cardinal is a wise man." Dahlia pondered Elinvar's question for a moment.

"He is. Not so nice as he is smart, though."

"To lose your way, you must first know where you are going."

Elinvar nodded.

"Only the gods know the end of the journey. Perhaps you should take direction from them." Gray Apple looked up questioningly at Dahlia. She stroked her mount's lean neck and pointed her forward.

"No one I know has heard the gods."

"The Thalass once said to me, 'Often, to hear the ocean, you must be underwater.' You cannot always hear the gods if you live fully in the world of men."

"Begging your pardon, Limnal, but if your family is hungry, there is no time for frolicking in the water. Not everyone lives behind the walls of a redan. Most have to fight and scrape, and they cannot hear the gods whispering. Besides, you cannot tell if you're going against the gods because there are no rules anymore. My father had land from long ago and farmed it like a good man. Never ran afoul of anyone. Then he found a cave with metal in it. Next thing, the Pelagines were there, and the Cabal, and the adepts. Everyone wanted a piece. They paid him nothing of what it was worth and then evicted him."

"Your father had no business mining."

"Only the Pelage and the Cabal can profit from the land?"

"Nobody profits from sanctifying metal. It is an expensive and time-consuming process. If the Pelage did not purify ore drawn from the ground, thousands would die."

"But it wasn't right for them to take his land. Laws are meaningless if they do not apply to everyone."

"You should speak up against injustice, if that is what you truly feel."

Elinvar rolled his eyes. "The only ones who would listen would be the Curials, and the next thing they'd want to hear would be my confession."

Dahlia realized how much Elinvar's skepticism gnawed at her own beliefs, and she resented his easy insolence. Had he been more thoroughly schooled, he would no doubt have had more trouble making such direct, vexing arguments.

21

Burnt Bridges

Any person who bears any device within for the
enhancement of the natural mental or physical abilities
bestowed by Bright Halo shall have no voice and no rights.
                                        −The Decree of Prohibition

Calx returned with Irae, carrying a stretcher that had survived the
fire in the foundry. Though little more than a swath of leather strung
between two poles, it would make transporting Rose much easier.

He pulled the ignition wire on one of his four remaining torches
and replaced the one he had left on the ground, now all but spent. He
felt Rose's forehead for fever and made sure she was warm enough,
tucking his cloak around her. The faint heat of her breath on his hand
reassured him.

Leaving the stretcher and Rose behind, he set off again with Irae to find a path to the surface.

Irae proved obedient but annoying, rambling endlessly as if silence were lethal. Calx suspected that Irae wanted to make his presence known to any allies within earshot. Perhaps some of his companions had survived. The threat of decapitation was the only thing that finally quieted the eclectic.

Despite his loquaciousness, Irae proved a competent guide. He walked awkwardly because of his injuries, but made no complaint.

Retracing their steps north to the foundry, they continued through the fire-ravaged room, through another set of doors, and along another gravel-paved corridor.

Calx found the entire complex disturbing, both for its vastness and for the bizarre mechanics evident in its construction.

"When was this place built?" Calx hated the thought of asking Irae anything, but in this case his curiosity overcame his pride.

Irae smiled as best he could, the blackened parchment skin of his face crackling. He neglected to stop the hole in his neck, so his voice was the slightest whisper. "A long time ago, before the rise of the Empire."

"By whom?"

"The Incognita."

"The men who left for the stars?" Calx laughed. "What would such people, if they ever really existed, want with this place?"

Irae shrugged. "Ask them."

"Shall I just shout to them in the heavens?"

"Is that not the way you speak to your gods?"

"Celebrants use a glass."

"Better still."

"And what would you have me ask?"

"Ask them why they have forsaken you."

Calx looked to Irae for further explanation, but got none.

The pair rounded a corner and came to an opening in the right hand wall of the corridor. Through the opening, a cramped room with a ladder leading up could be seen.

Irae put his finger to his blistered lips to indicate silence. From the intersection ahead emanated the orange glow of a portable lux, accompanied by the sound of feet crunching through the gravel.

They ducked into the small room as the sound drew closer.

Irae whispered something, but Calx could not hear him.

"What?"

Just beyond the doorway, the shadow of a man spread across the floor.

Again, Irae whispered something.

"I can't hear you!" Calx hissed back.

"I'm certain I saw a light," came a voice from without.

"Kill them!" Irae rasped.

Two men appeared in the corridor, each wearing a silver mask and a white haik.

His sword already drawn, Calx rushed the pair, hurling his torch to blind them. The first fell immediately, still trying to draw his blade as Calx drew his blood. The second stumbled backward and dropped his lux, which broke and spilled its effulgent liquid over the ground. Calx bore down on him. He recovered swiftly, readying his sword. The clarion of metal on metal rang through the passages as the man struggled to fend off Calx's blows.

They advanced farther from the light of the fallen torch with each thrust and parry. Calx suddenly found it quite difficult to see, while he, silhouetted by the glow behind him, became an easy mark. His opponent seized the initiative to counterattack and drove Calx back with skillful thrusts. With a bit of space between them, the masked adept elaborated his thoughts.

A gash opened in Calx's wrist.

Calx fumbled with his sword, now slick with his own blood.

Sweat rolled down the adept's face as he prepared for another mental assault. He pulled off his silver mask and wiped his eyes. Before he could complete his elaboration, Calx charged.

Their blades locked. The two men stared at each other for a moment. Then the adept saw nothing but Calx's fist hurtling toward his face. He reeled backward, fell to the ground, and died impaled, the alternate possibilities he'd hoped to realize dwindling with his breath.

Light-headed from loss of blood, Calx immediately wrapped his wrist in the few strips of cloth he had not used to bandage Rose. He recovered his torch, which was hissing away in the gravel, and sat down against the wall of the passage to catch his breath.

"You're lucky that adept was not very skilled," Irae said, emerging from the doorway. "You might have lost your hand."

"Those who study the blade and the mechanics seldom do both well." Calx grimaced as he flexed the hand below his injured wrist. "You weren't very helpful."

"Well, we never did establish whether I am your prisoner, your guide, or your companion. I would be loath to overstep my bounds."

Calx glared but did not feel disposed to participate in yet another argument. "Why did you urge me to kill them?"

"Because they would do the same to us, given the chance."

"These were the adepts who destroyed the foundry?"

"Two of the many."

"And the rest?"

"On the surface, I suspect. Fortunately, they fail to perceive the true nature of this place." Without further explanation, Irae gestured toward the ladder. "If they entered through the cave as you did, they may not have discovered the northern gate. You should be able to see the entire area from above."

Calx gazed at the faces of the two dead men and then at their silver masks. "It seems you were right about them masquerading as eclectics."

"Naturally. I am always right. It is part of my charm."

"You do not find it strange?"

"To direct the blame for your crimes toward someone else? No, I find it quite common."

"What would they have to gain from such a ruse?"

"Inspiring fear in their enemies and feeding misinformation to any survivors." Irae shrugged. "We are, however, unmoved by their relentless persecution. Their time will soon be past."

Calx felt an inexplicable sense of urgency. Something was not right. He stood up and approached the ladder.

"Where does this lead? I cannot see the top."

"It does not lead anywhere. There's a hole in the rock face above. Look for the north gate in the cul-de-sac to your lower left."

Calx nodded and climbed up the wooden rungs, which proved more difficult than expected. The cylindrical chimney was just wide enough for a thin man, and he could feel the stone against his back as he ascended. The heaviness of his limbs reminded him how long it had been since he had rested.

Sharp winds rushed in with the dawn through a cleft in the rock. Upon reaching the opening, Calx peered out across the jumble of snow-covered hills. Patches of morning sky were visible amid the dissolving storm. Sunlight was just beginning to clear the hilltops. To the southwest he could see a column of smoke reaching up from Tajo to the sky. It was not the pale smoke of hearth and home, but black and sooty, the color of ruin. Beneath the languorous fountain of ash, Tajo was afire.

In the shadow of a nearby cliff, Calx spied a large number of figures moving about. They looked like eclectics from afar, in their formal dress and silver battle masks, but he knew they were adepts. There were at least several hundred of them busily scurrying about. Some unlimbered eclectic siege machines, great wagon-sized devices with absurd contortions of tubes and gears, used to spit fire or projectiles or noxious chemicals. Others pitched tents and prepared their encampment. A steady trickle of men came from the direction of Tajo, looking worn and exhausted. Some passed through a door at the base of a small slope far below to the left. That would be the north gate. Further up the incline, he saw the mouth of the cave in which Rose and he had taken refuge, now viewed from the direction opposite their approach.

Calx watched the army unfold itself like a bottled spider. He could hear Irae calling up to him, but he did not answer. He could not, for the adepts had razed their own town in the guise of eclectic raiders. It was beyond belief. As one of the Caballine Azure, such treachery incensed him. Though most everyone in Sarcos hated the eclectics, he would not shirk from proclaiming their innocence in this matter if it would expose the adepts.

"Are you waiting to ripen up there?" Irae's rasping voice echoed from below.

Calx descended. "There are perhaps a thousand men encamped outside, with more arriving by the minute, fresh from torching Tajo."

Irae had shed his burnt rags for the clothing from one of the dead adepts. He looked surprised. It was a disturbing expression: the smoke-reddened whites of the eclectic's eyes open wide against the canvas of jet skin.

"It is a false army of eclectics, replete with siege machines." Calx walked into the corridor, visibly agitated. He thought upon the few friends with whom he served while posted to Tajo. He had not maintained contact with most of them, but the possibility of their deaths pained him, even if most had likely moved on.

"How convenient that they found time to destroy our foundry while murdering their countrymen." Irae steadied himself against the wall of the passage while he held his throat to speak.

"So bold a deception cannot work if there are any alive who know the truth."

"Enormous lies are the easiest to swallow. People find deception preferable to the truth. Consider the continued worship of your absent gods."

"Do not anger me, eclectic."

"Who is to blame for anger? The spark or the tinder? Perhaps it is your desiccated wit, thirsting for fresh thoughts, that burns too easily, caballine."

"The sound of your voice annoys me. If you cannot be silent of your own accord, I will help you to it."

"Tyranny is everywhere," Irae sighed.

Calx worried that he had left Rose alone too long. "We should return."

***

Like his brother, Shale, Gelt was in his twentieth year, though he believed himself to be the more mature twin. He had been accepted into the College Arcana at the age of twelve and proved himself an adequate student of the bright mechanics, while Shale spent his time carousing and laboring in the mines. It irritated him that not even their closest friends could tell them apart, especially when the differences were so pronounced. He was determined to establish the difference between himself and his wastrel brother, even if it meant dying to do it.

Gelt removed his angular, silvery mask, revealing a beardless face and eyes that shone like washed cherries. He knelt beside the shivering woman who lay on the ground beneath a delicate sword of silver and black. She looked like the one who had slain his comrade, though he had thought her to be a man at the time. He tucked his mask into his belt and checked to make sure his fulmin was secure in its holster, for one such weapon cost as much as a fair-sized sailing vessel, and to be entrusted with one meant protecting it with your life. He drew the ivory-handled hunting knife he always carried, not because he expected any resistance from the incapacitated redhead but because he was alone, in a dark place. From the slow rise and fall of her breast, he saw she was alive, but that only made the situation more complicated, for she would not make a particularly mobile prisoner in her condition.

Had he heard something? He turned.

***

Far away in Calda Rithil, a small coastal town near the border of Urgun, Shale, in the guise of his brother, entertained a young woman. In an old beached galley that had been converted into a tavern, she sat on his lap and listened as he regaled her with fictional tales of his exploits. She told him that she had always admired him more than Shale and that she continued to be impressed by his success as a student of the bright mechanics.

Shale found her so sweet and yet so passionate in her preference for his brother that he wondered whether she was aware of his ruse. Her professed admiration for Gelt might be intended as revenge for his attempt to deceive her. It certainly proved a more palatable explanation than the possibility of honesty. Ultimately, the truth did not matter to Shale. He enjoyed her company and she enjoyed his and the two were content to pass the evening with each other. Amid the whiskied revelry, in clouds of opium and tobacco, everyone in the tavern would remember raucous laughter in the wake of Gelt's lively orations while Gelt lay dying far away, blood pouring from his mouth in a final, terrified soliloquy.

***

Calx wiped his sword on the dead adept. He felt relieved that his approach had gone unnoticed. Weakened and exhausted, he doubted he could handle another engagement.

Rose seemed oblivious to what was going on nearby; her shallow breathing kept a quiet but respectable pace. Her strange sword lay atop her like a slender lover–the hilt held by both hands just below her chin, the blade stretching down to her knees, the arms of the crossguard too short to embrace her. An odd sight, thought Calx. He wondered how the blade had ended up thus.

Irae swayed unsteadily, having more difficulty with his damaged body than he would admit. "A quiet slash from behind. Such is the stuff of heroes."

Calx glared at Irae and walked around the corner toward the abyss.

"I do hope you'll give me some warning when you stab me in the back," croaked Irae. "It is the polite thing to do."

A rope dangled in front of the mouth of the passage.

"Gelt? Can you hear me?" someone asked from above.

Calx returned at once to the alcove.

"The adepts are everywhere." Glancing at the fallen adept, he noticed the dead man's holster was empty.

"Yes, all does seem lost. Perhaps I can purchase their favor by turning you two in." Irae grinned, though his facial expressions were far from clear. His tight skin clutched a rigid smile.

Calx smiled despite himself. "You must find yourself very amusing."

"When you resemble a carcass after the vultures have done with it, you must find humor where you can."

"We cannot return the way we came–nor, it seems, can we leave through the north gate. Is there another way out?"

"There is."

"Then lead on." Calx lifted his sword to Irae's neck. "But first I will take the fulmin you removed from our dead adversary."

Grumbling, Irae drew the strange weapon from the folds of his borrowed uniform and handed it to Calx. "You do not know how to work one, do you?"

"Actually, I do. An adept showed me once."

Irae shrugged. "They take too long to fire to be of much use at close quarters." He coughed, spitting up a bit of ash.

Though still mistrustful of the eclectic, Calx handed the fulmin back to Irae. "I need an ally more than a prisoner at the moment, and though I am sworn to destroy your kind, doing so would help none of us."

Irae bowed his head slightly. "Necessity, it seems, begets hypocrisy."

The two of them carefully shifted Rose onto the stretcher and set off back toward the foundry. Calx dragged the stretcher as a horse might pull a plow. In no condition to assist, Irae walked a length ahead. They passed through a small fissure midway between the abyss and the foundry and down a slick incline into one of the many natural caverns accessible from the central tunnel. Bathed in the colorful cast of the torch, it looked like the interior of a beating heart, with several connected chambers, deep red and wet.

They descended farther, through a scattered crop of boulders marbled with luminous moss, and came upon a small opening. Beyond lay a chasm, a continuation of the one where Rose had fallen, spanned by a rope bridge.

Irae told Calx to wait until he had scouted the opposite side, then crossed cautiously, his unsteadiness amplified by the undulating bridge. Upon reaching the far end, he disappeared into darkness.

The wind rushing into the chasm buffeted Calx as he waited. He set the stretcher down. His muscles ached. Removing his gloves, he wiped his clammy face, already in need of a shave. He flexed his arm and explored that strange feeling of new injury, with its hidden squalls of pain. He had been injured many times before, often more seriously, but each wound required its own negotiation. Some were undemanding, content to heal themselves without much attention; others were temperamental and querulous, constantly aggrieved. Yet, regardless of the terms established for the relationship, the end result was always a loss of freedom. Even in the absence of physical distress, the scars of injury wove themselves into a straitjacket of flesh and fear, constraining future actions with caution.

While Rose and he were bound by pain, Irae seemed unaffected. That was why he hated the eclectic: Irae was not a prisoner of his body; he did not suffer but by his own choosing. He was a kind of god, in complete control of his being.

Underground thunder shook the area, followed by another distant rumble. Calx did not know what to make of it, thinking perhaps it was a quake, even though quakes were not as percussive. The sound reminded him of the battery of massive cannons that once commanded the heights above Sansiso Sound. He had not heard them since he was a boy, before the restrictions on black powder.

Irae returned, walking like a newborn calf. "We must move on. They are sealing the cave."

A fine layer of dust settled on them. To Calx, it had the taste of the grave.

Irae growled, "The adepts would sooner destroy this place than see one survivor."

"The Pelagines will not be pleased to learn so magnificent a cavern has been desecrated."

"Perhaps, if they ever find out." Irae gestured toward the bridge. "I think you will be surprised how skeptical true believers can be when it suits them."

Calx lifted the stretcher and dragged it down the incline and across the swaying bridge. The unsupported end kept catching between the wooden slats of the bridge, but he managed to reach the far side with Rose still in tow.

Irae and two other men who appeared from nowhere greeted Calx. They were tall but similar to Irae in their lanky build, though both moved with greater ease. Silver skinned, their faces were hard and angular, like the masks of the adepts, though flexible enough for variations in expression. Each wore a loose-fitting charcoal uniform and jacket, ill suited for midwinter, with a sword and fusil. Further scrutiny did not differentiate the two. They were not mirror-image twins, yet they were as similar as an orange and a tangerine.

"Agar and Algin, meet Calx. " Irae quivered spasmodically, the physical damage he sustained in the foundry finally catching up with him. "The woman is Rose, not much of a talker as you can see."

"Irae, you should be rejuvenated as soon as possible," said Agar.

"Yield your weapons, caballine," Algin demanded.

"I think not." Calx set down the stretcher, but before he could draw his sword he was staring down the barrel of Algin's fusil.

Calx reluctantly allowed his sword to be taken from him. "I am your prisoner, then?"

"You are my unarmed guest," Irae said with evident pleasure.

As Algin reached down to take Rose's blade, Rose opened her eyes, yet was not behind them. The whites of her eyes were silver and as full of movement as the sea. While Calx and the three eclectics stepped back in awe, the sword shimmered and fused with Rose's hand, until flesh and metal were one.

"The sword become flesh!" Irae could barely form the words.

Agar stared, his mouth hanging open.

"How?" Algin asked. "I thought the sword had been lost."

Irae nodded. "Perhaps she was the one who slew Teal." He beckoned for silence. "Listen."

A thousand voices tumbled from Rose's open mouth, her lips never moving.

"Behold the Aver's Tongue."

Calx, eyes wide, observed the astonishing changes in his companion. He felt sure he had gone mad. Mind racing, he recalled the tales of Cruel Urizen he had heard as a child. His old fears were still there, slow to rouse but no less terrible for their sluggishness.

"What trickery is this?" he cried.

"Rose has become the Aver's Tongue," Irae replied. "She will speak his mind."

"You speak nonsense. She is mute." Calx gazed upon her silver eyes and despaired. "Can you not do something?" He reached out to touch her, but Irae stayed his arm.

"What would you have us do? Cut the god from her?"

Calx offered no reply. This was beyond his experience.

"We must correlate this great moment." Agar produced a slender cord from his pocket and stuck one end in his mouth. He moved it around, as a child might a stick of candy, then succeeded in attaching it somehow. He handed the other end of the cord to Irae.

"You drink from each other?" Calx made no effort to conceal his disgust.

"They are sharing memories," Algin explained.

"I have heard eclectics did such a thing, but I never believed it."

Algin nodded. "Not all of us can. It comes as the metal spreads within. It's really not all that different from verbal transmission."

"Except that our dinner conversation tends to suffer as a result," Irae added. He slipped the free end of the cord into his mouth, but his increasingly frequent spasms hampered his efforts. Agar offered to help, but Irae was determined to attach the cord on his own.

"Your lovemaking must be interesting," Calx said.

Algin smiled curiously. "As much as yours. If two eclectics correlate simultaneously, they create a feedback loop that renders both of them catatonic. Imagine holding two mirrors opposite each other. Each reflects the other into infinity. The transfer can flow in only one direction at a time."

Irae finally managed to attach the cord and announced his readiness. He and Agar both twitched in unison, then stood still. As the transfer proceeded, Irae's smallest movements were echoed by Agar.

Then it was done. Irae detached the cord and handed it to Algin, who took it in his mouth and repeated the procedure. Agar pocketed the detached cord and nothing more was said of the matter. It seemed quite an unceremonious ending for such a profound experience. Far better, thought Calx, that such wondrousness remain a cherished child of the mind than to issue forth unwanted and unappreciated.

Another thunderous rumbling shook the area, somewhat closer than before. The three eclectics conferred briefly and came swiftly to an agreement: Algin would stay behind in case any adepts still pursued them.

***

With Agar and Calx carrying Rose, and Irae somehow retaining enough balance to lead the way, they forged onward. The tunnel became smoother as they descended–the result of lava flows, if Agar was to be believed. The air smelled musty and used, almost intestinal.

Hours later, the passage they had been following came to a set of granite stairs. Though a trivial sign of habitation, it buoyed Calx's spirits. He had all but given up ever being able to retrace a path to the surface, which would likely be blocked were he ever to manage an escape.

As they descended the stairs, their footfalls ceased being the dominant ambient sound. Calx noticed a low murmur that grew louder with each step down, evolving into the sound of life, of voices rising above the dull hum of civilization.

"What is that?" Calx asked.

At the bottom of the stairs, the passage opened onto a vaulted cavern of frightening vastness. The ceiling lay lost in the darkness above, and the walls, where visible, seemed hours away.

Perched atop poles, hundreds of orange, green, and red luxes illuminated the road to an underground city beyond. Farther still, a broad stream of water fell from somewhere above into a lake of respectable dimensions, sending up a cloud of mist over sausage-shaped barges moored just offshore. Squat stone buildings, alien in their construction, with roofs and walls of layered slate, radiated from the edge of the water in a semicircular pattern. Along the serpentine streets, coaches pulled by tethered humans wheeled through the throng of foot traffic. Nearby, just outside the limits of the city, dozens of fires burned, while men in chains toiled in the shadows harvesting some crop scornful of the sun.

"Welcome to the city of Natal," Irae rasped. "You will be our guest here for the duration of your tragically short life."

22

Lake Caelum

"Strike a man to kill him now, strike his son to kill him later."

—attributed to the eclectics

Dahlia, Elinvar, and Cassia reached Lake Caelum in the late afternoon, before the setting sun could banish the shadows of the leafless elms. With wind-red noses, they crossed the bridge that marked the end of the wilds, passing over an ice-choked gorge where yet-unfrozen water wriggled from winter's grip, westward toward the sea.

The main road led directly through the center of town, amid clustered houses of colored timber and stone in the Prismal style, wherein each color represented an abstraction of a particular god. Old men in muddy dusters loitered about the town square, and some gathered to wager on a game of nine stones. They paid only a casual glance to the three riders, quite unwilling to let anyone think their lives were so bereft of interest that any traveler could command their attention.

Though no one in the town of a thousand could afford glass windows except the local Helion, the narrow, paneless windows remained unshuttered in all but the most extreme cold so that the women could supervise their men from inside, where it was warmer and conversation more intimate.

Passing through this gauntlet of feminine scrutiny, Dahlia and her companions tethered their mounts outside the ostler's and split up. While Elinvar set about gathering intelligence, Dahlia and Cassia headed down to the Albedo.

The structure faced a still lake, just below the hill where the town perched. It was modest by urban standards, but in the countryside, its stained-glass and its painted stonework made it a singular marvel. Here the worshippers of Halo gathered in the warmth of the goddess' gaze throughout the year to pray for a bountiful harvest and good health.

Dahlia rapped on the wooden door and was greeted by a tanned, muscular man in an orange robe embroidered with a golden sun.

"I seek an audience with the Helion Viola," Dahlia announced.

"The Helion is very busy today."

"Tell her it is Limnal Dahlia."

The man paused for a moment, making a quick assessment of the women before him. "You may wait inside." He strode across the atrium and through a door.

The chamber was completely open, punctuated only with stone pillars to support a roof riddled with skylights, while the expansive floor was covered by a worn carpet with intricate curving runes, now quite faded.

"It's so bright in here," Cassia observed.

Dahlia smiled, and for a moment saw in her attendant the innocent wonder that she had lost. "It is refreshing, but I daresay you'd miss the sepulchral atmosphere of the great Pelages after a while."

Cassia gazed about as if following the gyre of a bird.

From a chamber on the opposite side of the room, an elegant woman emerged, followed by her orange-clad attendant. Although she was no longer in her prime, she possessed a weathered sort of beauty. Like all the celebrants of Halo, she wore short platinum-blonde hair, as the goddess was depicted in the kinos. It seemed even to outshine her trailing gold robes.

"Dahlia! My dearest, what a pleasant surprise!"

Dahlia smiled. "Were your robes any brighter I would be blind."

The two women hugged. Dahlia glanced over at Cassia, who waited politely to be introduced.

"Cassia, meet Viola, Helion of Lake Caelum and an old friend of mine."

Cassia offered her wrist, but Viola, ignoring the custom, took her hand and clasped it.

"Let the men play with their daggers. It is good to meet you, Kyma Cassia."

"You are too gracious, Helion."

"What fair wind brings you to the house of Bright Halo?" Viola nodded to her attendant, who bowed his head and left.

"Both fair wind and foul."

"Then let us retire to my chambers." Viola took a woman on each arm and returned the way she had come, through pillars of stone and shafts of light. "You really do look well, Dahlia, though you seem far too thin."

"I travel too much."

"Then I will see that you get a fine meal tonight."

Viola led her two visitors into an unadorned stone chamber illuminated by a single skylight and ribbed with dark wood beams supporting the ceiling. An ill-fitted door of milky glass afforded a blurred view of the lake. Dahlia and Cassia sat on a cushioned bench, while Viola pulled a chair out from behind her desk, sitting nearer the small fireplace and her guests.

"I wish that this were a social call," Dahlia began. "But Deep Ekal in her wisdom has chosen otherwise. I travel to see the Thalass with news of the Aver."

Viola sat forward.

"He lives and will soon be in Sansiso to be confirmed."

"Though it lifts my heart to hear you say so, I almost do not believe it. In the nine moons since Ascension, not a day has gone by without some new rumor. He is alive; he is dead."

"I have seen him with my own eyes. He lives, though perhaps not for long. Cardinal Auric's men have taken to the field and there are rumors of war. I suspect Skye intends to use the conflict to force the Cabal to choose between Auric and Azo."

Viola thought about this for a moment. "I wonder how many in the Cabal will rally to Azo? Auric has many friends."

Dahlia shrugged. "Even among the eclectics, it is said. Open war with them will not help his cause."

"Speaking of eclectics," Viola said, "have you heard about Mere Saffron?"

"Is she ill?"

"Dead. Some months back, she had a vision that the Aver's Tongue lay buried on the isle of Farlon. With funds from the Pelage of Mecino, Mere Calico, Mere Teal, and she mounted an expedition. When they did not return, a group of caballines went to look for them. Calico and Saffron were found dead, and Teal is still missing."

Dahlia grimaced. "There was an eclectic hung to die at Stonesword who spoke of the Aver's Tongue. Do you believe her vision was true?"

Viola sighed. "It is difficult to say. Inquiries are under way."

"Pardon me," Cassia said, "but what is the Aver's Tongue?"

Dahlia weighed her words. "Though Urizen was slain in the Second War by Cardinal Gray, the metal inhabited by the dark son's essence remained. From the body of the dead god, artificers of old crafted the Tongue to remind them of their god. It has long been feared that Urizen used the Tongue as a place to hide when the gods cut the link between the world and Stardome. The blade has been sought in secret for years, that it might be kept from the eclectics. It is written that the blade will be found when the Aver again walks among us, and that he will die upon it."

"The eclectics believe as much, so prudence demands that we do too," said Viola gravely.

"Could not any sword harm the Aver just as well?"

"Not in the same way," Dahlia said, surprised her attendant showed interest in theological esoterica. "The Aver remembers the dreams lost to us since the Renunciation. When he dies, the dreams will pass to another yet unborn. Should he die by the Tongue, however, Urizen would taste his thoughts. He would understand the language of possibility and return from the ether stronger than before. As it was in the Dim Age, his thoughts would emanate from the swords and we would dwindle into him, our minds his. One weight, one measure, one God, one Law."

Cassia shivered. "Surely that would never come to pass?"

"The dream of the second skin is an old one. We have fought against it for a long time, but our gods give us little guidance. Let us hope that the Aver truly has the sight. Perhaps then we will prevail."

Dahlia forced a smile, though it was evident to the other two that she had doubts.

***

At sunset, Dahlia awoke from a brief nap, rose from her bed, and walked across the threadbare carpet to the washbasin. She stared at her reflection in the polished square of silvery ceramic that served as an affordable alternative to a mirror, then unplugged the waterspout until the basin was half filled, recalling when running water was found only in redans. Times were changing so swiftly.

She tried to imagine what Sarcos would be like if everyone carried a fulmin, if her father had owned a steamship instead of a skiff, if metal were as common as wood. Thus would the world be under Urizen. The thought sent a shiver up her spine.

Outside, she could hear the sound of many voices. She walked over to the only window in her room and opened the shutters. In the square below, a number of villagers stood around a man holding the reins of his horse. He appeared to be a lancer, or perhaps an impoverished caballine, clad in a white fur-lined anorak, soldier's fatigues, and high black boots partially covered with mud. His face looked dirty, though it was mostly due to the faded eye-black he wore to cut the sun's glare. From what Dahlia could hear, the man had been in a battle. Members of the crowd started shouting to friends and neighbors to come hear the man's tale.

Leaning out the window, Dahlia addressed a woman standing just below. "Kyma, what is the news?"

"The augmen have razed Tajo, he says," the woman replied.

Dahlia ducked back inside and hurriedly finished dressing. She rushed down the steep stairway, barely wider than her shoulders, through the entry hall and out into the crowd, breathless.

Elinvar stood nearby, his arms folded as he listened, and she jostled her way over to him.

"You heard this lancer, Limnal?" Elinvar inquired as soon as Dahlia was within earshot.

"No."

"A man by the name of Sim, he says the eclectics have come down from the northeast and massacred everyone."

Dahlia listened as Sim told his tale with the vigor of a seasoned showman.

". . . but Wild Brand did not favor us that night and we lost the woman and her companion in the snow. Fact is, we could not find our way back either. We must have been out there four or five hours, our dogs freezing to death, and us too if we didn't get back. But now I'm thinking Brand did hear our prayers and kept the seven of us lost to preserve us from what happened in Tajo while we were gone. We had almost given up hope when we saw a flash of light. Like the anger of Endless Gard, when the summer skies burst. So we head toward the light and soon we're outside Tajo, but the walls are breached and swarming with augmen, armed to the teeth with fusils and falchions. Then one of our dogs starts barking, and a group of them sees us and it's chaos. Three fell where they stood, torn to pieces by a fusillade. Two then make a run for a hole in the wall and duck in. I fear they met their ends soon after, for Tajo was burning and it was a hungry fire. That leaves me and Brake outside, and we're running back the way we came. We heard them kill the dogs before coming after us."

An angry murmur passed through the crowd.

"We've got a good enough head start that they can't see us in the storm, but we can hear them. Brake can't keep up, though, seeing as he's tired and all, so he wants to ambush the ones coming for us. I follow him east, through the gullies and hills, for at least a thousand lengths. I'm sweating and freezing at the same time and almost ready to lay down and die, but we arrive at this rope bridge over a ravine. Brake says he'll cross and get them to follow him, thinking they might expect us to cut the bridge from the far side but not the near one. So I stay back, just below the edge of the ravine under the near side of the bridge, and he waits on the other side. Sure enough, six of them—because augmen travel in groups of six—show up, following our tracks as if we were leaving a trail of string behind us. Brake, Halo bless him, hits one of them smack on the head with a fair-size rock, knocking the silver devil off the bridge. They discharge their fusils at him, but the bridge is unsteady and he's already behind cover and running as fast as he can on the other side. This gets them angry, and they're all hurrying after him, except the rear guard, who waits in the middle of the bridge and looks around, like he can smell me. But it's too late. Two hacks with my blade and I'm through the first rope. I see the silverface taking aim at me, then falling against the side as the bridge tilts. Three more hacks while he's trying to get back to my side and the bridge is cut, and he falls quiet as snow to his death. The others don't notice, being busy with chasing Brake.

"So that left me to make my way south, and with the storm blowing as hard as it was, my tracks disappeared soon after. Mind you, it's a day's march to the nearest farm under good conditions. I made it in two. Cold Gavo was tracking me better than the augmen. I was sure I was going to die. I prayed to Bright Halo and she led me once to a cave and once to a hot spring that I would not freeze at night. When I arrived under the warm gaze of the sun, I saw that the farm had been burned to the ground and the family that owned it put to the sword. It made me very sad, for they were good people and in the summer our patrols would sometimes stop there and drink with them. A stallion lingered on the terraced fields. I don't think he belonged to the farm, and why he was there I don't know, but he too seemed sad, for the mares all lay dead. Though I was starving, I felt I should not eat from the dead mares, and I think the stallion in the fields understood somehow. I was feverish at this point and I tried to get closer to the stallion, but he would not let me approach, and finally I collapsed in the melting snow. The stallion then came to me, and stood over me and when I rose, he stayed and allowed me to mount. I clung to his mane and directed him south, through the pines toward the Even River. By nightfall, I came upon a group of loggers camped on the river. The stallion left after they pulled me from his back. I rested and ate that night, and when I told them my tale, they loaned me one of their chargers so I could make report. So here I am a week after the fact, Sim, Lancer of the Fourth Hand, under Ordinal Amber, and if I lied but once may Cold Gavo catch up to me."

With the conclusion of Sim's tale, several indistinguishable men departed in a hurry—factors of the éclat, Dahlia assumed.

All at once, the assembled crowd began asking questions of Sim and conversing among themselves. For the past twenty years, there had been no open conflict with the eclectics, and many in Sarcos had no recollection of the last war. Though the eclectics were fewer than in the past, they had allies among the tribes of Urgun, eager to despoil the wealth of the south.

If war was something of a curiosity to the picayune, the éclat of Sarcos never ceased worrying, the result of keeping so tight a rein over the wild affairs of state. For each resident of Lake Caelum blindsided by Sim's news, there would be some official or dignitary ready to claim foreknowledge of the attack. Because those high in the Cast had so much to lose—in money and privilege—every conceivable scenario that might weaken their stranglehold on power was given hushed voice or quiet consideration, to the point where they predicted the future by the sheer volume of their paranoia.

***

As the evening light ebbed, so did the crowd.

Dahlia invited Sim to join her and her companions for dinner, an offer he accepted happily after so long a ride. Elinvar had wandered off somewhere, no doubt to steal a few moments with Cassia.

Returning to the inn's common room, where smoke from the fireplace mingled with the scent of ale and perfume, Dahlia ordered some tea and observed the other patrons. Several of the locals had gathered around the bar, intent on having a good time, news of a massacre or no. A pair of men, their brown beards matching their mud-colored cloaks, sat whispering, hunched beside a hookah that marked them as adepts as clearly as if they had worn sandwich boards. One of them gazed over at Dahlia with drowsy curiosity as he suckled smoke from a serpentine hose.

As Dahlia poured herself a second cup of tea, Viola arrived, followed a minute later by Sim, who immediately seemed uncomfortable sitting at a table with two high-ranking celebrants. The usual pleasantries were swiftly abandoned in order that Sim might repeat his tale for Viola.

After the second telling, Dahlia had a better idea of what happened at Tajo. Certain aspects of Sim's tale remained the same, while others he reported with more embellishment.

"By what good fortune were you outside the walls that night?" Dahlia asked.

"Therein lies a curious tale," Sim answered. "A good number of the lancers and hoplites had gathered in The Night's Rest to pass the evening by tavern fire rather than barracks chill. Next thing you know, this redhaired lad trips a member of my company by the name of Salt. Now, Salt is a big fellow, maybe twice the lad's size, and he's understandably angry. The lad only makes it worse by standing there and smiling, not saying a word. So Salt grabs a mug and hurls it at the lad and, seeing as he had a few mugs himself, hits the wrong man and next thing you know everyone is brawling. Then one of Salt's friends grabs the lad from behind, but the lad breaks the man's nose and squirms free, only it's not a lad but a lady, dressed for the wild. When he realizes this, Salt gets even more angry, knowing he'll never live down being shown up by a woman, and he goes for his blade. Now it's serious. The tavern falls quiet. The redhead draws her sword and doesn't back down. Now I've seen a few duels in my time, but this woman was something special. She took Salt apart in the blink of an eye. Salt slashes at her, and the next thing I see a white flash and Salt's hand lying on the floor, still gripping his sword. So then, while we're keeping Salt from bleeding to death, the woman runs out the back into the storm. As soon as we can gather our gear, seven of us head out in pursuit. That's how we ended up out there in the first place. You know the rest."

"A white flash?" Viola said. "I have heard tales that warriors of righteous cause sometimes see a white flash, a sign of Halo's favor."

Sim scratched his head. "Could be, I suppose. Could've been an adept's trick. Could also have been a spark, like you get sometimes with metal on metal."

"Can you describe the sword?" Dahlia leaned closer to Sim.

"'Twas a fine long sword–pretty though, with an emerald the size of cherry in the pommel."

Dahlia played with her hair absentmindedly. Ordina Rose might have such a weapon. She certainly had the skill, and it would make sense for her to travel as a man.

Viola looked at Dahlia questioningly.

"There is a pattern forming in the threads of the past few days that I sense but cannot divine."

Viola nodded almost imperceptibly, then turned toward the door that led out to the town square. A faint rumble quickly resolved itself into the thunder of horse hooves.

"Soldiers," Sim said. "A great number of them."

The arrival of hundreds of caballines set drinks aquiver in their tankards and brought most everyone to a window or door. Men clad in the finery of the Caballine Azure rode into town astride their glistening cavals, the mounts' gray skin numbed with oily anesthetic in preparation for battle and the cold. The riders sat proudly in their saddles, wearing plumed helms and azure uniforms emblazoned with a golden sun, a tribute to their patron goddess. Each wore a blade at his side and rested a light lance across the neck of his steed. Dahlia noticed no black-powder or energy weapons, though soldiers high in the Cast wore vests of ceramic brigandine that glittered under their surcoats.

While most of them continued toward the lake, some forty dismounted in the town square, tethering their cavals to anything that didn't move.

"People of Lake Caelum," cried one of the riders. "By order of Cardinal Azo, you shall render aid, assistance, and lodging to the soldiers of the Fifth Hand until such time as we depart tomorrow. Furthermore, all able-bodied men beyond fifteen winters shall assemble here within one hour. Noncompliance will be punished. The Cardinal or one of his adjutants will be available here for audience until we depart."

With the completion of the rider's announcement, silence seized the town, except for the fearful shuttering of windows and the futile locking of doors.

At the inn, all eyes fell on Viola, the spiritual leader of Lake Caelum and one of the few residents immune from Caballine Azure intimidation. With Dahlia following, Viola headed out to the square, her platinum hair and golden robe a repudiation of the night. She strode to the center of the square and shouted, "Cardinal Azo, let us have words."

The caballines gave Viola their full attention, for most had never heard their commander challenged openly. The man who had made the public address approached the two women and, recognizing the authority signified by their raiment, offered his hand. Viola drew a small knife she always carried with her and completed the ritual, placing the handle against the man's palm for a moment.

"Your future," said Viola in an abridgment of the proper words.

"I thank you for it. I am Spinel, Caballine of the Fifth Hand and adjutant to Cardinal Azo."

"Viola, Helion of Lake Caelum, and beside me is Dahlia, Limnal of the Pelage Deep. Explain the presence of Azo and his herd."

Spinel's eyes grew wider and wider, as if milk were spilling out from his pupils. Clearly distressed to hear such an epithet applied to the Cabal, he stammered, "We ride in defense of Sarcos."

"On whose authority?" Viola fumed.

"On my own authority as a Hierophant," came a voice from behind. "And in the name of the Aver, may Halo protect him."

The two women turned to find a muscular man of considerable height approaching, his helm carried under his arm. He had an air of meticulousness about him, from his well-laundered garments of azure and gold to his neatly trimmed beard. He had a peculiar bowlegged walk that made him seem uncomfortable on foot. Though he was not overly charismatic, his matter-of-fact voice and brusque manner amplified his authority.

"Even a Cardinal cannot declare martial law without good reason." Dahlia knew she would not prevail, though the law was on her side.

"I should think an eclectic invasion reason enough for you, Limnal." Azo grinned unctuously as he shifted about, stretching sore muscles.

"Aye, we have heard," Viola snapped, "though it is a poor pretense. Where are the eclectic soldiers? Where are their great machines, full of fire and death?"

"Helion, you surprise me. Have your forgotten the Caballine Azure and the Lucifal are allies?"

"No, I have not forgotten. Nor will I forget this slight. These are my people, and you know well that you should have come first to me before descending with your men."

"Decades of peace have made you too enamored of ceremony and protocol. Were we to proceed as you wish, we would be sipping tea with our heads on pikes. The silver army is but a few days' march from here, and if they are not contained in the mountains, all of southern Sarcos is threatened."

Viola rolled her eyes.

"Let him be, Viola," Dahlia broke in. "The fifteen-minute ride from Chine Redan appears to have left poor Azo exhausted beyond coherence."

Azo looked down at Dahlia and sneered. "If I am tired, it is because we have been two days upon the road. My properties are a good deal farther away than Ordinal Chine's. Now, if you will excuse me, I have business to attend to." Turning abruptly, he walked away.

Dahlia put her arm around Viola and guided her back toward the tavern. "Save your anger for another day. I will discuss the matter among the Council of Hierophants."

"He is almost as bad as Auric, a law unto himself. I doubt our censure will bother him."

Passing among the bustling caballines and townsfolk, the two women moved as if walking through deep snow, without care or hurry it seemed. "What made you believe Azo and his caballines had ridden from Chine Redan? Ordinal Chine is a good man and wants little to do with Azo or his allies."

Dahlia smiled broadly. "I wanted to know how long he had been on the road. Had I asked him directly, he would not have told me. I guessed he would not miss an opportunity to correct me."

"Why would it matter where he came from?"

Dahlia glanced about and whispered, "It took Sim seven days to reach us: three on foot, four on horse. With the poor weather, even if another soldier escaped Tajo mounted, which seems unlikely given that horses are scarce in the mountains, it would take at least five days to travel from Tajo to Lake Caelum. Then, as the Cardinal said, another two to reach Azo Redan. Even allowing only four days coming out of the mountains, the earliest Azo could have known about the attack would be last night. Yet he had time to muster his lancers and set off two days ago? It seems to me he must have known of the attack a full day or more before he says."

Viola pondered for a moment, her platinum hair swaying listlessly in the evening breeze. "Perhaps he anticipates the confirmation of the Aver, and sets forth before ordered otherwise. I find it interesting as well that Azo and Auric should find themselves both mustered for war. There is little love between the old guard and the new."

Dahlia nodded. "The future is being forged before our eyes, but who wields the hammer?"

***

Night passed uneasily in Lake Caelum. In each house, caballines were sprawled on floors amid the clutter of their armaments while the residents of the town slept poorly, if at all. The promises of peace and progress that had teased the townsfolk into contentment were too easily withdrawn. The young did not mind so much, finding the splendor of the riders as engaging a pageant as the rites of Halo held each spring by the glassy lake. But those who remembered the wars knew the martial courtship of the populace moved quickly from embrace to rape. Lying awake with each other, husbands and wives whispered about traveling west toward the coast, though the work to be had in and around the cities was nothing to desire. There crouched the smoke-shrouded foundries that lived on flesh and bone and sinew, but spit out the mind. The new millennium belonged to the gear and wheel, to steam and metal. In the end, most would stay despite their fears, even if it meant being butchered.

The caballines departed just before dawn beneath a damp mist of silver and gray. From the Albedo, Viola watched the soldiers water their mounts at the lake. Amid the tall pines, the cavals leaned down and kissed their reflections into a burst of ripples.

With the coming of the sun, Dahlia made her obeisance, welcoming Halo's rise and thanking Ekal for assuring her bright daughter's safe return. The expected storm had never arrived. She was almost dressed when she heard a frantic knock at her door.

It was Cassia, her eyes red with tears.

"Limnal," Cassia sobbed, "Elinvar is gone! The caballines have pressed him into service."

Dahlia beckoned the distraught aspirant into her room and closed the door. From the chill of Cassia's hands, it seemed she had been outside, searching for Elinvar. "Cassia, Elinvar is gone at my request. I have asked him to return to Skye Redan with a message for the Cardinal."

Cassia stiffened, sniffling. "Could you not have told me before you sent him away?"

"Aye, I could have." Dahlia reached to wipe away a tear.

Cassia recoiled from Dahlia's touch, brushing her hand aside and turning away. Grabbing her attendant squarely by the shoulders, Dahlia spun her back around.

"Kyma Cassia, the price for laying a hand upon one of the éclat is thirty lashes, and to so touch a Limnal merits death. Do you need to be reminded of this?"

Cassia shook her head and stood very still, sniffling.

"Good. You are here as my attendant. I have been very tolerant of your desire to spend time with Elinvar at the expense of my needs, but there is a limit."

"Aye, Limnal."

Dahlia gazed upon the chastened young woman, whose face was as red as if it had been slapped, and could not sustain her annoyance. In Cassia, she saw her own youthful folly and her regret for paths not taken.

Softly she said, "Cassia, if you wish to be with him, he is but one hour ahead of you on the road. An aspirant must love Ekal above all others, and it is clear where your affections lie. I would not stand in the way of your happiness."

Cassia sniffled and smiled broadly. She hugged Dahlia and ran back to her room to gather her belongings.

Dahlia sighed and continued packing.

While the stable boy readied Gray Apple, Dahlia dined on bread, cheese, and apples. She thanked the innkeeper for his hospitality and offered his establishment the blessing of Ekal, which he greatly appreciated.

Outside, the town square looked well trampled. A few members of the Fifth Hand rearguard lingered.

Dahlia walked down the dirt road toward Lake Caelum and the Albedo to bid Viola farewell. Standing outside on the path to the main door, the two women embraced and promised to keep one another informed if either should learn anything of note concerning recent events. Viola's orange-robed attendant lingered nearby, his eyes watchful for some hidden danger.

"I wish I could stay with you longer," Dahlia said. "But in serving Ekal I must be restless like the tide."

"You would like it here, though I daresay, knowing you, that you would miss the sea."

Dahlia nodded, listening to the tiny waves of the lake tickling the shore. "I think I would miss it less here. It reminds me of the Pelage at Tabron, a small town half a day's ride north of Sansiso. The only thing missing is the song of the gulls."

"I am not surprised. This was once the site of a Pelage, about a century ago, before it was razed by marauders."

"If the eclectics defeat Azo, make sure you are not here when their armies arrive. You are not so easily rebuilt as the Albedo."

"There are perhaps some eclectics who disagree with you, but if you wish to worry, worry about those here who have forgotten the purpose of devotion. An empty Albedo might as well be destroyed."

Wearing a cynical grin, Dahlia clasped Viola's hand. "Do not give up hope. Nothing inspires devotion among a people better than fear."

Viola nodded and grew flushed. "I know. I still have hope, and though it is crass, you are right. When I say my evening obeisance, the Albedo will be full for the first time in months. The challenge is weaving commitment from fear, for it is the most fragile of threads."

Dahlia kissed Viola on the cheek. "It is also the easiest to manipulate. Though I hate to say it, Azo has done you a favor."

After yet another series of good-byes, the two women parted, and Dahlia returned to town. Checking Gray Apple's saddle to make sure the groom had secured it properly, she mounted and started up the northern road.

Not more than five minutes outside town, she heard a horse galloping behind her. Turning in her saddle, she saw Cassia, clinging to her mount's mane for dear life. Dahlia reined Gray Apple to a halt.

Breathless but exhilarated, Cassia panted, "I would have joined you sooner, Limnal, but I could not get this stupid beast to turn around."

23

Enmity

Conscience is but a word that cowards use,
Devised at first to keep the strong in awe:
Our strong arms be our conscience, swords our law.

–The Bard of Avon

The Certain Ministry stood out like a bully held back too many years in school. Composed of slabs of granite so tightly interlocked a hair could not fit between them, it was the most imposing structure in Sansiso save the Redan Inviolate. It was almost a sovereign state, out in the middle of Sansiso Sound on its own island. The fishermen who lived on the island referred to the ministry as "the Block."

Skye watched the Certain Ministry draw closer while his oarsman faced astern. He did not relish this trip, but it was necessary, as it was to walk among bees for honey.

The bay was winter clear, and at times he could see the white sand below. It was almost like flying. He imagined the balloonist had seen as much, at least while rising. The sky's reflection shone in the water. Somewhere above, the Incognita were looking down at him. They would fall too some day. But Auric first.

Landfall came, and Skye proceeded through the village that ringed the shore of the island. One good storm and the ramshackle huts would be indistinguishable from debris washed ashore. But the marginal existence was what drew the fishermen. They seemed to find vitality in being balanced between land and sea. They were awash in possibilities, but, unlike the adepts, they had no control over their fate.

He traveled without a guard, as much for the convenience as for the dare. Since his face had appeared on the counterfeit currency, he was more well known than ever—and less well liked. The picayune and the pith feared adepts, but they knew well enough what would happen if they offered violence.

Which made the incident inexplicable.

Something smashed into the side of Skye's face, and for a moment he thought he had been shot. His hand went to his head and came down wet and red. And slick with seeds?

A broken tomato lay on the ground. It had a piece of paper stuffed inside, a decale.

Wheeling about, Skye saw fishermen, oblivious in their sealskin leathers, empty windows and doorways, no sign of an assailant. Behind his back, someone snickered. On another day, he might have killed them all. But he had more pressing business. Better to let them burn themselves out, as Pelagines did with their vast arrays of votives, than to snuff them one by one.

He wiped the drippings from his face and stalked up the sandy path toward the Certain Ministry in such a state that the sentries at the gate let him pass without a word.

The interior of the ministry was as spartan as the exterior was ugly. Skye surmised that the decorator had followed regulations rather than aesthetics. Light, it seemed, was admitted by permit instead of design. Long, rectangular halls, straight stairs, and rigid soldiers led finally to the Office of the Verifex.

The officious clerk showed him in at once.

At the far end of yet another rectilinear chamber, behind a desk of marble too heavy for ten men to lift, sat the Verifex. He had the face of a fox, with reddish sideburns, prominent cheekbones, and a pointy nose. He sat motionless in his pressed suit, his high collar making his head appear detachable.

"Cardinal Skye," he said dryly, "you are early."

Skye approached. To either side, tapestries hung over alcoves, where sentries stood as if in upright coffins. The luxes above radiated a cold blue glow.

"Do you wish me to leave?" Skye asked with forced politeness.

"No, you are here. Sit, sit," the Verifex said, waving Skye closer. "I am surprised you came, Cardinal."

"Are you?" Skye remained standing.

"Yes, I had thought you would remain safe at home."

Skye grinned. "Because of Auric's threats? I have more to fear from the fishermen below."

The Verifex smiled too, but the effect was wholly unsettling. On him, it was an expression of discomfort, more a happy sort of wince. "Mmmn. Your face has become a symbol of their suffering."

"A target for their vegetables," Skye said sourly.

"The picayune on my island are a truculent bunch, but the blame is as much yours as it is theirs, Cardinal. Your face appears on the forged notes."

"Do you imagine I would be so foolish as to print counterfeits with my portrait?"

"It would be unexpected, certainly. But it would fit with your aspirations to rule."

"The notes are Auric's doing," Skye fumed. "Surely, you can see that!"

"Perhaps, but it was you who seized the Aver."

"It was necessary to ensure his safety."

The Verifex caught his reflection in a ceramic desk mirror, touched his finger to his tongue, then reached up to flatten his eyebrows. "Likewise," he said, "my investigation is necessary to ensure the safety of the Empire. Someone has been buying up large tracts of forest and farmland—on the strength of your face. I want to know why."

"By letting it be known that the notes are forged, you have given Auric the means to question the Aver's legitimacy because of the boy's association with me. Worse still, you have weakened my position on the Council."

"Perhaps you should resign."

Skye clenched his teeth. Auric's support went deeper than he had expected. He wondered if he could kill the Verifex before the sentries reacted. They would expect him to use the mechanics, but a paper-weight would be sufficient. In his mind, he played out the permutations. Regrettably, anger would not serve his ends. Without a word, he turned and walked out.

The Verifex rose. "Your time has passed, adept!"

Just before leaving, Skye looked back, his tall frame filling the doorway. The Verifex had the look of a hungry man whose meal had just been taken from him. "Tell Auric he is a poor puppeteer," Skye said. "I can see his hand on your strings."

24

Vejas

Beware the Pelagines. They will not meet you on the field
for a contest of arms, and are more dangerous enemies for it.
—A saying among the adepts

A day's ride outside Lake Caelum, Dahlia and Cassia approached
the edge of the Sarsen Plateau, where the land southeast of the lake
region fell away, down to the rain-shadowed steppes and Vejas beyond.
Amid the ash and debris left by previous travelers, they made camp at
the top of the switchback that snaked down through the rocks, preferring to wait until their horses were fresh before descending.

By the stingy twilight of midwinter, Cassia hurriedly gathered tinder
for a fire. The cold, dry breeze that had been at their backs most of the
day retired, leaving only a few frail clouds aglow in the claret sunset.

Another group of travelers had likewise chosen to rest nearby, as did most of those heading east. From the look of them, Dahlia guessed they were farmers eager to stay clear of troops of any kind. She walked over to the neighboring camp and introduced herself.

The father, a fit if not particularly imposing man by the name of Huck, with graying hair and few teeth, rubbed his hands together like a raccoon. He responded politely and introduced his small doll of a wife, Tulle, and their two daughters, Acacia, cute at five, and Dulse, awkward at fifteen and fond of the heavy theatrical make-up popular among the lower Cast. A second man in a leper's swath—a servant, presumably—tended a small fire a few lengths back.

"A fine night for traveling," Dahlia said.

Huck nodded. "Aye, so it is." The sky had cooled down to an ashen blue. Cinders rode the rising air to usurp the glory of Stardome, until they died.

"You make for Vejas?"

"Aye, if they will have us there."

The sullen elder daughter turned away and moved back toward the figure tending the fire.

"I take it you flee the silver army?"

Huck glanced for a moment at his wife, then shook his head. "Like many around the lake, we sold our lands recently. The price was more than fair. We have been planning to move east, where the winters are milder and the growing season longer. The silver army merely hastened our packing."

From a satchel on the ground, Huck withdrew several decales and handed them furtively to Dahlia.

"What are these for?"

Huck grinned awkwardly and winked. "For the favor of the gods."

"Really, that is not necessary," Dahlia said, shaking her head. She was about to return the money when she recognized Skye's face on the decales. Counterfeits. The poor wretch was hoping to pay a little instead of being robbed of a lot, unaware he had already been taken.

"Please permit me," Huck said, worried that he had offended.

"As you wish. May you meet at the end of your journey such generosity as you have shown here." Perhaps the best thing she could do for him was sustain his delusions.

"Are there others who have sold their lands recently?"

Huck nodded. "Among those pith who own, aye."

"Who was the buyer?" It seemed odd to Dahlia that anyone would acquire property around Lake Caelum in a time of such uncertainty.

Huck shook his head. "Someone interested in birch trees more than good soil," he said, then added with an air of pride, "The factor I dealt with bade me be silent about the sale."

"Yet you have told me. Why?"

"It is said you cannot deceive a Limnal, for Deep Ekal can follow a lie to its roots," Huck replied, rubbing his hands together.

The faintest curl of a smile formed on Dahlia's lips. "True enough. May the gods favor you on your journey."

She excused herself and returned to camp, where Cassia crouched over a pile of sticks and twigs.

"The wood is damp," Cassia lamented. "Fire will not take to it."

Dahlia gazed down at her young aspirant and wondered how the maiden could be at once so incompetent and endearing. She knelt down slowly beside Cassia and rearranged the tinder to allow the flames to breath more easily. "Fortunately, you have chosen to serve the Pelagines. We do not make as much of a fuss about fire as the Lucifal."

"I am hopeless, aren't I?"

Dahlia took the tinderbox from Cassia and struck a spark onto the dry grass at the base of the tiny pyre. She blew softly upon the smoldering tinder and the flames awoke, sending out antennae of smoke to explore the world into which they had just been born. "No, I think you are used to being taken care of. That will pass."

Dahlia stood and retrieved her bedroll from Gray Apple, who nuzzled her a bit too forcefully, nearly knocking her over.

"Thank you for being so kind to me, Limnal," Cassia said.

Dahlia nodded. "Why do you suppose someone would wish to buy up land around Lake Caelum? It's not a particularly fertile area."

"Perhaps it is of military value?"

"Perhaps. What makes you think so?"

"I don't know really. I was just thinking of the boy over there, and then all the soldiers we saw."

"Which boy?"

"Among the other travelers."

"A boy? I believe you mean their elder daughter?"

"Oh. I did not see his face under his cloak, but he did look like a boy when I saw him standing in the brush relieving himself," Cassia said earnestly.

"Really?" Dahlia laughed, then said aloud to herself, "So they wish to protect their son from impressment?" It seemed a more truthful answer than their avowed desire to farm in the dry east.

"Are you going to report them?"

Dahlia shook her head. "Wanting to protect their son is no crime, and it is not my task to do the work of the Curia. By their deception, they are a danger to no one but themselves."

Cassia seemed relieved.

***

The following morning Dahlia and Cassia rose at first light. They packed quickly, having no reason to linger. The family from Lake Caelum had already broken camp. Had they left before dawn to avoid further questions?

By noon, they reached the point where the torturous path down from the Sarsen Plateau, tired of turning back on itself, finally relaxed into a straight road east.

Taking respite from the strenuous descent in dappled sunlight beneath an oak ready for its new leaves, the two women ate dried apples and tangy goat's-milk cheese from Aqal. Against the murmur of a stream flush with melted snowfall, they spoke of the future of the Pelagines in Sarcos. Cassia, despite her naïveté, argued persuasively that the Pelagines held Sarcos together, and that the old traditions ought to be maintained regardless of the whims of the éclat, the pith, or the picayune. Dahlia expressed her cynicism, half because she knew the rising mercantile class of Sarcos saw themselves as the heirs of the faded gods, and half to sound Cassia, who had been previously too shy to voice her opinions. Though none of the weighty matters discussed were resolved, Dahlia found much to respect in her attendant.

Later that afternoon, under the weary winter sun, Gray Apple flattened her ears and turned skittish. Stroking the animal's velvety neck, Dahlia gently urged her mare into the brush.

Amid the stubby bushes that bordered the dirt road, the corpses of the family from Lake Caelum lay sprawled behind some rocks. The husband, wife, daughter, and disguised son had each had their throats slit.

Apart from the others, the servant had been dismembered. Even before she saw the tufts of severed wires sprouting from the litter of limbs, Dahlia realized these were the remains of an eclectic. Judging by rope remnants on its arms and legs, the eclectic had been tied up before being dismembered and pilfered for parts. It would not have taken too many men to restrain this particular eclectic, given the limited extent of his conversion.

Cassia had remained on the road, unable to coax her horse to follow. "What do you see, Limnal?" she called out.

The work of the Caballine Azure, Dahlia thought to herself.

"Limnal?" Cassia called again.

"It appears our neighbors from last night had a secret beyond the masquerade of their son. They kept a thrall."

"A bound eclectic?"

"Aye, he wears the old collar of obedience."

"I don't understand, Limnal. Are they back there?"

"They are dead. Dismount and tie your horse. We must commend them properly."

***

Two days later Dahlia and Cassia saw the spires of Vejas towering on the edge of the Testing Desert, where Deep Ekal manifested herself in an ocean of dust. The eastern jewel of Sarcos covered a vaguely conical hill, as if the city were a hat of stone towers on a head of rock and clay. Citizens of Sarcos saw Sansiso as the heart of the Empire and Vejas as its mind, the point from which the ripples of thought spread. From Vejas came the voice of the Thalass, who spoke for the Pelagines, the Lucifal, and other religious organizations of lesser significance. Like the sea, like Deep Ekal, the words of the Thalass were calm and reasoned most of the time, in contrast to the martial, incendiary rumblings of the Council, with all their petty squabbling. But when roused, the Thalass could not be denied. In the absence of the Aver, she had the authority to nullify the vote of the Council. It remained to be seen how her role would change in the coming months.

The two travelers rode through the gates of the walled city unchallenged, which surprised Dahlia, given the heightened tensions in the north and west. They followed the heavily traveled Avenue Ascendant, which coiled around and up, past the ornate facades of government and private buildings set into the hillside, ever higher toward the tower of the Thalass.

Most of the shops were closed, in observance of one of the multitude of sacred days that peppered shopkeepers' calendars. An exemption extended to itinerant vendors meant that most of the city's holiday commerce happened in the streets. Lines of robed celebrants broke and reformed amid the jostling of merchants. From above, the swell of people appeared very much like the white foam of breaking waves so visibly absent against the backdrop of sand.

At the pinnacle of Vejas stood the Tower Abatis, a gloriously absurd stronghold of stone and timber built to resemble the trunk of a great oak. Flying buttresses extended from the central structure into the sky like branches of stone. Mirroring the roots of an oak, massive columns plunged from the base of the tower into the hill, down underground to the deep, sacred places.

The Matron of the Tower greeted Dahlia and Cassia at the gate and, upon hearing their business, immediately flew into a paroxysm. It would be hours, even days, she said, as if the mere thought of an audience was an unkind burden. The demands upon the Thalass were formidable, she explained, and one could not arrive unannounced.

Dahlia preferred not to exploit her rank, but it would be necessary to clear the weeds of bureaucracy. She whispered in the ear of the Matron, then passed through the gate to the grounds of the Tower Abatis. The Matron remained, trembling, holding her tongue and the reins of their horses.

Though expedited by her position, Dahlia waited in the courtyard garden, abloom even in midwinter, for several hours with Cassia and other supplicants. The Thalass intended that her visitors wait long enough that they might gain some appreciation of the eternal power she served. There were larger, more impressive gardens elsewhere in Sarcos, but none so perfectly balanced between the chaos of life and the still rigor of death.

Dahlia recognized a few of the waiting éclat, but there was no one she knew well. She would not have spoken to anyone in the gardens regardless, out of respect for the sanctity of the place.

Servants of the Tower saw to it that those waiting were comfortable. After two hours and some light refreshment of nectar and spice cakes, Dahlia was escorted in by an attendant. Cassia remained in the garden.

At the base of the great spiral stairway, beneath the strangely contorted wooden support beams that defied architectural norms, stood four of the twelve Abdica, the fierce women who guarded the Thalass. Like the Screen, they had the faces of fanatics.

Dahlia submitted to a thorough search and was finally escorted into the Stygian chamber where the Thalass received visitors.

She waited in complete darkness for several minutes. She could hear the dry breathing of the Thalass nearby, just above the threshold of silence. During her only previous audience with the Thalass, when she sought the Old Woman's blessing after being elevated to the rank of Limnal, she had been exceedingly nervous, to the point that the darkness made her hallucinate. The Thalass had asked her what she saw in the absence of light and, being afraid, she had replied, "Urizen." She had seen something that day, she was sure, but it could have been anything–her own mind feeding on itself–and perhaps that was the point. Now she was bored. She missed her fear and felt guilty that it had fled with her youthful zeal.

A mellifluous voice inquired, "Limnal Dahlia, is it?"

"Aye, Thalass. Thank you for granting me audience. I bring news from Skye Redan."

"Mmmn. The Aver lives."

"Then you have heard." It troubled Dahlia that she had come so far to repeat old news.

"On some matters, I am well informed."

Dahlia waited for some further explanation, but none came. Unable to see the reaction on the Thalass's face, she felt lost, but such was the purpose of a Blind Audience. It was said the Thalass could see perfectly in darkness.

"I would have you confirm his Ascension come the first day of Musca," the Thalass added, almost as an afterthought. "Make my wishes known to the Council."

Dahlia was shocked. "I would be honored, Thalass, though some may resent your faith in me. I know I speak for the other Limnals in desiring your presence at the ceremony."

"It is a long journey to Sansiso, and I am old," the Thalass replied wistfully. "Are you afraid?"

Dahlia took a moment to reply. "Aye, I suppose I am. Afraid I counterfeit my faith."

"Even I have had such fears." The disembodied voice of the Thalass floated like a dandelion seed. "In darkness, doubts can be seen more clearly. Tell me what you see."

"I have felt for some time now that I am not alone. I had a dream, Thalass. I sat with a living reflection of myself, but I could not tell who reflected who."

"A dream? You are certain?"

Dahlia nodded. "As near as I can be. It woke me. I believe it was due to my proximity to the Aver at the time."

The Thalass paused for a moment. "Urizen senses your doubts, my child. He finds comfort in the shadows of your mind, on the other side of you."

She blames me, Dahlia thought. But have I no reason to despair? "I came across an eclectic, hung up to die at Stonesword. He said the Aver's Tongue would speak of the forgotten memories and we would be whole again."

"You have heard, then."

"Of the fate of Mere Saffron? I have."

"You understand, then, the peril to the Aver? The reason the boy has been hidden for so long?"

"I know the lore, but … " Dahlia paused to think how best to articulate her doubts.

"But you have difficulty believing that Urizen could return," the Thalass said in a mixture of accusation and pity.

"Aye," Dahlia admitted. "I suppose I am unused to miracles."

"No, you allow them to become debased in your eyes! Thus it is that Urizen blinds. You look upon the works of artificers and see divinity."

Taken aback by so stern a rebuke, Dahlia stammered, "Forgive me. My mind too easily betrays my heart."

"From what thread is love woven?"

Dahlia thought for a moment. "There are many answers."

"There is one. Different words, perhaps, but one answer: sacrifice. Seldom is it given willingly, but when it is, it binds us together. There are a few such patriots still."

"Do you count me among them?"

The Thalass laughed softly. "That is the question, isn't it? You are not here out of chance. By your future actions you will have to answer that question. You say there are many answers; I say there is one."

"Is there nothing, then, to criticize in Sarcos?"

"To criticize is to poison. It is not done out of love. Rather strive to transform, to guide, to reveal. Only Deep Ekal has the right to destroy."

"Yet even now we prepare for war." Dahlia recalled her orations before the Curia. She knew this was not the time or place for argument, but she had always preferred her own answers.

"War is not such pure hatred as criticism. It is closer to the fire of Bright Halo, both baleful and beneficial. Out of the ashes of war comes fertility. It is not an easy paradox, but one we live and die with."

"Are we then in support of the adepts?" Dahlia asked in astonishment. "I came at Skye's behest to convince you of the wisdom of his war, and instead *you* question *my* zeal. How is it my work was done before I arrived?"

Dahlia felt a cold hand brush through her hair in the blackness, and she nearly jumped from her skin in fright.

"We travel now in the same direction as the adepts," the Thalass continued, her voice drifting slowly in the void as the old woman passed behind Dahlia. "But our destination is not the same. Who do you believe most threatens our interests?"

Dahlia thought about it for a moment. Eclectics? That was the obvious answer. "Cardinal Auric," she replied finally, "who maintains the largest standing army among the éclat. Were he of a mind to do it, he could rule Sarcos."

"Cardinal Skye has more friends among the éclat and could with a few words achieve such ends with less bloodshed."

"Skye has no such ambitions." Dahlia said, though she really had not considered the possibility. "He believes in the Aver."

"It is as you say, for Cardinal Skye is perhaps our greatest ally in this."

In this? It seemed an odd choice of words to Dahlia. It suggested a relationship already extant, as opposed to a future alliance. "I do not understand," Dahlia said.

"The power of the adepts is fading. There are only a few left truly skilled in the bright mechanics."

"Has it not always been thus? It is a difficult art."

"But it grows more difficult with each passing day. Each year fewer of their students leave the College Arcana with any real ability. The children of the éclat are graduated because their families have paid well. For most, the title of adept is the rank purchased when Cardinal and Ordinal proved too expensive. The truly gifted are rare, and soon I fear they may disappear entirely."

Dahlia was stunned. "How can it be I knew nothing of this?" Yet, she did know. She had ridiculed Skye for denying how debased the art had become. Skye's reaction had said as much as the Thalass had just said. It must be agony, she thought, for Skye to watch the bright mechanics fade.

"Few do, and I would have it remain thus. None of the adepts will admit it, certainly."

"Does anyone know the cause of the adepts' decline?"

"The ability of the bright mechanics to circumscribe what is possible depends upon belief, and people are putting their belief elsewhere. Beyond that I must be silent."

For a moment Dahlia said nothing. Disparate thoughts raced through her head without resolution. With whom would the Thalass be enjoined in silence? Skye was involved somehow. Intrigued, she asked, "Why have you entrusted this knowledge to me?"

There was a pause. "I am told trust freely given is most often returned, though in truth it was not my decision to open this door for you."

"You know that you have my loyalty, Thalass."

"You are in a position of great delicacy, though just how much so is not yet clear to you. Your belief in the Aver must be strong for the Council to accept the boy. I would have you remember in the coming weeks whom you serve, and about the sacrifices love requires. Think upon our words in the coming days, and be wary of Cardinal Auric. Take with you the blessing of Deep Ekal, my child."

With that the Thalass walked slowly away, her feet scuffing the dirt floor. One of the Abdica opened the door and pale light diluted the darkness. Disoriented and confused, Dahlia departed.

***

While Cassia attended to the necessary washing of clothes, Dahlia spent the remainder of the day meditating, composing a letter to her old friend Curial Dure, and viewing fragments of the sacred kinos in the reliquary of the Tower Abatis. She had her own pair of white linen gloves for handling the fragile strips, and often spent hours holding them over the light box to better analyze the tiny images. The pictures, so lovingly translated onto strips of translucent sheepskin, might have been bruises with their muted browns, greens, and reds. Though the original strips had long since turned to dust, these illuminated copies, themselves taken from earlier reproductions, retained something of the sacred, something of life.

Though she dearly loved the fragments where Gard and Ekal appeared together, the majority of her time was consumed in her search for a particular kino of Urizen on which she had written an exegesis years ago. When she found it, filed under *T2*, she reviewed the images and the assorted annotations, paying particular attention to the sequences where Urizen could be seen changing his flesh to metal—the dream of the second skin. The kinographers who offered their interpretations disagreed on the meaning of the transformation. The commonly accepted position took the association of Urizen and mayhem with transmutation as evidence that what the eclectics advocated was inherently profane and destructive.

Dahlia had published a similar interpretation, though more as a show of orthodoxy than true conviction. She carefully reread the few annotations by obscure Pelagines and Lucifal that suggested—though quite obtusely, to avoid a scandal—that the synthesis of flesh and machine might once and for all bring peace, a sort of divine family reunion. The notion intrigued Dahlia because in each case, the authors of these borderline heresies cited the dual nature of the sword as a symbol of conquest and reconciliation. In flesh, giver of life and death.

Suppose the Aver were slain with the Tongue? Urizen would feast upon the forgotten memories, and his dreams alone would rule. The eclectics would take on his image, and they would be gods. People would shed their skin to be thus, and as it was in the Dim Age, there would be but one mind for all. It was a seductive future, in a way—to disappear. Was that not what she did when she walked around in disguise?

Dahlia clutched her head. Madness this way lies, she thought. In her mind, Urizen seemed close, almost beside her. Why did no one seem to care? Surely the Thalass realized the danger? Was there nothing more to be done to safeguard the Aver? All the armies of the éclat should surround him. Instead, Skye played hide and seek with the boy's life. There was madness aplenty, but it was not hers.

The miniature silver sword that Auric had given her as a gift for the Aver still hung around her neck. It was strangely comforting, like a tiny one-legged sentry guarding her against despair. "Ask him of his dreams," Auric had said. That was the way out of her maze of worries. Seek the Aver.

***

The following morning Dahlia delivered the Labor of Limnal Myx to its creator, one of the most beloved senior Limnals in Vejas and certainly the most joyful at the moment of the tapestry's return.

Standing outside Myx's modest whitewashed row house, Dahlia and Cassia shared the graying woman's elation, each embracing her in turn.

"You have greatly eased my conscience, Dahlia," said Myx, omitting Dahlia's proper title as a sign of friendship. She tried to stifle her tears, but did not entirely succeed. Gently setting the huge swath of silk on the ground, she unrolled it carefully and regarded the astonishing patterns of blood-dyed thread that had no rival but in nature itself.

"I heard you had been ill, and I would not have you stand before Silent Gavo without your Labor to protect you."

Myx beamed, "May Ekal favor you for your thoughtfulness. How ever did you find it?"

"Cardinal Skye heard of the theft months ago, and one of his factors managed to locate your Labor among other stolen goods." Dahlia preferred not to lie, especially to another Limnal, but she could not bear to sully her old friend's name by implying he saw Myx's Labor as an expedient form of currency.

As she watched the bony Limnal checking her work, nodding and unrolling a bit more, she felt justified in her deceit. Out of the corner of her eye, she saw Cassia watching a group of young women in the black habits of Mere aspirants outside. She nudged her attendant, lest Myx take offense at Cassia's distraction.

When Myx was satisfied that her Labor remained intact, she looked up at Dahlia, still dew-eyed. "Might I offer you some refreshment before you go?"

"Regrettably, I must decline, but there is a favor I would ask of you, if you'll hear it, Limnal."

"Myx, if you please."

Dahlia smiled. "Of course, Myx. My attendant, Kyma Cassia, aspires to enter our sisterhood. I was wondering whether you might have a place for her among your students?"

Myx nodded happily. "With a recommendation from so esteemed a Limnal—a Hierophant of the Council, no less—I could not refuse." She looked Cassia up and down, still nodding. "Is it your wish now to begin the great labor?"

Cassia hesitated only for a moment, but Dahlia knew her mind returned to Elinvar. "Aye, Limnal Myx. I wish it more than anything in the world."

"Excellent. Then perhaps you will break your fast with me?"

Cassia looked to Dahlia. "You will not have further need of me?"

Dahlia shook her head. "Not as much as the world needs the fine celebrant you will become. I have some affairs to deal with, and then I must make for Sansiso."

After a brief exchange of farewells, Dahlia departed out onto the Avenue Ascendant, alone with her thoughts.

25

The Old City

To reach so very high, you break the sheltering sky
And bring a rain of tears that flower into lies
                                        —The Creed of Ekal

999, Year of the Chameleon, Under Musca

After four weeks in a dank cell, Calx began to despair, his spirits
buoyed only by the overhead lux that kept the darkness at bay. He had
heard nothing from his captors since his arrival. His voice was hoarse
from shouting at inattentive guards and his fingers were raw from
scratching at the mortar in the walls. Each day two meals were delivered to him through a slot, but his hunger for contact went unsatisfied,
despite his taunts and pleas.

Relief came unexpectedly with the simple click of a lock. The door opened and there stood Irae–no longer burnt or scarred, but a fit, lanky man clad in a white button-down shirt with black vest and matching pants. There was not a trace of silver in his skin. He had a roguish look about him, amplified by his nascent smirk. With him was another man, presumably also an eclectic, armed with a fusil and wearing black fatigues, which Calx could only assume represented the informal military dress of the eclectics.

Calx could not help but be amazed by Irae's transformation. He had heard tales about the eclectics and their skill as artificers, but to actually see someone so grievously burned restored to health seemed miraculous.

"How is Rose?" Calx asked.

"You reek, caballine," Irae replied, making no effort to conceal his distaste. "Bevel here will see that you are washed and provided with new clothes. Then we can chat. Make sure you do something about that scruffy beard, too. You look like an itinerant shrub." He wheeled about and walked quickly away.

***

Rose felt as if she had been sleeping for years, and she remained unsure that she had really awakened. Her arms bore the marks of dozens of injections intended to facilitate her recovery, while her mind harbored the real trauma. Sleep felt like falling, and she awoke thinking of impalement. She remembered Calx standing over her, full of worry. Beyond a dull ache in her chest, there was barely a scar to corroborate her recollections.

Her arm. Her right arm was a sword. It was not a sudden revelation. More a creeping revulsion. A hallucination that would not fade. The blade sprouted from her hand like a silver tree with finger-sized roots that faded from pink to silver. She could move the sword as if she held it. But it held her.

For the first few days, when the shock still showed on her face, the eclectics had treated her kindly, and she welcomed the opportunity to learn more about them, anything to take her mind from the abomination she had become. She spent hours listening to her timepiece. Its constancy gave some comfort.

During her marriage, she'd had little contact with anyone except other éclat, and though she'd heard the hatred with which eclectics were discussed, she'd never been conversant enough in the issues to come to her own conclusions. It was strange to become what she had been taught to loathe.

Her awkwardly scrawled inquiries about Calx were dismissed with terse reassurances. Other questions about where she was and what had happened during her coma received equally curt replies. The sword, she was assured, would not remain attached permanently, but further explanation was not forthcoming. Though physical therapy kept her occupied, her appetite for answers grew with her strength.

For six days, Rose had risen early in the morning and gone for a walk, accompanied by Irae, who proved surprisingly sympathetic, as if the improvement of his physical state repaired his disposition. He walked her up and down the colonnade and all over the grounds of the convalere to speed her recovery. He appeared to be genuinely concerned about her well-being, and Rose found it particularly easy to listen to him. He steered clear of personal subjects, discussing such innocuous topics as the difficulties of underground agriculture or tales of the Dim Age.

On the seventh morning after her awakening, Irae arrived and said, "Now that you are well enough, it is time we speak in earnest about your future and that of your companion."

***

After bathing, Calx followed Bevel out of his oubliette to a courtyard awash in multihued light beneath a black sky. The ambience of the convalere seemed more military than medical, though the attention to aesthetics—large windows and low walls—made it unsuitable for defense. As if he had an army to besiege the place. He turned his thoughts toward freedom—puzzling out a means of escape seemed, under the circumstances, more productive than resistance.

Fountains of water and steam sprouted and trickled everywhere, and Calx noted several odd stone sculptures depicting vaguely human figures. They passed through a round assembly chamber featuring a semicircle of benches facing a dissection table complete with leather restraints. A variety of odd mechanisms perched beside it, some made entirely of metal.

They came out into the open again along a colonnade bisecting a knobby mushroom garden. Instead of the ambient sound of birds, the fleshy wings of bats churned the air, flitting after insects drawn by the luxes. In the distance, the din of Natal could be heard.

Bevel stopped outside a set of double doors twice his height. "They await you within."

Calx entered the ornate chamber warily, followed by Bevel, who remained by the door, arms folded.

Seated before him around a circular table of polished mahogany were Rose, Irae, Agar, and a third man, silver from head to toe. His heart leaped, though he reined his emotions in, lest his captors see his feelings toward Rose as a means of coercing him. He allowed himself a smile.

Rose smiled back and absently waved with her transformed sword-arm.

Calx gazed upon the slight redhead with amazement. She seemed to have completely recovered from her injury, though she appeared thinner, even in her baggy black tunic and fatigues. Her restrained, silent anger seemed likewise to have been attenuated.

"Hello, Rose," he said, feeling no need to address her with her proper honorific after all they had been through together. "I am pleased to see you alive."

Rose made a reciprocal gesture, signing with her left hand that she owed Calx her heart.

"She seems to believe that she owes you her life," Irae quipped.

"She owes me nothing," Calx said flatly. "It is I who owe her." For a moment, the two stared at each other. Rose seemed somehow more subdued, less edgy, though perhaps her injury still weighed upon her.

His eyes returned to the sword that blended into her arm. "You are somewhat changed."

Rose nodded, clearly distraught.

"Calx," Irae continued, "meet Anan. He is one of the Recast."

Calx looked upon the bizarre man of metal with hatred. "Then it is you I have to thank for my imprisonment."

"Rather it is I you have to thank for your life," Anan replied, adding pointedly, "caballine."

Rose looked questioningly at Anan and then at Calx. She angrily traced the sign of the Caballine Azure, then looked at Calx expectantly.

His face flushing, Calx replied, "He speaks the truth. I serve the Cabal."

Rose's eyes narrowed, and her expression grew cold.

"Rose, allow me to explain . . ."

Rose held her left hand up to silence Calx, then gestured at him.

"She curses you as a bounty hunter," Irae interpreted. "She is signing rather quickly, but I believe she's calling you a two-legged rat."

"Spare me your translation," Calx spat. "Rose, it is not that simple—"

Interrupting, Irae barked, "Bevel, return Calx to his cell. He is upsetting our guest."

Bevel advanced toward Calx.

Calx tried to back away, only to feel Irae seize his arm. Though he struggled, Irae's unnatural strength proved irresistible. He tried to cry out to Rose several times, but Bevel and Irae managed to keep their hands over his mouth. He bit into the tepid flesh of Irae's palm, and his teeth gnashed against the eclectic's artificed bones.

"He is filled with hate for our kind!" Anan exclaimed. "Take him away."

Once outside, Irae grabbed Calx's jaw and hissed, "Though my skin knits quickly, I do not enjoy being bitten. Do it again and I'll snap your fingers like crisp beans."

Calx relented. Without a weapon, he was helpless against the two eclectics, each of whom had twice his strength.

"You may walk if you will be cooperative," Irae said curtly. "Otherwise, we will have to fold you into a less cumbersome form."

Out along the colonnade, they planted Calx on his feet, then each took an arm.

"Do you intend to keep me here indefinitely?" Calx demanded.

"Oh no. Now that you have served your purpose, there's no reason to keep you here at all." Irae flashed a wry smile.

"My purpose?"

"Once we learned that Rose was in fact Ordina Rose of Fin Redan, it was clear she did not know you served the Caballine Azure. Destroying her trust in you pushes her into our arms, and where else can she go looking like she does?"

Calx seethed with anger at having been used so, but he knew he had himself to blame. He felt certain that he could explain his actions to Rose's satisfaction if only he could speak with her alone, but Irae would never give him that chance.

His captors guided him through a low door and into an isolated portion of the convalere. It was a large room, with fifteen beds—some of which appeared occupied—beside which were curious metal boxes that radiated odd lights and sounds. Plain stone walls offered no distraction from the slow silence of the dying. A woman in a white robe emblazoned with a red sword attended a patient.

Irae spoke, his voice more hushed. "I had thought the destruction of our foundry to merely be a sideshow to the razing of Tajo, but it seems I was wrong, if you can believe me capable of such misjudgment. Since your arrival, our factors have been disappearing all over the Empire. This imaginary eclectic invasion is but a pretense to eliminate us and our allies."

"I cannot say I am saddened to hear such news," Calx remarked.

Irae stopped and grasped Calx by the shoulders. "You have the foresight of a turtle cowering in his shell. We alone have kept the ancient wisdom alive, though the great machines fail, though the libraries have burned, though our dreams dwindle into darkness."

"Our dreams? We share nothing except hatred," Calx said.

Irae laughed. "Once, we were one, man and machine and god, changing the course of rivers, controlling the weather. We worked miracles. You can see it in the kinos from the Dim Age. It was a marvelous and frightening world. The devastation that followed came from those who think as you do, from those who could not bear childhood's end."

"Childhood ends only in death. Such is our nature."

Irae approached one of the beds. "If you wish to live as a child, under your gods, know that Urizen will hold you accountable for your actions." He carefully withdrew a stained sheet, revealing the mangled torso of a naked woman still somehow clinging to life.

Though he had witnessed much butchery, Calx turned away. "Enough. Leave her some dignity."

"The adepts took that from her already." Irae replaced the sheet, but could not conceal his anger. "They assumed she would die after they tore her arms and legs from her. We may yet be able to save her, providing we can find the proper parts."

"If you would be my god," Calx said wearily, "then punish me. I tire of your prattle."

Irae nodded to the attendant and then led Calx away, with Bevel close behind. Instead of returning to the oubliettes, they headed out the portcullis of the convalere, and down toward central Natal.

"Ordina Rose cares for you, though you deceived her," Irae said as he walked beside Calx. "I would know why. For her sake, I might even spare you, provided I see that you are capable of learning."

It occurred to Calx that Irae might have feelings for Rose. That would explain the eclectic's reluctance to execute him. Though there was something uncomfortable about crediting Irae with compassion, his lingering humanity might well prove his undoing.

The three men proceeded along a narrow gravel road toward a more residential area of town. Stuccoed houses, few inhabited, pressed up against the edge of the street, their facades like curious faces with peering windows and tight-lipped doors.

"We are not abominations. Our minds are like yours. We eat and breathe like you, up until the last stages of the transformation. We each are different, like you. You could become an eclectic if you so chose, and you would be the same person. Would your death matter less if you had an artificed limb?"

"I am content with the lot the gods have given me, and for those who are ungrateful, they deserve their fate." Calx remained wary of Irae's sophistry.

"This is what you would protect? Ignorance and prejudice?" Irae's face twitched with frustration. "You are pathetic. We have far more support than you can imagine in your closed little mind, even among the Caballine Azure. Of course, the adepts, the celebrants, and the Cabal's old guard are terrified. Mind tricks are no match for fulmins and fusils. When Urizen returns, those who do not take up the second skin will die."

Irae's zeal frightened Calx. It mirrored his own passion, as if his devotion to the gods were turned inside out.

Rounding another corner, the three men came upon an open square with a burbling fountain at the center. Four stone benches cordoned the fountain, one of which was occupied by young couple. Calx stared at them for a moment, not wanting to believe the pair to be eclectics, though he knew that down in this sunless world, everyone had abdicated humanity.

Bevel nodded to the couple and the young man acknowledged the greeting.

They had reached the heart of Natal, and moved among the other eclectics as if mingling with the crowds in Sansiso. There were tradesmen and laborers, and merchants and professionals dressed in the latest fashions, albeit without parasols. The myriad faces displayed a strange tranquility, mirroring the still lake located only a few blocks away. People, seemingly content but curiously devoid of energy, moved in and out of slate cottages that resembled bristling hedgehogs hunkered down in the gravel. Beneath the multihued night, Calx wondered if perhaps it was desperation they lacked.

Or uniformity. For all Irae's talk about being one with Urizen, the eclectics Calx had seen were as distinctive as different species of birds. Tall and short, with flesh of all tones, they displayed an astonishing variety of artificial limbs and other body parts. There were legs of wood and of metal, some of which looked nothing like human appendages.

"What think you of our city, caballine?" inquired Bevel with evident pride.

"It is astounding," Calx admitted. "Though your people are more so. It is a shame they must live in darkness."

"We will not live in darkness forever."

"It is time," Irae announced. "You have seen something of our kind. Now you have a choice to make. Before you stands the Quiet House." He gestured at a drab stone building with but a single door and no windows. "It may not be evident to you here, outside in the ambient noise, just how quiet it is inside, despite the occasional screaming. You may continue forward and languish there until you rot. Or you may partake of the living metal, and become one with us."

Calx glanced about, observing the curving alleyways and the plumes of steam and smoke that rose above the lake to mark the passage of a steamship. The passersby did not share his curiosity. They barely took note of him.

Irae cleared his throat. "I await your answer."

"First tell me what will become of Rose."

"Become? A revealing choice of words." Irae paused for a moment. "You needn't worry about her becoming one of us. She was an eclectic since before you knew her, probably since she was a child. A mere human could not survive an injury such as hers. I am surprised you never suspected."

Calx closed his eyes. He had seen only what he wanted.

Irae grinned. "We had to further her transformation to repair her injuries. We replaced her heart and modified her immune system. She has recovered far more quickly than we had hoped. While the sword is part of her, the living metal will not take, but soon she will be as shiny as she is beautiful."

"Does she know?"

"No, not yet."

Unbalanced by his despair, Calx drifted backward into the path of a horse-drawn cart. The driver shouted angrily and swerved to avoid running Calx down, then stopped. Something brushed Calx's shoulder. It was the handle of a shovel that hung over the side of the cart.

Bevel slapped the side of the wagon. "Look where you're going."

Lunging, Calx grabbed the shovel. He pivoted, delivering a vicious slash to Irae's throat—one of the few vulnerable areas on an eclectic. Irae fell, gasping for breath. Calx aimed for Bevel on the back swing, but the muscular eclectic batted the shovel from Calx's hands and charged at him.

Calx fought vainly to keep his arms from being pinned, but he was unable to resist his assailant's strength. He crumpled to the ground beneath the cart, grappling with Bevel. The eclectic's arms felt like a pair of pythons. Allow me to live, Bright Halo, Calx prayed, to see your face once more.

The shovel clattered to the ground next to the horses.

The cart lurched and Bevel's grip loosened. The eclectic bellowed angrily. One of the wheels had rolled onto his legs. The driver struggled to calm his horses, but they were not bred for war and reacted badly to the fracas.

Though his arms remained trapped by Bevel's bear hug, Calx kicked frantically at the ground, trying to keep Bevel beneath the rocking wheel. The panicked horses finally bolted, and the heavily laden cart rolled forward.

Unable to restrain Calx and hold his ground, Bevel slipped beneath the wheel, his leg bursting like hammered sausage. The composite bone remained intact, but dislocated at the knee. He shuddered and lost his grip.

Calx flopped inelegantly beneath the cart as it passed over him and away. He emerged bruised but intact and sprinted away, unnoticed in the confusion.

Natal became a blur as he ran. He feared that somehow being observed by one would make him known to all. The men and women he passed watched with curiosity, but did not pursue.

Skidding to a halt in the gravel road as he reached the edge of the great underground lake, he ducked into a building apparently used by boatwrights.

Behind the upturned hulls of rowboats, he made his way to the opposite end of the warehouse and slipped out the back door into a deserted alley.

Commotion followed in his footsteps. Irae could not be far behind.

Calx leapt up on an abandoned wagon, clambered onto the roof of the warehouse and began crawling through the shadows toward the adjacent building, a taller, sturdier structure of mortar and stone. He could hear Irae shouting below.

Lying flat on the roof, Calx saw a vent that led inside. He removed a warped grate and squeezed through.

Inside, sprawled on a catwalk beside some disassembled cylindrical tubing, he looked down upon a massive machine entangled with a bewildering array of gears, fan belts, pulleys, and levers. Directly below him lay an idle furnace the size of a small whale. Judging from the angle of the partial exhaust duct that stood atop the furnace like a cowlick, he guessed his point of entry normally spewed smoke and steam.

The machine, with its linked furnace, reminded him of the gigantic bones on display in the Sansiso Museum, thought to be the skeletal remains of long-dead dragons.

With the unattended contraption slumbering peacefully, Calx made his way down from the catwalk on a rope ladder. The wooden floor where his feet finally came to rest was warped and mottled with colorful stains.

As he scanned the area for a place to hide, a piece of paper on the floor caught his eye. Bending over to pick it up, he recognized it as a decale, with the distinctive image of Cardinal Skye on the front. A good omen, he thought, until he realized the back of the bill was blank. Flipping the decale back to its face, he doubted for a moment what he had just seen. It was an incomplete counterfeit.

Calx had stumbled across one of the eclectics' printing presses. He knew, through his work with the Verifex, the havoc they wreaked.

The realization that the counterfeiters were more subversive than pamphleteers was slow in coming among the upper echelons. Calx had been among those who had urged the point of view that counterfeiting undermined the trust holding society together, but until the extent of the problem became apparent, the Verifex had squandered considerable resources silencing only those who challenged the Council of Hierophants with printed words.

While the majority of illicit presses had been found and destroyed, those possessed by the eclectics had long remained out of reach.

A rare opportunity presented itself.

Among the drums of ink, he found a noxious-smelling chemical he felt sure would burn easily, and proceeded to douse the press with it. The fumes were very strong and he soon felt dizzy. He retreated to the far side of the chamber to clear his head and to find a means of ignition that would allow him to reach the exit once the fire was alight.

In the narrow space between shelves sloughing stacks of parchment, Calx discovered a small room beside the closed door that led outside. A lux lay partially covered on the desk beside an open crate. He stepped in and looked about, finding nothing of note beyond the usual office paraphernalia: a quill pen, an inkwell, a blotter, and a few musty books.

A tuft of decales sprouted from the crate. His curiosity aroused, Calx wrenched the box open and found it filled with stacks of money, each tied neatly with twine. He exhaled deeply and shook his head. The forces of the genuine fought a losing battle. The forgers would prevail by weight of numbers. He would need both currency and evidence if he ever escaped, so he grabbed a bundle of decales and tucked it into the pocket of his trousers.

A ledger lay open on the desk in the center of the room. Rows of figures were generally not of interest to Calx, but one of the names listed in the meticulously kept leather volume caught his eye. From the look of it, Cardinal Auric had taken delivery of a considerable sum. Grabbing the book, he headed back toward the press.

He emerged from between the shelves to discover an eclectic, armed with a fusil, standing by the press and staring up at the vent by which Calx had entered. Startled, Calx backed up, knocking a stack of parchment to the floor.

The eclectic turned, leveled his weapon, and fired.

The projectile struck the wall just above Calx's head. Suddenly, the air around the press erupted into an inferno, the accelerant-drenched floor ignited by the muzzle flash.

The eclectic whirled about in a frenzied dance of panic and fell gasping for breath as the conflagration drank the air dry.

The gluttonous fire spread quickly. Calx, doubting this eclectic would have Irae's luck and survive, retreated toward the exit. Flames followed in his footsteps, thirsting for the air that rushed in the moment he crashed through the exterior door.

He emerged breathless to find himself on a quay by the lake. A series of explosions followed and the fire pushed its way past him, out onto the stone promenade, knocking down everyone in its path and setting his clothes aflame in several places.

The eclectics along the water's edge scattered.

In the confusion, Calx stumbled toward the water and threw himself in, extinguishing the patches of fire on his garments. He swam from pier to pier beneath the crescent quay. His strokes were clumsy, hindered by the ledger and a stack of now soggy decales, but no one noticed his passage. The eclectics were watching their city burn.

Waiting beneath the pier, his thoughts returned to Rose as she'd lain in the cavern, sweat drenched and feverish. He longed to go back to her, to explain, but he knew better.

The fire spread to the neighboring warehouse despite the efforts of a growing crowd of volunteers. Those charged with fire prevention were slowly wheeling their pumps into place. The massive machines resembled skeletal elephants with two trunks, one for drinking and one for spraying. The eclectics handling these beasts turned the hoses on the flames and the blaze sputtered smoke and steam.

It was a beautiful sight, the first dawn in sunless Natal.

Calx paddled clumsily toward a strange boat moored a short distance away. It sat low in the water, on the threshold between floating and sinking, and resembled an artificial whale, being completely enclosed and without sail or mast. The mooring line hung low enough for him to reach. Hand over hand, he climbed ashore.

A few hundred lengths out, to Calx's astonishment, the lake disgorged a second whale from its depths. Instead of water from a blowhole, a man emerged from a hatch and seemed to direct the movement of the submersible ship while the rest of the crew presumably remained inside. It moved languidly toward the opposite end of the harbor.

Soaked and bedraggled, Calx thanked Halo no one stood nearby to note his emergence from the lake. He dangled his legs over the edge of the promenade and rested for a moment. If only Rose knew the truth, he thought. He had never intended to turn her in, at least not after her injury. With a frustrated sigh, Calx stifled his self-pity and set his mind on returning to the world he knew.

He had once heard Ordinal Fin mock the notion of underwater ships, decrying the cowardly use of submersibles. It occurred to him that these floating cylinders were just such vessels. Though Calx understood the contempt of those heavily invested in the might of surface vessels, he would welcome the mantel of coward if the submersible offered freedom. Looking upon the strange vessel in the glow of the fire, he concluded that the underwater passage between Natal and the outside world was his best hope.

A plank stretched from the quay to the vessel's spine. Warily, Calx crept aboard.

The hatch of the vessel opened easily. In the shadows, the control room proved treacherous. The luxes below provided the bare minimum of light to navigate the tangle of pipes, consoles, gears, and cords. The interior reminded him of a cadaverous hand he had once seen in a physician's chambers, the flesh peeled back and pinned to a wooden frame, revealing a miraculous assembly of tendon and sinew. He imagined himself as a giant seizing the submersible from the depths and opening it up with a knife, finding therein a crew of little men pulling levers, and being likewise amazed at the hidden workings of the world.

Though he would have liked to study the controls further, he needed a place to hide, not knowing when the crew would return. He had to stoop as he made his way down an access corridor toward the rear of the vessel, which clearly had been built with comfort as an afterthought.

The air smelled of oil and peat as he moved further back. Wishing he could leave Natal on foot, Calx nevertheless pushed on, passing several small chambers, each of which seemed intended to house two of the crew. Finally, he found a storage room.

A brief search revealed a variety of useful items, and within minutes he had a sack for his ledger and decales, along with an ample supply of dried beef, a sailor's coat, and a wooden baton he found lying on the floor. He drank from one of the room's water barrels and, making sure he had not left any obvious signs of his presence, proceeded to bury himself behind several large sacks of grain. All that remained was to wait.

***

When Irae returned, his neck bandaged, Rose was still angry. It was rare enough that she tendered her trust to anyone, and to have her goodwill repaid thus proved too much to bear.

"Humans are just deceitful," Irae ventured.

Rose, in an uncharitable mood, agreed.

The two sat on a flat rock just south of the convalere. Irae said nothing, perhaps sensing Rose's confusion. The point where her sword joined her arm, where her right hand had been, fascinated her. It swiveled just as her wrist had done. To the touch, it was warm, yet numb.

Rose began to cry.

She felt ashamed and turned away. But it was not weakness that brought her tears, it was becoming the freak she had always believed herself to be.

Irae spoke, explaining how the eclectics were better than the humans from which they were descended, and how centuries of subjugation had strengthened their community. He told of strange arts, the dark mechanics gleaned from the Dim Age.

"The humans hoped to hide their black hearts in their machines, to free themselves of their legacy of violence. In so doing, humankind grew weak and dependent, losing the ability to dream. They took direction from the stars that appeared in their walls of glass. By renouncing their power, their long-foreseen apotheosis, humankind gave Urizen life. He had lived in the shadows for ages, under many different names: Man's Son and Polpot, Fewrer and Kolera. But the ether fed him, until he became aware. Then began the Skin War, when man and machine fought for dominion. Many of our kind perished on the battlefield and in the thinning camps.

"Urizen created the living metal to bring peace, for it would unite man and machine. But the humans feared the union of metal and flesh, so they drained the ether and encoded its secrets in the body of the first Aver. Urizen failed and many of our kind went insane once the uplink was broken. It was thought then that Urizen had died, but those who fled to the stars carried Urizen's seed, and through their work he lives again. Soon the Tongue they made for him will give him voice."

Having been hunted herself, Rose found Irae's tale compelling. When she looked upon the wiry eclectic, she saw a soulmate in persecution and an end to her flight. She had been told to be afraid of the followers of Urizen, and perhaps once she believed that advice to be wise, but just as the boundary between flesh and metal had blurred, she could no longer distinguish between fear and faith. She knew then she would betray her past in much the same way Calx had betrayed their future. Perhaps she had been hasty in her indignation.

"You were dying when you arrived," Irae said, "and we decided to take you across the threshold. However, it appears someone else beat us to it. You have been one of us for a long time, perhaps since your birth. Your nervous system bears several innovative additions, including a spatial-imaging coprocessor unlike any I've come across."

Rose placed her hand on her breast. The tempo of her heart felt unnaturally steady as it kept pace with her timepiece. Sixty beats a minute at rest. It was the first time she had recognized the strangeness of the synchronicity.

"We replaced your heart. We used a better one, if I may say so. Your circulatory system has been regenerated through telomeric reconstitution as well. We would have continued with muscular and skeletal alterations, but because of your weakened condition, we thought it better to wait. We have found incremental transitions work best."

Rose took a deep breath to dispel her creeping sense of bewilderment. Her mother and father had only alluded to the nature of her childhood illness, but Gauss knew. He had tried to tell her in his peculiar way. She reached instinctively to her vest pocket, where she kept her timepiece, a cherished sibling of sorts.

Unlike the Tongue. Though she had seen a variety of prosthetics on maimed soldiers, none were quite so singular in nature. There was no mistaking the purpose of the long blade. She tried to imagine herself at a formal dinner, slicing venison with her blade-hand. Or running the wrong hand through her hair.

"Has the sword sent you any visions?" Irae asked, noting Rose's discomfiture.

Rose nodded. She signed in reply with her left hand. There was a boy. Long ago.

Irae's eyes widened. "It is he for whom you are destined. He is the Aver. In him, the dreams of the Dim Age are encoded. He is Urizen's prison, and you are the key. Like the great swords of the Pelagines, yours, the Aver's Tongue, is a broadsword. It broadcasts thought. You have become the Aver's Tongue. You must now tell him of his death. When the sword becomes flesh, when you join with him, it will give voice to the one mind, the one law, under one god."

Rose stared at Irae, She heard his words, but did not understand.

"It will become clear in time," Irae said. "Now that you and the sword are one, it will guide you to the Aver. It will tell you what is expected."

Gazing at the blade growing from her wrist, she wished it were so. The Tongue, like her own, was still.

26

Confirmation

Power lies in the ability to change enough that things remain the same.

−Cardinal Skye

The mist that had settled over Sansiso did nothing to mute the din
of activity in the capital. It was the first day of Musca, when the éclat
arrived from near and far for their annual obeisance.

At Hangman's Circus, by the gates of the Redan Inviolate, a tide of
humanity had rolled in. Officials of import from throughout the Empire
disembarked from tribute-laden coaches, while those of lesser rank
pushed their way through the clog of vehicles and servants, hoping not
to be trampled. Soldiers of the Screen−the protectors of the Hierophants,
clad in ceremonial crimson dusters, gold-buttoned vests, and black fatigues−

slowed the procession by questioning every arrival. At the edges of the crowd, street vendors, thieves, and entertainers of all sorts plied their trades, hoping for some small kindness to trickle down to their pockets.

Inside the courtyard, the visiting éclat relaxed. A great table had been laid out on the damp grass like a miniature battlefield, with a carnage of meats heaped high on huge platters, legions of loaves, fresh-baked and armored in thick crust, and salients of plump pastries bleeding cream as they yielded to the grip of soft hands. Elephantine casks of wine were assailed relentlessly from all sides. Everyone indulged in the splendid fare, provided in the name of the Aver, paid for by last year's tribute, and–if the lineage of the funds were traced back far enough–originating in the pockets of the picayune.

While they waited, the guests hurriedly made and broke alliances among themselves, hoping to advance the positions of their families. Each guest dressed to best frame his or her station, but the combined effect of so much calculated coverage was anxiety. Between the lines on the faces of those present, despite the accretion of powder and makeup, the signs of fear were evident. The troubles with the eclectics could soon fester into open warfare and no one was certain about the Aver. Secret enmities, subtle poisons, and silent assassins, that was how the éclat preferred it, a tidy little game in which positions changed but no one really ever lost. Full-scale war meant a fundamental shift in the balance of power, and in the finish of each glass of wine was the hint of a more personal end.

There was talk too of Skye's loss of face. The Verifex had made it known that the notes bearing the Cardinal's image were forgeries. The pith and the picayune, who relied on paper currency more than the éclat, were particularly hard-hit. While it was said the Council planned to redeem the counterfeits, most believed such a thing would not come to pass for a long time, if ever.

In the auditorium of the Redan Inviolate, a meeting was already under way. Beneath the vaulted stone arches of the tremendous chamber, the twelve Hierophants had gathered to end their rule of Sarcos. There was but one issue before them: the confirmation of the Aver.

When the various procedural questions had been thoroughly discussed, Dahlia headed backstage.

"I will come with you, Limnal," Skye said.

Without looking back, Dahlia said, "No, Cardinal, you won't. The right is mine alone." She would not often see the Aver in a private audience and the question Auric had asked her to put to the boy remained unanswered.

Backstage stood the boy, slight, in a white robe, guarded by two of the Screen. His protectors seemed more attentive than usual. Dahlia guessed they had heard of the recovery of the Aver's Tongue. She carefully shifted her black gown and kneeled. "Aver," she began, her voice breaking, "I am Limnal Dahlia. I will be officiating today."

The boy stared past her and smiled. "You are the one who foresaw my coming."

"Aye, Aver. The memory is with me still." For all her doubts, the boy filled Dahlia's heart with hope. Something about his blindness drew her, as if he understood the darkness worshipped by the Pelagines.

"Am I as you imagined me?"

Dahlia thought about it for a moment. "No, you are more real, if that makes any sense."

The boy laughed. "You speak like a politician, but I am glad you find me so."

More real, and less sacred, she thought. Perhaps anyone who encountered someone so richly imagined would react thus. "Forgive me. My words fail me."

"To tell you a secret, I am in awe myself. I feel as if I have risen from the dead and everything has been made new. It was a long fall from the hilt of the sword."

Lies seldom escaped any Limnal, so attuned to sound in a world of darkness, and Dahlia heard only the most appealing honesty. Though her heart had already confirmed the boy, the tiny silver sword that she removed from her neck threw its weight behind Auric's doubts. "Cardinal Auric asked me to give you this," she said as she handed the charm to the Aver.

"Thank him for me."

"Before we proceed with the ceremony, I would hear something of your dreams. Many fear your dreams will not be to their benefit."

The boy turned his clouded eyes toward Dahlia. "I have seen a woman, not unlike you, in love with a man yet apart from him, separated by the confluence of events. Her heart belongs to the past and the future at once, and thus is rent."

The boy continued describing his dream, but Dahlia did not hear him. She had recognized *The House of White* immediately, or thought she did. It was her story. It had been since she first saw the iconography as a child. It was her dilemma, torn between Cardinal Skye and the gods. She knew the dream called for sacrifice. Had she not sacrificed enough for the love of the gods? Did her doubts have to die too? What more could she give up but her secret desires? Her imaginings of what might have been? Had she no right to those?

"Limnal?"

Dahlia banished the thoughts from her mind. "My apologies. I am distracted of late."

"Was that what you wanted to hear?"

Strangely, it was exactly that. No doubt the boy sensed as much. She expected no less from the Aver. "You dream of sacrifice. Whose will it be? The Caballine Azure? The adepts, perhaps? The eclectics?"

The Aver stared into space. "That battle is yet to be fought, though the adepts are weak. Ask me when I wake tomorrow."

Auric would be pleased to hear that. But could she tell him in good conscience? Doing so would embolden him and his sympathizers.

Without further ado, Dahlia led the boy back into the auditorium. Bathed in theatrical light, he glowed in his white robe.

"All kneel before the Aver of Sarcos!" bellowed the captain of the Screen.

The Hierophants kneeled. The Soldiers of the Screen did not. It was their privilege and their doom. If ever the Aver fell, they would fall too, upon their swords.

The Aver walked cautiously across the stage, as if he were a sleepwalker, and stood before the Council. With the fluid motions of one steeped in ritual, he drew a ceremonial dagger across his wrist and coaxed a few drops of blood from the shallow cut. He displayed his wound for all to see, receiving nods of approval that he bled as a human should. "Your future flows through me," he said.

He regarded those kneeling before him, though his eyes did not meet the astonished stares of his subjects. He passed before each of the Hierophants and each offered up his or her wrist.

Though he could not make out the faces before him, he seemed to recognize each and every one.

"Preceptor Nard," he began, his voice quavering, "Cardinal Skye, Cardinal Auric, Ordinal Mallow, Limnal Dahlia, Helion Sika, Helion Xanthe, Cardinal Lilac, Cardinal Ocher, Curial Clove, Ordinal Ash, and Cardinal Azo. I take you as my Hierophants. As you serve me, so serve Sarcos."

"In you are the memories of our tomorrows," Dahlia answered solemnly. "Lead and we will follow."

"Follow and I will lead."

"In the name of the Thalass, stand confirmed before your people."

The Aver moved to the pool of light at the center of the stage, arms behind his back. The éclat filed in silently, slowly filling the seats of the auditorium. Though he trembled, his audience saw only that for which they had long hoped.

And the Pelagine girls' choir sang, "Deus ex corpus!"

***

Skye slipped away from the ceremony during a reprise of the "Song of the Chimney Sweep." He was smiling. For all the miracles he had worked with the bright mechanics, he considered the resurrection of the Aver his greatest achievement.

Outside, he straightened his stiff jacket and headed toward the Aver's chambers. He walked for several minutes, past curtained alcoves and long-locked rooms only recently refurbished for the Aver. Though there were eyes and ears everywhere, Skye had to see the boy one more time. The die was already cast, but he could not shake the feeling that he had not prepared the boy sufficiently.

In order to maintain the perception of the Aver's divinity, only the Soldiers of the Screen were permitted to see him eat and sleep. Private audiences were to be cleared at the highest levels, and, while the boy remained underage, a celebrant was to attend all his meetings.

Elinvar stood on guard outside the Aver's chambers, a fulmin lance in hand.

"All is well?" Skye asked.

Elinvar nodded.

"No second thoughts?"

"You know me better than that, Cardinal. It is never easy wearing two faces. But if the boy can manage, so can I."

Skye paused for a moment. "You are a good man, Elinvar."

"Your enemies think so too."

Skye put his hand on Elinvar's shoulder, then continued on to the Aver's chambers. He passed through the Hall of Deeds wherein the devotional treasures of the Empire hung in the modesty of near-darkness. Though time had muted the colors of many of the paintings and tapestries, the adoration infusing the works remained undiminished. Here, among works of the imagination, he waited for the Aver.

A short time later, Flux arrived, after dismissing his escort as the Cardinal had instructed. He looked pale, as if he had lost too much blood from the cut on his wrist. But the bandage he held to his arm was barely stained.

"You did remarkably well," Skye said quietly, taking a seat on a claw-foot stool covered in leather that was worn and wrinkled like an old man's palm.

The boy stared blankly at the wall. "I am scared, éclat."

"I know. I have enough fear for both of us." The Cardinal looked the boy up and down and was satisfied with the transformation. "You must not refer to me thus, however. Even in private. The Aver would use no honorific, even addressing his Hierophants. Your old life as Flux is no more. You are now truly the Aver of Sarcos and you must adapt swiftly, for our sake and for the sake of the Empire."

"They will know. I cannot fool everyone."

Skye regarded the boy with sympathy. Using the bright mechanics in place of one's eyes had to be exhausting. "You only have to fool yourself, and everyone else will follow. They want to believe in you.

Give them no reason not to. I will help you as much as I can, but I too am your servant now, and I must not be seen to influence you unduly or our ruse will be discovered. Sarcos is ready for war. You have only to declare it."

"I fear it will become apparent that I have never commanded an army."

"Leave that to Cardinal Auric. You must remain in the Redan Inviolate until there is a decisive engagement."

"But I thought—"

"When we discussed your command of the army, my spies had not reported the recovery of the Aver's Tongue. Do you recall the legend?"

"It is the broadsword forged from the body of Urizen."

"Aye, that which can break the Aver's cycle of reincarnation, if legends prove true."

"But as I am not the true Aver, how can it harm me?"

"If you are unmasked in death, before events have taken their proper course, we are undone. You must remain safe until our work is complete. Give Auric command of the army. Dream of the passing of the adepts. Give him what he wants." Skye tried not to think about what would become of the boy once the charade ended.

"I find it amusing," he continued in levity forced upon him by guilt, "that your blindness enhances the illusion so much. The Pelagines adore you because of it."

"Aye, though they are in darkness by choice."

"Of course." With fatherly assurance, Skye put his hand on the boy's head. "The fear will pass. Think only of the great miracle you will work."

"Will the eclectics come for me?"

"I am counting on it. They will try, once the army is afield, and there are fewer troops in the city."

"I will try to be brave."

"Among the Screen, only Elinvar knows your true identity. It is he who waits outside. He is one of my factors, though no one knows this. He will look after you. There are others too, who will make themselves known if the need arises."

Flux nodded and as Skye turned to go, he asked, "Cardinal? If I should live, what will become of me when my role is done?"

"Once we have recovered the Tongue and the true Aver is restored, you will be free to do as you wish. You will not lack for means, if that is your question."

Flux smiled awkwardly. "I wonder if the true Aver will want me as his shadow?"

"Worry first about the present," Skye said.

The Cardinal departed in the company of his uneasy conscience. How could he be asking too much when he was giving the boy divinity?

Elinvar stood outside, still as stone.

"Have you informed Anan of the army's route?" the Cardinal whispered.

The stoic sentry nodded.

"Be certain they take the bait before springing the trap. Do not worry about the boy. He is prepared."

"I know how to deal with augmen," Elinvar said, shifting his grip on his fulmin lance.

Skye chuckled. "Your hate is showing."

"Only in private, when I dwell upon what they did to me."

"Your vengeance will not be long in coming."

Skye waved and headed back the way he had come. His footfall echoed through strangely empty corridors. An open window admitted a cold breeze. Careless, he thought. The servants and sentries had gone to catch a glimpse of their Aver.

He walked over and bolted the window.

Rounding the corner, he came upon a decale lying at the top of a short stairway. He picked it up and saw that it bore his face. Had he missed seeing it when he passed by earlier?

Something scuffed the gritty tile floor. He spun around.

A hooded man with a long knife was almost upon him.

Having no time for a more elaborate defense, Skye named the sun in the language of possibilities and from his words came a brilliant flash of light.

The hooded man stumbled, slashing wildly, striking Skye's leg as he fell.

"Assassin!" Skye cried out. Blood poured from a gash in his thigh. The disoriented assassin scrambled to his feet.

Skye could not control his rage. To be so abused here, in the Redan Inviolate! It was too much. He focused his mind on his assailant and upon the words that were the seeds of his wishes. From the hooded man arose a horrible scream as the gentle eddies of air surrounding him turned sharp as razors. The swirling breeze that so placidly carried motes of dust became a vortex of blades honed with anger. Like water from a dog shaking itself dry, ribbons of blood showered the walls, and a moment later the hooded man collapsed, a quivering mass of torn flesh.

Skye looked down upon the dead man, exhausted from forcing so potent an alteration upon the world. A narrow escape, he mused.

Then came thunder.

In agony, Skye turned. A second assassin stood before him, smoke rising from the fusil in his outstretched arm.

Skye's back felt as if it were afire. Blood rose in his throat and the floor rose to meet him. It cradled him as his mother had before she lay him down to sleep. He would fall no further.

"Your worthless money was my ruin," the fusilleer said. "Now the debt is paid." Then he ran as the boots of approaching guards drummed the corridors of the Redan Inviolate.

Death came but Skye turned a blind eye. As darkness closed around him, the dying adept began one final elaboration. His hourglass almost empty, he wished it full.

Time is a river that never stands still. Yet, its wellspring is always refilled. Time that has passed returns to the till, and flows out again, down some other hill.

This rhyme he learned as a child returned to him and he made it his own, mining the essence of the words as he denied his fate with all his will. The body is strong and the mind is stronger. Thought survives. I survive. Though my body dies, I am, still.

Then the pain was gone and he opened his eyes.

He was home.

***

News of the Cardinal's death spread quickly among the assembled guests. At once there were whispers that the eclectics had infiltrated the Redan Inviolate, allowing soft men to boast of great deeds soon to come in defense of the realm.

Among the Caballine Azure, public mourning and private delight were the order of the evening, for the adepts had lost a key advocate. The Aver would certainly endorse their security recommendations, or so they believed.

The few who knew Skye well were genuinely distressed, both for the loss of a friend and for Sarcos.

When Elinvar reported the news to the Hierophants, Dahlia wept.

Elinvar remained close by Flux, ready to help him deal with whatever situation arose. He knew he was a poor substitute for the Cardinal, but clearly the boy needed someone with whom to share the burden of so great a deception. Both the Cardinal and he shared a common concern for the future of Sarcos, which now lay upon the shoulders of an impostor.

***

The ceremony to commend the Cardinal lasted all night, beneath a thick swath of incense. Many among the éclat came and went, but Dahlia remained in the bare stone chamber throughout, joining in the mourning dirge while her voice held. She could not recall a time when the mood among the celebrants was darker. Skye's death left a void, in her heart and in that of the Empire.

In the still hours at the edge of sleep, when she alone remained, she thought she saw a hooded figure. Startled, she turned, but saw no one. A flock of geese flew north, past the narrow window, while the stars faded with the coming sun.

At dawn, the celebrants moved the corpse outside so Bright Halo might gaze upon Skye before the ascension of his spirit.

Flux paid his respects when the light topped the curtain wall. He arrived flanked by two of the Screen, both wary of further violence. He knelt beside Dahlia and leaned his head on her shoulder.

***

Shortly before noon, the business of war began in earnest. The Council and the éclat met in the auditorium, with the Aver in attendance. With the adepts in disarray, and Azo's troops still up north, Auric was tapped to provide the bulk of the army. While most of the éclat could spare but a few hundred men each, the ambitious Cardinal had over six thousand in his service and at least as many more in the service of his supporters. Had Ordinal Amber's men escaped Tajo, he would have had more.

For hours, Auric felt the noose tightening around him as the logistics of fielding an army were hashed out. He had been poised to rule the Empire, until the coming of this boy had ruined everything. Though it galled him, there was nothing he could do. His fair-weather allies would desert him as soon as the chance presented itself. Open rebellion would turn him into a pariah. There was one option. He could side with the eclectics. But would they have him? He could not be certain. Since the destruction of Tajo he had heard nothing from them.

***

After a long day of meetings, Dahlia retired to the sitting room in the west wing of the Redan Inviolate to gather her thoughts. To her surprise, she found Curial Dure waiting for her by the glow of a slow fire.

He had been infatuated with her years before. There had never been anything between them but glances. He was too old, even then. But as a celebrant, she appreciated worship from afar and had always looked kindly upon the old man.

Well into his eighties, he still seemed alert and contented. His eyes were enormous, like green plums, such that conversing with him had always given her the sense of engaging someone through a fish bowl.

He looked up from the chair where he sat, leaning against his own knee, which he had pulled up to his chest like a jackknife.

"Hello, Limnal," he said, "I am pleased to see you again."

"Thank you, Curial. You brighten my evening as well." Dahlia took a seat on the plain wooden chair opposite the old man.

"Excepting your company, I cannot recall a time more grim."

Dahlia sighed. "Skye was a good friend."

"A man of worth," said Dure, nodding as he tugged his shirtsleeve a bit farther out of his stiff coat. "I grow tired of attending funerals." He withdrew a long, curved pipe from his pocket and began filling it with a blackish tar from a walnut-sized container.

"It is my least favorite task," Dahlia remarked, not quite honestly, given that the Pelagines were known for the beauty of their death rituals and indeed took pride in their devotions. She watched as Dure lit his pipe and sucked hungrily at the fumes from the tar, a resin called sloe, named both for its dark color and its qualities as a tranquilizer. She had seen Skye use it on several occasions to counter the effects of more potent hallucinogens.

"Has the cremation been . . . er . . . scheduled?"

Dahlia smiled. "Your name is on the list. The ceremony will be held at Skye Redan in a few days."

Dure looked relieved. "When you are old, too many people forget to include you among the living. Are you the executor, then?"

Dahlia nodded. "I am not sure if I should be honored or resentful. Liquidating his estate will be something of a chore."

"Sadly, his passing will leave many questions unanswered."

Dahlia suspected the old man wanted the answer to a particular question. She remained silent. She could wait.

"Did Skye ever mention an artificer named Peregrine?" Dure ventured after a few moments.

"Not in my presence. Why?"

"He was released from the Sanos Asylum, shortly after Pavo's Day, on the basis of a falsified writ. The man had a reputation as a skinrunner. Friends among the eclectics and such. The Verifex would like to speak with him."

"Skye despised such men."

Dure shrugged. "Even so, he knew their world well. More so, in his youth."

"What has Skye to do with this artificer?"

"Nothing, I imagine. The writ bears the signature of one of Auric's factors, who happened to be dead on the date the writ was executed. So we are casting a wider net, beyond Auric and his friends."

"I see," Dahlia said. "Enemies too."

"Skye kept an eclectic in his employ, you know," Dure said, clearly dubious of such things.

"Handel? He's harmless."

"Are the Pelagines going to follow the Cabal into sympathy with these abominations?"

"You are too hasty in your condemnations, Curial. He is not like the rest. He would not harm anyone."

"Still, this Handel fellow spent time at Sanos." Dure rubbed his aged hands together, as if trying to polish some particularly ugly parcel of truth into salability.

"Surely it is coincidence, nothing more." But Dahlia could not even convince herself. Her doubts grew like weeds.

"Even so, were I to find myself, like Cardinal Auric, with my allies deserting me, I would look for something more damning than coincidence."

"Speak plainly, Curial. Is there something you wish to tell me?"

"You loved Skye dearly, as I once did. I think it only right that you hear what is whispered, that you make up your own mind about the man."

Dahlia sat forward and listened, her look unforgiving.

"Some say the Aver is a fraud."

"Heretics, perhaps. Who else?"

"Curial Sine. Others too."

"Impossible. You saw him make the ascension."

Dure shrugged, his bones moving visibly beneath his pale skin like fish below ice. "There are always whispers. Perhaps Auric's ambitions collapsed under their own weight and nothing else. Perhaps Skye's seizure of the boy was completely selfless. I meant no offense, Limnal. I will leave you in peace." Curial Dure rose slowly and ambled out.

Dahlia watched the embers die and thought of her lost lover. Through her tears, the light sparkled like the stellar reveille she had seen as a child.

27

Within

Because we have no means to feed the fire Halo lit within us, we burn from the inside and are in time consumed. Yet we strive to honor Halo by tending the sacred fire, by setting it alight within our children.

—The Creed of the Lucifal

Rose lay on the narrow bed, listening to the underwater song of the submersible's engine as the curious vessel slipped away from Natal.

With her wound almost healed, she felt ready to practice swordplay once again. Though the cramped quarters left no room for such activity, the shock she felt on being joined with her blade had given way to a compulsion to test her keen-edged prosthetic. Its silence unnerved her. Irae had said it would guide her, but she felt nothing from it.

The realization that she was an eclectic was only beginning to sink in. Over and over again, she felt the new hole in her soft palate with her tongue, moving the flap of skin covering it back and forth as she sometimes did when trying to dislodge food caught in her teeth. The dark tales she had heard huddled around summer bonfires, about the eclectics and their abominable blood rituals, had proven completely unfounded. She had expected some transformation, some kind of rebirth. But she remained the same misfit she had always believed herself to be—only now it was more evident.

Shortly after the vessel's departure, Irae asked her if she would share memories with him, but she was not ready to be so generous with her thoughts. Perhaps that was where the nature of the change lay.

A while later, Rose gripped the oval door frame and passed into the corridor that was the hollow spine of the submersible. She walked slowly past similar doors toward the control room, where she saw Irae directing the vessel as if he were an orchestra conductor. She watched silently so as not to disrupt the rhythm of his directives. He appeared unduly frantic for what seemed so languid a voyage. Four other eclectics kept time with his commands, turning wheels, pulling levers, speaking into funnels attached to tubes that piped the voices elsewhere. There was something vaguely amusing about seeing such primitive histrionics from those supposedly so well integrated with machines.

Glancing at a glass level, Irae issued orders to the helmsman. "Ahead one-half, down fifteen degrees right rudder," he said. "Vent port chamber and repressurize."

Rose waved her good hand at Irae during a lull in the litany of his staccato commands.

"The currents are particularly rough here," Irae replied. "I am trying to keep us from being smashed against the walls."

Rose made the sign of inquiry.

"You want to know where we are?"

Rose nodded.

"Beneath the mountains southwest of Tajo, in an underground conduit that connects with Lake Dulcora and the Even River farther toward the sea."

Rose watched the team of eclectics navigate the submersible for a while, then headed forward to the observation chamber, which was nothing more than a closet with three seats and a window into the darkness. It was the potential of a view that brought her. Could it have been a month since she had last seen the face of Bright Halo shining against the azure sky? She missed the wind that set the great oaks dancing, and the solitude of the road.

When she thought about the brief adventure she had shared with Calx she realized how much she had come to rely upon her silence as a means of controlling her life. It was both solitary confinement and a fortress of self-determination.

Soon, Irae would expect her to open her mind to the thoughts of the other eclectics. They were so eager to taste her knowledge, to know what she knew of their god. Just thinking about it made Rose feel possessive. Already the memories of those slain by the Tongue drove her to distraction. Where, she wondered, would she find silence in the thoughts of thousands?

28

Who By Fire

An offer that cannot be refused may yet bring a reply that
cannot be accepted. Therefore, situate yourself such that all
roads lead to your offer, and any reply will be acceptable.
                                                    –Curial Alder

Flux stood atop the parapet of the high tower of the Redan Inviolate, and a tear fell, lost in the shimmering sheets of rain. It passed
through the drainpipe at his feet and out into the air again, swept in a
broken stream toward the cobblestones below.

Despite months of preparation, he was overwhelmed by the demands of his role. As the Aver, he was the voice of the gods. His power
was near absolute. Though the meetings he attended and audiences he
gave seldom required anything more than a nod of approval for deci-

sions already made, doling out his permission to the finely attired clerks and recorders of his word became as tiring as if he were transfusing some spent adept with his blood.

His desire to justify Cardinal Skye's trust had helped him endure the first few days after his mentor's death, but it was not enough. Even Elinvar's secret sympathy proved insufficient to buoy his spirits. Only fear kept him in character.

The day before he was to see the army off, he stared out the window of his bedchamber, not to survey the gray landscape he could not see, but to feel the warmth of the sun on his face. A bird landed on the sill, feathers aflutter. A pigeon, he thought. Too small for a gull. The soft cooing of pigeons echoed through his youth. His father had kept them, to pull from his sleeve—or to eat when money was scarce. He remembered the sound from visits to the asylum, and he realized that he too had become a prisoner.

***

In the pinched row houses that lined the residential streets of Sansiso, fathers and daughters hid their few precious works of metal, while mothers hid their sons. The foundries were already increasing their production of weaponry, and rather than levy a new tax to finance the military, impressment gangs would soon be visiting each house in turn, seizing human and material resources as needed. The hardships of the last war had taught the picayune to be reluctant patriots.

The vast bureaucratic apparatus of Sarcos had been awakened, and the coming bloodshed would at least irrigate a modest crop of profitable permits and arms contracts. The death futures market never looked brighter.

The éclat took advantage of the "unfortunate opportunity" that was the war. Behind the flurry of lavish dinners following the confirmation of the Aver, the éclat could barely restrain their ambition. Alliances formed and dissolved in a wary political ballet as each family of note maneuvered, bent its honor, broke its word, and forged it anew to secure a better seat at the postwar table, closer to the Pelagines and farther from the likes of Cardinal Auric.

***

A week later, Flux sat on his pale caval, beneath the weight of his black-and-gold ceremonial armor and the burden of pretense. He waited for his army to pass before him in review just outside the gate that opened onto Hangman's Circus. He would offer his blessing and the soldiers would think themselves protected. When the light of Bright Halo first struck his helm, the march began.

Fifty hands presented themselves before the Aver, some twenty-five thousand men, representing half of the professional soldiers in the Empire. Of these, half of those served Cardinal Auric or one of his allies. Among the lesser éclat, those who maintained only a handful of soldiers, smiles were everywhere. Auric was finally being brought to heel.

First came the adepts, solemn and lightly armed, in long overcoats and loose fatigues. They shunned the hindrance of armor and took only falchions in the event their minds failed them as weapons. A few carried fulmins or packs laden with odd siege devices. They regarded the Aver as they passed on foot, proud men all.

Among those observing the progress of the adepts, however, there were questions about why so few of them paraded by. One thousand strong, the marching column represented only one tenth of the registered practitioners of the bright mechanics.

Next came the footmen, nearly five thousand of them, in the service of the lesser éclat. They inclined their spears and heads in salute as they passed.

A wave of six thousand lancers followed, riding their light chargers. The fluttering banners tied below the tips of their lances snapped as if they were drumming the air. These were the troops who served the wealthy, culled from the garrisons of dozens of redans.

Last came over thirteen thousand of the Caballine Azure, perched like peacocks atop their oiled cavals. The great families of the éclat were all represented, either by sons or fathers, each bearing the standards of the Cabal and his lineage upon his tunic.

The schism in the Cabal could be seen in the weaponry of the riders: a few bore the traditional sword and lance, but most shouldered muskets and fusils. Despite the respect many held for Cardinal Azo and the old ways, he and his army were far away. Despite the prevailing belief that killing at a distance was cowardly, despite the generous servings of contempt heaped upon the adherents of black-powder weapons for allowing the valorous art of hand-to-hand combat to devolve into an exchange of lead projectiles between two points, Auric and his men knew they were the future.

Without warning, one of the Cabal broke ranks, prodding his mount into a canter, to where Flux stood amid a knot of soldiers. Elinvar and the other Screen reacted swiftly, encircling the Aver as two of them leveled their fulmin lances.

"Keep your distance!" bellowed the old Seneschal, standing beside Flux's mount.

A murmur coursed through the crowd. The rider was Cardinal Auric.

"Glorious Aver, I come before you as a supplicant. Will you hear my petition?"

In the laconic persona of the Aver, Flux nodded.

"Divine Aver," Auric cried to the assembled host, "behold the swords of Sarcos. On your dreams, we shall ride to victory!"

A great cheer erupted.

"Tell us what you see!"

All eyes turned toward Flux, his billowing white cloak tugging at him like a sail. For a moment, the birds roosting in the eaves of nearby houses could be heard again.

Flux felt his inner turmoil dissolve. He would no longer cower from assassins. The people needed him.

"Cardinal Auric," he began, with a slight tremor in his voice, "I have dreamt only of the sounds of battle these past nights. My place is with my soldiers."

Auric grew flushed and seemed to shrink in his saddle, manifesting his demotion in his posture.

Flux stammered on through the awkward silence. "So let it be known . . ." His voice trailed off, and he could not craft the right words. He felt suddenly as if every questioning face in the crowd judged him a fraud.

The old Seneschal stepped forth, bellowing, "So let it be known that on this day, the Aver takes command of the army of Sarcos!"

The crowd roared.

Elinvar looked stupefied.

Auric smiled graciously, and offered his wrist to Flux.

The gesture went unnoticed.

Caught up in the excitement, Flux kicked his heels into the flanks of his mount. Instead of launching itself into a dramatic gallop, his caval trotted through the Screen, then stopped.

The crowd erupted again.

The Soldiers of the Screen were taken aback by their Aver's advance and scrambled to reposition themselves.

Unhappy with his mount's recalcitrance, Flux drew his sword and held it aloft, eliciting another cheer from the crowd. A curious euphoria possessed him. His decisions were finally his own.

His voice rang out, "In the name of Ekal, Brand, and Gard, victory for Sarcos!" He brought the flat of his blade down on his caval's backside and the somnolent animal took off, with Flux clinging desperately to its mane.

The soldiers lifted their weapons. "Aver! Aver! Aver!"

Galloping past his men, all he could see were flashes of light and dark, as if he were caught beneath an angry breaking wave. He did not know where he was going, but that hardly seemed to matter. He knew who he was, and that was enough.

29

Thorns

To take a thing is to change it. By keeping us at a distance,
thorns are the keepers of beauty and the sharp factors of
eternity.

—Lucifal Jasmine

Without the daily march of the sun, Calx lost track of time. He had
been hiding on the submersible for several days, and was eager to stand
beneath Gard's sky again. This confined, isolated existence, cut off from
the physical world he knew, represented everything he feared about
the eclectics.

Rose's proximity compounded his discomfiture, her footfall audible on occasion in the corridor beyond. She had no reason to enter
his sanctuary, but her disembodied presence only served to remind him

of the distance between them. He loved her, yet could not fathom her abjurement of humanity. Though her apostasy had been nurtured by his own deceit, he blamed the eclectics. They were easy to hate.

A draft of winter pine told Calx the submersible had surfaced. He waited while several of the crew removed supplies from the storeroom, praying he would not be discovered.

In time, silence spread through the vessel, but for the intermittent sound of hammering in the induction room. Calx emerged from his burlap cocoon, stiff and irritable. He retrieved the sack with the ledger he had gone to such trouble to retain, to which he added as much dried meat as he could carry. He worried his rations would draw wolves, but he had no alternative.

He slipped into the submersible's deserted control room and hid among a bundle of leather tubes, each the size of his arm. They were warm and slightly greasy from the lubricant used to keep the leather supple. The sensation recalled a surgical delivery he had once witnessed, where a glistening baby was extricated from a gash in the mother's stomach. The child's umbilical cord was wrapped around the boy's neck like some lunatic's cravat, at once feeding and choking him.

At dusk, Calx emerged headfirst into the world again, between a deep blue sky and its watery reflection. He descended the narrow gangplank, leaving the submersible moored to a moss-covered pier of stone while it tugged against its tether in a futile effort to join the free-floating ice.

Just beyond the far end of the pier, he noticed a sentinel standing beneath a willow, guarding against approach by land. Rather than trying to divert the eclectic's attention, he decided he would just walk by, hoping he would be taken as one of the crew.

As he advanced, fear overcame him. Had the sentinel shared memories with Irae and the others? His bluff would surely fail. He slipped the wooden baton he had taken into the sleeve of his overcoat and closed with the sentinel as casually as his accelerating heart would allow.

"I believe you left this on board," Calx said, holding up his sack.

Startled, the sentinel turned to take a blow to the face. He dropped to the ground slowly, the bridge of his nose driven deep into his brain.

Luckily, this fellow didn't have Irae's metal skull. Calx armed himself with the dead sentry's fusil and falchion, and found that the corpse was surprisingly heavy. Dragging the sentinel to the middle of the pier, he rolled the body into the cold water of Lake Dulcora. It sank with unnatural swiftness.

As the sky went dark, Calx crept ashore, into the shadows of tall pines. He followed a path from the pier that led to a lichen-covered stone house. Lights spilled from within, and Calx heard voices.

Circling around back, he crouched below an open window, where he could listen to the subdued voices within. To his disappointment, nothing said that night was of any consequence. It seemed nothing more than a reunion of old friends and aged wine. He wondered which footfall voiced Rose's presence.

Finally, exhaustion overcame him and he moved deeper into the woods to sleep, lest some eclectic stumble across him dozing behind the house.

When morning came he was numb. Despite the heavy coat he had taken, the frigid air cleaved to him like syrup. The lumpy mattress on which he had spent the night in Tajo while waiting for Rose now seemed like a bower in paradise. He roused himself, shaking off bits of dirt and a few surprised insects, crestfallen at the departure of the warm, fleshy hill that seemed too good to be true.

At the far side of the house, the eclectics had gathered to saddle their horses.

From his hiding place, Calx recognized Rose, Irae, and Agar. The remaining men and women were strangers to him. While most of the riders appeared human, a few resembled mosaics of flesh and metal, some with chromed limbs, others with silvery partial faceplates. They were all well dressed and well armed, with fulmin lances, sophisticated fusils, and swords of brilliant steel.

Barely within earshot, he caught only fragments of Irae's orders. It sounded as if they made for Sansiso, likely as assassins. Under normal circumstances, he felt certain the eclectics would be apprehended. But he had come to suspect that some among the Council might look the other way for the sake of personal gain. If only he could be certain.

Caught in a knot of speculation, he resolved to follow Irae's party until he could ascertain its purpose.

An hour later, the house was shuttered. The eclectics followed the Even River southward, away from the lake. Four of them remained, one tending a riderless horse. After a brief consultation, three of them headed off in the direction of the submersible while the fourth lingered by the house, calling for someone named Tusah.

Calx guessed it was Tusah he had commended to the bottom of the lake, and who now had no use for a horse. Emerging from his hiding place, he maneuvered around the back of the house. He readied his falchion, preferring not to announce his presence with his fusil. Cautiously moving into position, he found the horse alone, tied to a sapling. The open front door suggested the whereabouts of the remaining eclectic. He thought for a moment about a line from the Creed of the Pelagines, one he learned as a child: With each door Wild Brand opens, let others pass through.

Soon astride the rust-colored horse, he laughed for the first time in weeks as he galloped off in pursuit of Rose.

***

After two days in the saddle, Rose was eager to rely on her own legs again. She was a fine rider, but she preferred to be on foot. She wondered if her new brothers and sisters, with their artificed limbs, felt the same way. She listened to several of them recall their adjustment to their altered forms. The eclectics seemed rather surprised by her interest, and generally tried to allay her concerns, dismissing the diminution of sensation as trivial. When she protested in her frantic sign language that losing such pleasures as a warm bath was a great sacrifice, they generally nodded sympathetically.

Though her companions were, with the exception of Irae, uniformly laconic, Rose sensed no lack of camaraderie. The common ancestry of oppression that tied the eclectics together colored their occasional stories and quips. The repeated incidents of abuse recounted by those willing to speak openly made it easier for Rose to contemplate killing the Aver.

On the evening of the second day, Rose succumbed to her nagging desire to be accepted into the group and indicated to Irae that she was ready to share his memories.

She had seen Pelagines perform their elaborate remembrance of the dead, and as Irae uncoiled the cord that would serve as a conduit for his memories, the contrast between the two rituals gave her pause. It seemed something so intimate ought to require ceremonial foreplay.

Cautiously, Rose accepted the unattached end of the cord from Irae, and as she placed it into her mouth, she convulsed with silent laughter. The cord tickled as it clicked into the connection port.

There was no fire in the camp, to avoid advertising their presence–only the light of Gavo's silvery eye and Brand's million dreams above. Rose reminded herself that the eclectics called them "moon" and "stars," but old habits, like weeds, have strong roots.

The transfer began and ended in what seemed no time at all. It reminded her of drinking a glass of water with a peculiar taste that one recognizes only later. She had hoped for a revelation, only to find under each new memory another layer of complication. Where she had only her own point of view before, she now had dozens, as irreconcilable as the warring gods.

Rose yanked the cord from her mouth in horror. The confusion written across her face asked, "What have you done to me?" She fell slowly to the ground, her head spinning.

Irae tried to comfort her, but she recoiled from his touch. "It will pass," he said. "All of us are with you now. You must separate our thoughts from yours, like wheat from chaff."

Rose knew he spoke the truth. She remembered he had said it before to others over the years. Still, it was not easy for one used to isolation.

Irae left her alone and she lay on her back, gazing up at the stars. She imagined each one an eye looking out from the firmament of her head onto the vista of some eclectic's past. In these dreamscapes she saw too many truths. There was the warm southern seashore where a sailor had fallen in love–the same shiny sand where a mother had watched her son swept away, little hands clutching at the waves like five-fingered fins. There were the green hills overlooking Sansiso where one man's solitude was another's loneliness. There were so many sights and sounds and scents recalled with near-equal portions of pain and pleasure.

In those memories was a hint of what might have been, a hint of all the dreams denied. She remembered now for hundreds, perhaps thousands. What must it be like for the Aver, she thought? To carry the burden of billions long gone within? Killing him seemed almost an act of mercy.

Eventually, her own experiences surfaced as irrepressibly as debris from a sinking ship, and she was able to salvage the boundary between thoughts of hers and those of others. She wondered then whether, as the Lucifal said, all memories began long ago in a single great sun, white as an unscattered rainbow. She had longed to belong, to be part of a greater whole, but now she was not so sure. What if being an outcast was not a punishment but a reward?

***

The following day, the eclectics turned west, away from the Even River and into the hills of Scoria. Though it was not the most direct route to Sansiso, Calx, following behind, surmised the eclectics wanted to keep their distance from Skye Redan, just to the south.

The land turned greener as they neared the sea, and farms became more common. Stones piled in undulating lines fenced the land, making the fields more difficult to traverse. It would be only a matter of time before the eclectics were forced to take to the roads.

Calx had little trouble tracking Irae and company, but the foliage thinned and he had to drop further and further back to avoid detection.

At midafternoon, Irae called his group to a halt.

Calx tied off his mount and approached cautiously on foot.

The eclectics waited in silence for almost an hour, until a hooded rider emerged from the forest. They greeted the rider warily, lowering their weapons only after they had ascertained the newcomer's identity.

A heated discussion ensued.

Calx slithered closer, pressed up against the pungent earth and pine needles. There was something familiar about the rider. He handled his horse like a caballine.

It was his former comrade-in-arms, Elinvar.

***

Elinvar shook his head, drawing back his hood. "I urged the Aver to remain in the city, but he would not listen."

Irac fumed. "You were paid to make him listen."

"You vastly overrate the value of your decales," Elinvar snapped.

Irae drew his fusil.

Holding his hands up in front of his scarred face, Elinvar flinched. "Let us be reasonable, Irae," he said. "There may be a way."

"I am listening. It will be fascinating to hear how we can seize the Aver from an army of twenty-five thousand."

"The encampment is poorly guarded to the south. Tomorrow, there will be an opportunity for you to infiltrate unnoticed."

"An opportunity?" Irae said impatiently. "Explain."

"I have said too much already. Let it suffice that an opening will present itself."

Irae leaned forward, his eyes narrowing. "Perhaps if we shared memories, your inability to find the right words would be less troubling."

"Come now, Irae," Elinvar answered with a nervous laugh. "You sound as if you do not trust me."

Irae grinned. "I don't."

With a nod to Agar, the other eclectics closed around Elinvar and dragged him from his horse.

Elinvar struggled violently, pulling his captors to the ground with him, but he could not break free. They brought him to his knees and restrained him, stretching his arms between them. His wide-set eyes burned with anger.

Irae produced a cord from his pocket, his memory conduit. "You understand now why it was necessary to have the port installed when you offered to provide us with intelligence."

Hard hands pinched Elinvar's jaw until it opened wide enough for the cord to be attached. He fought still. Veins bulged like adrenaline etchings. It was futile.

Irae smiled as he slipped the other end of the cord into his mouth. "Sharing is good for the soul," he quipped cheerfully.

Irae and Elinvar moved for a moment in unison, just as a fusil fired from somewhere nearby.

Elinvar collapsed with a hole in his head.

Irae seized and twitched like a beached fish.

The eclectics turned, horses panicked. The sniper fled through the trees. Agar and three others took off in pursuit.

Rose slid from her mount. Her first instinct was to comfort Irae, to try to still his shuddering. She held back, not wanting to cut him accidentally.

Another eclectic, meanwhile, had the presence of mind to detach the cord, and Irae relaxed. Though shaken, he appeared stable.

The eclectics waited for him to recover. Rose knelt beside him and stroked his synthetic hair.

Finally, he said, "I saw the moment of death. Overwhelming. Little else got through. Betrayals upon betrayals." Staring at the ground, he added, "They're all going to die."

***

Calx rode hard through the trees, branches whipping his face. His legs ached. It had been a long time since he had ridden so vigorously. But he had not forgotten how to do so. Horse and man had a bond unknown among the eclectics.

Through icy stream and thick brush, Calx widened his lead. He stopped at the top of a ridge, lips cracked, mouth dry, and laughed. No one followed. He turned south, hoping to find the army Elinvar had spoken of. The only way to free Rose was with the help of the Cabal. He hoped he would not have to liberate her against her will.

Calx regretted killing Elinvar, though he had proved a traitor. He would have preferred to shoot Irae, but another would have taken his place. Life offered too few clear shots.

Several hours later, beneath the heavy cloud cover of an approaching storm, the darkness was almost complete. As Calx emerged from the forest onto the plains west of Skye Redan, rain began to fall.

He dismounted beside a jumble of rocks and secured his horse. Soaked and exhausted, he took shelter beneath the overhang of a boulder. He slept poorly. Rose weighed heavily on his mind. What would it be like, he wondered, to be an eclectic?

In the middle of the night, he awoke suddenly.

Above him loomed a sneering lancer. A black boot hurtled toward his face.

30

Sanos

Each year, I learn more and am less certain about it, the
ultimate result of which will be omniscience, limitless
possibilities, and death. This seems peculiarly bad timing.
                                                    –Curial Dure

Following the departure of the army, Dahlia wrapped up her affairs in Sansiso. She was due back at Skye Redan by the end of the
week to pay her respects to Cardinal Skye. She did not relish making
the journey in the coming rain. When she last traveled north it was
snowing. Perhaps the time had come to give up the saddle for a coach.
Still, faith without hardship verged on hypocrisy.

While perusing the sparse winter fare displayed in the market stalls
outside the Pelage Deep, she ran into Limnal Henna, a colleague who

presided over a Pelage in the southeast. They embraced amid the rowdy morning crowds, gathered for warmth around the chestnut roasters.

Henna remained the same fleshy cherub she had been in her youth, and was evidently without complaint serving the Thalass on the border of sleepy Aqal. The southern sun left her tanned like the picayune who labored in the fields, but she professed not to mind.

The two women left the shadow of the great Pelage, fighting the tide of worshippers who came for the morning projection. Though it would have been easy enough to find a private chamber in the catacombs below, both Dahlia and Henna preferred to break their fast at a nearby tavern.

Over hot cider, the two Limnals discussed the activities of various celebrants and the latest political maneuverings among the Pelagines.

"The search for the Tongue goes poorly," Henna said. "Our factors have been scouring the countryside, but no one has seen the blade."

Dahlia nodded. The eclectics would do their utmost to keep the blade hidden.

After reminiscing about Mere Calico and her tragic end, the conversation turned to other subjects.

"I wanted to ask," said Dahlia, "whether your Pelage had recorded an unusual number of land transactions recently."

Henna looked surprised. "Aye, a number of farmers recently sold their lands. The buyer was a man with whom I am not familiar."

"A factor for one of the éclat?"

"Almost certainly."

"On my way to Vejas, I encountered a family who had sold their lands to an unnamed buyer. They were paid with forged notes. I suspect the same is true down south."

"Likely the ubiquity of the false notes is what prompted the Verifex to intervene."

Dahlia shrugged. "Suppose it is not the land that is valuable, but something on it?"

"Unsanctified metal?" Henna asked. "You think perhaps Auric seeks a way around our cartel?"

"I wonder."

***

Dahlia spent the afternoon searching fruitlessly among the dusty stacks of land deeds stored in the Pelage Deep. The dismal state of the records finally led her to despair. Between land schemes, wars, and dire prophecies, she felt drawn in too many directions at once. She had become suspicious of everyone, as if she alone had been excluded from some great conspiracy. Or was her mind making connections where there were none?

Frustrated, she left the vaults and walked back along the dark corridors to the heart of the Pelage to meditate. She stood for a time by the altar, contemplating the golden statuette of Cardinal Osker, perhaps the Pelage's most sacred artifact from the Dim Age. Lost in thought, she ran her finger along the hieroglyphic translations of the kinos that had been carved in the walls.

When she reached one of the dreams of unexpected paths, she paused. There was something in the tale that reminded her of her own situation, though it was one of Gard's dreams. What was he trying to explain by describing how a quest for justice became a contest to acquire a treasured bird? The orthodox interpretation, that curiosity leads to unexpected paths, did not seem to fully capture the essence of the dream. Examining the tangle of symbols carefully, she noted that a man of the lesser Cast called Gutman had praised Gard "for plain speaking and clear understanding." If she could not determine her own path, as it had seemed since she first received the summons to Skye Redan, perhaps understanding was the most she could ask for. It seemed to her that the was really a dream of diminished expectations.

But then Dure's words returned to her. He had asked about an artificer named Peregrine. The name of a bird. A kind of falcon, wasn't it? A curious coincidence, if nothing else.

***

Old trees claimed the land north of Sansiso, beneath lolling tongues of fog that rolled in from the sea. For all their evident might, the moss-covered boughs offered travelers no serenity.

Riding along the neglected path to Sanos, Dahlia felt vulnerable. Only the most desperate of men would waylay a Limnal, but these were desperate times. Time to start carrying a fusil. Skye would have scolded her for traveling alone. Other Limnals rode with soldiers, but she preferred her own company. Perhaps others knew that too.

Neither Skye nor Auric trusted her fully, not really. Not even the Thalass. Had she been foolish to think that she could achieve some measure of understanding without taking sides? They wanted her allegiance without letting her understand. They wanted faith, and she had none to spare.

From the corner of her eye, she thought she saw someone. A figure in a brown mantle? No. Just the wind through the leaves. She shivered and urged Gray Apple onward.

Late in the day, Sanos Asylum showed itself through the trees. The old rectangular manor stood five stories tall and perhaps three times as wide, with two additional wings extending still further. The walls were so thick with ivy that it seemed the sloping roof had only vines for support. Barely visible through the foliage were dozens of slit windows no wider than three fingers. Birds slipped in and out of the ivy like bees from a hive.

The asylum was eerily silent and the gravel courtyard was poorly tended, with branches and leaves scattered about. Dahlia tied Gray Apple to a tree at the edge of the clearing. It surprised her there was no attendant to greet her.

She knocked on the door and waited.

A bony young man in a shabby suit opened the door just enough to present his goateed face. "If you've come for treatment, there is no one here to see you," he said wearily.

Behind him, a burly sentry armed with a half-eaten baguette peered out at Dahlia, then retreated to a bench in the foyer.

Dahlia grinned. "I wish to speak with the director. Is he in?"

"And who are you?"

When Dahlia identified herself, the doorman became a fountain of apologies. He heaved the door open and roused the sentry from the bench so she might have a place to sit until the director could be summoned.

Still saddle-sore, Dahlia preferred to stand.

The foyer had seen better days. It was not much more than a gray corridor, devoid of decoration, that made adjacent rooms inviting by its sheer blandness. To the left, a stairway climbed to the second floor. Further on, small doors offered access to the rest of the asylum. A single lux, barely glowing, hung overhead.

After a minute spent scanning the courtyard, the sentry asked, despite the evident lack of such conveyance, "D'you come by coach, éclat?" Bits of bread crust flew from his lips.

"By horse."

The sentry craned his neck. "Don't see one."

"I tied her to a tree over there." Dahlia pointed through the doorway.

The sentry furrowed his brow. "Best I move her. Bad mushrooms around the silver birch. Amanitas."

"She has a keen enough nose to know what's good for her." Didn't she? Dahlia shrugged. "Perhaps you should, to be safe."

The sentry nodded and lumbered out.

A door opened at the far end of the hall and the doorman reappeared, beckoning. "The director will see you now."

Dahlia followed the doorman, who kept looking back over his shoulder every few steps, as if he were afraid of losing his guest en route. After rounding a corner and ascending a short flight of uneven steps, they arrived at another door.

The doorman knocked.

"Come in, come in."

After ushering Dahlia in, the doorman perfunctorily offered up his wrist before hurrying out, whistling as he went.

The director's windowless office reeked of pipe tobacco and mildew, the latter scent emanating from yellowed stacks of paper rising precariously from the damp floor. Crammed into the office between the desk and two chairs were several trunks stuffed with papers and books.

"Welcome, Limnal," the director said. Wax lined the nails of his upturned hand, presumably from scraping candle drippings off his desk.

He had the rumpled look of a scholar, long in wear but sharp still. Hair clung to the sides of his head, a gray frame for his rosy ears. "Director Citrine at your service."

"Perhaps I have come at a bad time," Dahlia replied, glancing askance at the trunks.

Citrine nearly fell trying to get around the clutter to offer Dahlia a chair. "No, no, no. I always have time for so esteemed a guest. You see, you caught us rather off-guard, coming alone as you have. Most everyone has gone. Us too, by week's end."

Dahlia eased herself into her chair, afraid it would prove as fragile as it looked.

Citrine rushed back behind his desk and sat, then stood again as he realized he had not offered the Limnal any refreshment.

"Porter!" he cried, then turned to Dahlia. "Would you like anything? We have ... er ..."

Porter entered immediately, as if he had been just on the other side of the door.

"Porter, do we have anything for the Limnal?"

"Naught but water, kame, and it smells of old leaves."

"Nothing?" he gasped.

"Dove has some bread." Porter grinned, revealing a mouth looted of teeth.

Citrine shook his head and waved Porter away. "That won't do at all. I have a flask here somewhere."

"It's all right, kame. I came well provisioned."

Citrine looked up from his rummaging and shrugged. "As you wish, éclat. What can I do for you?"

"Did you say you were leaving by week's end?"

The director nodded sadly. "Aye, not much point in staying, really."

"Why is that?"

"No more patients."

"None? What happened to them?"

"All dead. Tragic accident. Poisoned, a month ago yesterday. Gruesome business. Best I can tell, the cook decided to experiment with the local mushrooms. Probably saw a rabbit nibbling and thought they were safe."

"Your sentry mentioned amanitas. The adepts use those for their visions. They are not lethal, so far as I'm aware."

"You are thinking of the one called the Fly Agaric, the muscaria," Citrine cautioned. "We have the amanita verna around here. Far less fun. The only vision that comes is death."

"How many?" Dahlia's imagination was already inflating the tragedy to genocidal proportions.

"All ten," Citrine said cheerily. "Most of our patients left with the transport order from the Thalass last year. Our eclectics went to the adept's facility at Davas. Security issues and such. Those who remained were mostly picayune malcontents and the occasional artificer."

"Was a man named Peregrine among them?"

Citrine's smile froze. "Oh, I wouldn't know about that."

"Your remaining ten patients die, and you cannot name them?" Dahlia sat forward in her chair as Citrine leaned back.

"Well, no, he was not among the ten."

"But he was here before the incident?" Dahlia brushed her hair back and looked into Citrine's eyes. "You cannot deceive me, kame," she said, knowing he believed as much.

The director laughed nervously. "Why would I do such a thing, Limnal?"

"That is precisely the question I would put to you, kame. You are, after all, a civil servant. I ask you, in the name of the Aver and the Council, why would you lie to me?"

Dahlia knew how to put steel in her voice.

Citrine bowed his head in supplication, his hands clasped together. "Please, Limnal," he blubbered, "they told me to lie. They said I was not to mention his name on pain of death."

"Who said?"

"The Cabal."

"Cardinal Auric?"

"Near enough. One of the late Ordinal Fin's factors."

Dahlia nodded. "He was the one who presented the writ of release to you?"

Trying not to tremble, Citrine nodded. "I remember thinking it was rather odd, Peregrine having a reputation with skins more than metals. Usually, the Cabal looks for the metalworkers. Pays well too."

"Would you know Fin's man by sight?"

"He wore a hood, so I saw little of his face. Likely ashamed of his looks. Had a scar, if I recall."

"Here?" Dahlia pointed just below her left eye. "Like a crescent?"

Citrine nodded, uncertain but eager to please.

Elinvar? That made no sense. Yet, he had served Fin, Skye, and now the Screen. He had ties to the Council, without doubt. But on whose behalf had he been acting?

"Do you have a log of some sort?" Dahlia asked. "Records of your patients, and your visitors?"

Citrine, anxious to end his interrogation, led Dahlia to a drafty room where the records were kept. The chamber had once served as a recreation area for the staff. Rough stone walls shone with patches of color, the result of a well-intentioned but incomplete effort to liven the atmosphere with paint. A variety of plain chairs offered nothing but discomfort.

"I will fetch Porter to make the room agreeable." Citrine hurried out.

Porter's arrival brought candles and a crackling fire, and the room's ambience improved from dreary to tolerable. Dahlia, reluctant to travel back to Sansiso in darkness, inquired about the possibility of remaining for the evening. Happy to oblige, Porter trotted off to prepare a bed, whistling a chirpy tune.

By sunset, Dahlia had grown weary of scouring the asylum's records. She wasn't even sure what she looked for, or why. To set her own mind at ease? There were rumors, Dure had said. Nothing tied Peregrine to the Aver. His release during Serpens, the month after Pavo, was likely coincidental. If it was Elinvar who had served the forged writ, that was hardly conclusive. Was Ekal testing her faith? Or was she trying to justify her doubts?

Her vision beginning to blur, Dahlia set down the Director's log, the crisp pages crackling like fire. With birdsong echoing through the asylum, she set off in search of Porter to see whether her room had been readied.

Her lodgings left much to be desired, but she made no complaint. A lumpy mattress had been dragged into a room recently stripped by the departing staff. Its path remained traced in dust. Beyond bed, night table, washbasin, and fireplace, there were no amenities. A tattered square of brown velvet hung immodestly over the slit window.

Dinner came via Porter. He mumbled an apology for the director, who he said had urgent business elsewhere. She did not press the matter, willing to let Citrine cower in his chambers. Fear made for poor conversation, in any event. After handing her a bowl of spiced potatoes, Porter offered to taste her meal.

"That will not be necessary," Dahlia said. "You seem pious enough not to poison a Limnal without good reason."

Porter blanched. "You know I would never do such a thing."

Dahlia nodded. "Of course."

"Before I turn in, is there any other way I can be of service?" he asked earnestly. "Something to stuff in the window perhaps?"

"The draft is not that bad, thank you."

"For the birds, I mean. They can be rather loud."

"I heard them earlier. Do they nest in the eaves?"

"We had a patient for many years who called himself Cuckold," Porter said, still amused by the name. "Sad man—nice though. Fell on hard times, and his wife left him, if I recall. A real showman, he was. Died about a year ago. Kept birds—to pull out of hats, you know. They just stuck around. Easy food, I guess."

Dahlia furrowed her brow. Why was that name familiar? "I did not see him on the list of patients. Did his family pay for him privately?"

"Charity case. Cardinal Skye paid his upkeep. Heard he died recently too. Quite a shame. He was a kind man."

"You knew Skye?" Dahlia said, eyes wide.

"Aye, he used to come every month or two, though not much in the last year. Took Cuckold for walks. I think he felt sorry for him. Never did say why."

"What kind of birds did Cuckold keep?" Dahlia asked, thinking back to Skye's words when she rebuffed him.

"Why, cuckoos, of course," Porter said with a laugh. "Him being crazy and all. We used to trap them for him. There were others too—pigeons and such."

"Did Cuckold have any family?"

***

The next day, Dahlia arrived at Byfield Way, having changed her horse for a day-hire coach. The street ran through one of the rougher neighborhoods on the periphery of Sansiso, and the coachman kept his whip ready as Dahlia disembarked. Telluria loomed in the distance, shrouded in smoke. The filth of the great foundry had worked its way into the soil, giving rise to twisted trees and birds that croaked. Picayune squatters watched from the shadows, just beyond a weed-choked well.

Near an abandoned Albedo, she found the house she sought: the crumbling hut where Cuckold, or Jet, had once lived. It appeared to have been part of a larger farm, now subdivided to accommodate the expanding urban population. The thatched roof sagged in the middle, frozen in suggestion of imminent collapse. Shuttered windows and an overgrown garden told of an occupant absent or dead.

Nonetheless, Dahlia knocked and waited.

When no one answered she wandered around the back of the house. Though the yard was small, hedges blocked the view of the adjacent lots. Behind the house stood the remains of a fire-scarred shed, its door hanging open like some lack-wit's mouth.

Inside, the wooden floorboards had long since rotted through and the gray sky was the only roof. Dahlia walked carefully. After a casual perusal of the debris revealed nothing of interest, she returned to the street.

She was about to leave when she noticed someone watching her from the shambles of a house across the way. A moment later, the surveiller drew the drapes. Her curiosity piqued, she approached the neighboring house and knocked on the door.

After a minute of waiting, Dahlia grew impatient. "Open the door or I will fetch a sentinel!" she exclaimed.

The door opened a crack and a prune of a woman peered out. "I meant no disrespect, éclat," she sputtered between violent spasms of coughing.

"You were watching me. Why?"

The old woman hesitated. "I heard you mucking around across the way. I thought it might be the boy."

"The boy?"

"Cuckold's boy. Been away for years, though," the old woman said, pointing with a skeletal finger at a stack of letters on the dingy side table. "I have these parcels for his father. They say not to discard them."

Dahlia stepped inside, to the evident dismay of the woman, and took one of the many identical letters. On the envelope, addressed to "Jet of Byfield Way," was the seal of the Curia and the admonition, "Destroying, discarding, or otherwise hindering the delivery of this letter to the listed recipient(s) is a crime under the Civil Codex of Sarcos."

Opening it, she read:

Jet of Byfield Way, or any living heir(s),

Our records show a balance due the Sansiso Postal Authority in the amount of seven hundred thirty-three decales for storage of a payment-on-delivery parcel. We cannot release this parcel until payment is received. Please come to the Central Postal Authority in Sansiso to pay the amount due and collect your parcel. Failure to comply will result in further charges.

At Your Service,

Collections Office, The Central Postal Authority

Dahlia laughed aloud when she read the date. "This is over two years old."

"The expressman brings me one every month. He's afraid that if he declares the address invalid he'll be fined, because the man who had the route before him failed to say anything when he had the chance."

The old woman wrung her hands nervously and gazed at the pile of letters. "I'm quite anxious to be rid of them."

***

Dahlia stepped from her coach in Tel Square. Across the plaza, the Central Postal Authority stood in one of the city's oldest buildings. Clutching her stack of letters, now bound with twine, she walked briskly through the flocks of mottled pigeons scouring the street offal for food, through the somberly clad bustle of men and women, and into the atrium where the factors of the Central Postal Authority rushed madly about. The constant shouting, jostling, and surliness of the main-floor expressmen, busy routing their packages and dealing with customers, was matched only by the lethargy evident among the senior managers on the upper floors.

After several misdirections, Dahlia finally arrived at the fourth-floor Collections Office where, after some bitter wrangling and a discreet payment, she finally obtained the long-held parcel.

She walked to the end of the dimly lit hall, where a shuttered window begrudgingly admitted a sliver of light, and examined the wax-sealed envelope. It was quite unremarkable, and did not come from anyone of means, if the quality of the paper was any indication. More-over, the wax seal was a thumbprint rather than the mark of any of the great families.

Opening the envelope, she withdrew a single sheet of thick paper bearing a smudged charcoal rendering. She recognized the Aver's face. Incredulous, she held it up to the light. It was truly a fine likeness. She was amazed any artist would risk such heresy.

On the back of the rendering, she saw someone had written, "Your son is well. One of the éclat saw fit to look after him, and he will soon be leaving Telluria for a better life. He asked if I would write and let you know he is well. Though he values pictures not at all, I have drawn this image of him from memory, hoping it might please you as the image of my son pleases me."

The note was signed "Morphine."

Though he values pictures not at all? Because he could not see? Curial Dure had been right. The Aver was dead. The boy was a fake. She closed her eyes, but the truth did not, like ugliness, disappear in darkness.

31

The Defile

The hand of Fate is easily seen if you but pry it from your eyes.

−A saying among the eclectics

The land became increasingly empty as the army moved into the countryside. The field hands took refuge in bushes and barns. Houses were shuttered. Women and children hid in basements. Spring had almost bested winter, but no one was planting when the Aver's army passed. Occasionally, when the light was right, the soldiers saw eyes peering from knotholes, or between the boards of homes. Everyone knew the treatment they could expect during wartime, but it was said the Aver rode with the army, and that was a sight worth seeing.

Flux tried to imagine what the stars saw when they looked down upon the great army of Sarcos marching off to war, a winding line of soldiers with oiled leather helms glinting like the scales of a serpent. He'd had a snake once. To his dull eyes it was a wriggling ribbon of light. He remembered it because it offered him the sensation of control that eluded him as he held the lifeless reins of his caval. He imagined that some would revel in the experience of heading up a serpentine column of soldiers, but he had never felt more constrained. The lives of all these men were a crushing burden.

***

By the fourth day out of Sansiso, scouts returned with news relayed from the northern redans. Several conflicting reports reached the command staff about the position of the eclectic army, which had either moved west from Tajo or southwest toward Lake Dulcora. What appeared more certain was the status of the bridge over Noto Gorge, which remained unoccupied.

Taking the recommendation of his strategists, Flux ordered the army of Sarcos to turn toward the bridge double-time. By nightfall, the bridge would be secured, thereby cutting off one of the three routes toward Sansiso. With Azo's forces already to the northeast between Tajo and Lake Caelum, the eclectics would either be hindered by the hills or forced to move west toward the farmlands near the coast, where they would be caught in a web of well-defended redans.

At noon, as was customary in the Caballine Azure, Cardinal Auric called the army to a halt so that his men might observe the height of Bright Halo's ascension. The caballines dismounted and lay upon their backs in the tall grass of the plain to make their obeisance. Most of the other soldiers did the same, not wishing to offend the gods on the eve of battle.

It seemed to Flux that Auric had become more assiduous in his observance of religious custom to make his embrace of the dark mechanics seem more wholesome.

Later that afternoon, Flux attended a briefing with his senior officers. The meeting place—four walls of billowing silk, stretched between stout wooden posts—offered little shelter from the wind.

Ordinal Sepia, a sallow adept who looked like he had forgotten to eat for several weeks, warned of foul weather before dawn. The wind trilled the silk walls in confirmation of his words.

"How is it we were not forewarned?" Auric demanded angrily. "You would think among hundreds of adepts, at least one would have the weather sense of a field hand!"

"To predict the whims of Endless Gard is to know him," Sepia replied, "and, unlike our judgmental Azure friends, we do not pretend to know the mind of a god."

Auric glared. "I am tempted to believe that the adepts themselves called the coming storm that they might later dismiss it to earn favor."

Several of the other strategists chuckled.

Sepia offered only a peculiar smile.

Flux held up his hand. "Speak no more of such things, Cardinal. You will divide our army before the enemy does."

"Your pardon, Aver," Auric said, his voice strained. The others took the cue and went back to discussing the logistics of encampment.

Come darkness, the army of Sarcos had turned the Noto Plain into a city of cloth. Gusty winds challenged the tents on the flatlands, but could not drive them away. To the north, above the line of tree and hill, the storm-bruised sky threatened.

Flux sat alone in his tent, listening to the rise and fall of the wind. He feared for Elinvar, who had not been seen for hours. The remaining Soldiers of the Screen were making quiet inquiries throughout the camp, in case an assassin had infiltrated.

"Your grace, may I have leave to enter?"

It was the voice of Din, his taster. "Come," Flux said.

"Your meal is on its way," he said in the clipped accent of the south. He was a whippet of a man. Toxins showed up sooner in the frail.

"I am not hungry, Din," Flux said with a sigh.

"You should worry less and eat more."

The scent of lamb stew preceded the arrival of the cook, accompanied by Pica, one of the Screen.

The cook delivered his clay pot to Din. He had changed into a fresh suit and a pristine white apron to deliver the meal, lest the slightest grease stain suggest inattention. He offered his wrist. "To your health, Aver," he said.

Flux thanked the cook nonchalantly, as he had been trained, and waved the man away. Pica remained to witness the tasting, and Din immediately commenced his ritual. He pulled a polished hardwood spoon from his coat and displayed it with a flourish before asking, "May I die for you this night, Aver?"

Flux nodded. How weary he had grown of that question, posed to him three times each day. It was he who had given his life for a lie. To let another risk death for him seemed wrong. What would Din think, Flux wondered, if he knew the truth?

Din helped himself to a spoonful of stew and pronounced it fit for consumption. He compared it favorably to several previous meals, as if tracing its lineage.

Flux waved the men away and Pica escorted Din out, closing the tent flap behind him. Flux didn't touch the stew.

With the wind picking up, he stepped outside. Pica and the other Soldiers of the Screen waited nearby. Poor though his vision was, he could see the lightning cracking the dark sky.

"Pica," Flux said, "can you see the army?"

"No, Aver, the cordon of silk around your tent blocks my sight." Pica stepped forward to better hear the youth speak. "It is dark, besides."

"Any word of Elinvar?"

"No, Aver. But do not worry."

***

Calx regained consciousness to find an owl-faced caballine shaking him. His head throbbed. Somehow, he had arrived in a tent that stank of mud and wet canvas. He sat bound and gagged on a crate, in the glow of a lux, under the scrutiny of two lancers and the caballine.

"Good," said the caballine as Calx stirred, "he wakes." He removed the gag from Calx's mouth.

"I must speak with the Screen," Calx said between coughs. The blow to his head had left him nauseated.

"You must speak with me first." The caballine gripped Calx by the face and tilted his head up. "You do not look like an eclectic."

"I am Calx, of the Caballine Azure, on assignment for the Verifex." The three men glanced at one another.

"Are there any among the éclat who know you?" asked the caballine.

"My commission comes from Ordinal Celadon."

"Wild Brand favors you," said the caballine. "The Ordinal rides with us." He nodded to the second lancer, who ducked out of the tent and into the rain.

"I am grateful," Calx said. "What is your name?"

"Welt of Navar. Enough talking for now." Welt replaced the gag, ignoring Calx's protestations. He gazed at the remaining lancer, who had taken a seat on the ground. "You look pathetic, kame," he said.

The lancer looked up, pushing against the damp canvas beneath him in a losing battle against gravity. There was a hollow look in his eyes, and his skin shone with sweat. "I fear I would fall were I to remain standing."

Welt smirked. He then turned toward Calx and looked him over, fitting him with a new identity. "If you are a caballine, you will understand my caution. Some say eclectics can kill with voice alone. Not the way adepts can, but with sound so sharp it cuts like a blade. Seems unlikely, if you ask me, but no more strange than eclectics themselves."

Calx tried to speak through his gag, but his muffled grunts only irritated Welt.

"Be silent," he said, raising his hand in threat. "We will wait for the Ordinal."

Ten minutes passed. The storm gathered strength and the lancer weakened. He clutched at his stomach and shivered in agony. Welt, looking rather faint himself, covered the lancer with a blanket.

"Something is wrong," the lancer whispered.

Welt glanced nervously about. "I will fetch a physician. Watch the prisoner." He stepped out into the rain.

Shortly thereafter, the lancer began vomiting blood.

For almost an hour, Calx watched the lancer's harrowing decline. To keep his mind from the man's suffering, he struggled with his bonds and had nearly worked his right hand free. Outside, but for the downpour, it was strangely silent.

By the time he managed to escape, the lancer was dead. In the absence of a celebrant, Calx mumbled a hasty commendation, figuring the man deserved some measure of respect. His duty done, he grabbed the dead man's sword and set off to find someone who knew what was going on.

A flash of lightning showed a great pool of water on the plain. The tents looked like they were floating on a brown lake. Like houseboats on the Lake of Salt, he thought, though he had only heard tales of the place. Nearby, the crack of several fusils briefly challenged the thunder.

The Noto Plain had become a place of nightmares. From what Calx could see, the army had turned on itself. Groups of men fought one another because they were there to fight. It seemed the adepts had the upper hand, but the caballines fought on.

Dawn was only an hour away, and he could barely make out shapes in the gloom. There were bodies everywhere, many still alive, though in wretched pain. Horses and cavals wandered through the labyrinth of tents gazing curiously at the men dying in the mud.

Calx slogged through the encampment, his breath hanging in the air. He kept his eyes to the ground to avoid stepping on dying soldiers. Urizen has come, he thought, though he knew the signs of poisoning. He wanted to believe the adepts were incapable of such barbarism, but the proof lay before him.

Just beyond a nearby tent, he heard the hissing of a torch and then saw three adepts in the magnesium glow. They walked among the bodies, checking the fallen for signs of life. Where they found it, they swiftly snuffed it out.

He stole away, lest his revulsion drive him to fury. He could not serve the Aver dead. He had to survive, to remember what passed this night. As he had survived Tajo? By flight? The brave lay at his feet, he told himself, and what good were they now?

***

The eclectics waited for hours in the rain. Concealed within the forest at the edge of the plain, they could just make out the Sarcosian army. In the distance, its barbed silhouette of lances and standards looked frail, more whiskers than quills.

Shortly before dawn, Irae approached Rose, who sat alone under a sycamore tree. She was huddled in a damp blanket, her sword arm protruding.

"You look like a different person when you are wet," Irae observed.

Rose gazed quizzically at Irae, her eyes asking if that was good or bad.

"Has the sword told you nothing?"

Rose shook her head. Not as it once had, she thought.

Irae turned his eyes to the dark sky. "Urizen is stingy with his signs," he said bitterly and sat beside Rose.

She leaned up against him. There was no need for words. She remembered Irae's thoughts about such moments, words he had said to others—strange comfort, to be sure, but comfort nonetheless. His thoughts gave her a sense of her place. For an outcast, that was everything.

A few minutes later, Agar returned from reconnaissance. "It is just as you foresaw, Irae. The humans are dying."

32

Prison and Palace and Reverberation

And the Sword shall become flesh and dwell within us, and
we shall behold the Aver's glory long-forgotten, written in
shadow on the white road.

—The Old Prophet

The day of the funeral, Skye's body lay in the garden of his cherished home on a makeshift bier beneath a slack cerulean awning that
recalled brighter days. In attendance were his few close friends and a
selection of the elderly éclat, the young being too busy dying on the
battlefield. The light drizzle hid what tears there were and masked the

eager sweat of those few who had come with veiled hopes of some material remembrance by way of Skye's will.

There were whispers that the tribesmen of Urgun had allied themselves with the eclectics and that a great host lay but a few days north. Following the completion of the service, a hundred adepts and several hands of militia made ready to occupy Skye Redan. The enemy was to be allowed no further south.

Dahlia approached Curial Sine as the service concluded. If anyone knew of Skye's relation to Jet, he would. Though he had no reason to help her, many of the elderly éclat seemed eager to bare their secrets to attractive young women. She supposed it was a sort of penitence for youthful misbehavior now long forgotten by all but their consciences, or perhaps usefulness reminded them of potence.

Sine was an exacting skeleton of a man, his features as sharp as his mind. He wore the traditional hooded pallium, a square-cut mantle that clad the Curials of a century past. He had a reputation as a difficult man, due in no small part to his irritating habit of telling the truth when it was least wanted. He was visibly pleased when Dahlia suggested they speak in private, and for almost an hour they strolled through the damp topiary menagerie which, strangely, seemed as well maintained as when Skye had personally directed his gardeners.

Having exhausted the pleasantries and sensing the time was right, Dahlia asked, "Curial, did Skye ever speak to you about a man named Jet, or Cuckold?"

Sine rubbed his hands together for warmth. "What makes you think that he did?"

"He was your friend," Dahlia said with a shrug, "and you oversaw the administration of Sanos."

"You have been studying. Skye said you would."

"It is a matter of vital import to me."

Sine stared at Dahlia for a moment, shifting his bony jaw from side to side. "Aye, I know. Handel has the answers you are looking for."

"Handel?"

"He waits in the library."

Dahlia stopped and stared at Sine. "Skye never allowed Handel in his library."

"Nonetheless, he awaits you there," Sine insisted.

Dahlia headed up to the house. The light rain gave the stone walls a silvery sheen. Inside, the warmth had already drawn many of those who had come for the funeral. Upon reaching the library, she found the door locked.

She knocked, and the door opened.

Handel stood in the doorway, dressed in his formal uniform. He was smiling. It was an expression that seemed out of place on someone so disfigured. "I have no gift for your labor. I hope my presence will suffice."

Those were not Handel's words. Dahlia looked into his dark eyes. He had changed. "Skye?"

Handel nodded. "I am here."

"How?" Dahlia entered as if in a trance. "You died."

Handel shut the door and took a seat in Skye's favorite chair. Dahlia did sat as well, her gaze fixed.

"Yes, I did. I am only a memory now, kept alive by your love and Handel's. I tied a knot in the stream of time. It will come undone soon, and I will be gone again. But for now, I am as you remember me. Perhaps less handsome."

Dahlia laughed, though her eyes welled with tears. "No man should have such power."

"I am the last." Handel leaned back in his chair. "Among my fellow adepts, doubt is rife. They see the power of the dark mechanics and they are eaten from the inside. Just as the people look for their gods in the machine, anywhere but in themselves."

"And so you gave us the Aver?"

"Yes."

"And you called me because I had seen the reveille, all those years ago?"

Handel nodded. "Because you wanted to believe more than anyone. And because love blinds."

Dahlia rose. "It was not enough to use a blind boy for your game? You had to use me, too?"

"Had I not, you would have unmasked the false Aver. I know you, Dahlia. You and Auric are the only two unafraid of opposing me in the Council."

"Why couldn't you trust me?" Dahlia demanded.

"Because you did not trust yourself. I have followed your career. I have seen your reluctance to do what is necessary."

"Was it necessary to burn Tajo?"

"In siding with Auric, Ordinal Amber sealed the fate of his men."

"And to poison the inmates at Sanos? That was your work, was it not?"

"Better you should be indignant about the fate of Auric's men."

"Why so?"

"They have suffered the same fate."

"Poisoned by mushrooms?" Dahlia's mouth hung open, aghast.

Handel nodded. "My factors had to buy acres of birch trees to obtain an adequate supply. Who would've thought Auric's counterfeit notes would prove so useful?"

"The Aver is with them."

Handel paused for a moment. "The Aver is safe in the Redan Inviolate."

"No," Dahlia said. "He stripped Auric of command. He rides with the army. Perhaps he is dead already."

Handel took a moment to steady himself. "Elinvar will keep him safe," he insisted. "The boy is not without resources."

Dahlia backed away. The horror of what Skye had done filled her with revulsion. "Only now, in Handel's scarred body, do you have the face you deserve." She turned to go, though the cruelty of her words made her wonder if she was not the same as him.

"It is the face of fear, and it is not mine alone. Look at me, Dahlia, and tell me if you do not see yourself in my eyes."

Trembling, Dahlia faced Handel.

"Our war is not with the eclectics. It is with those in between. It is with Auric and his ilk, the apologists and the compromisers. You have heard about the waning power of the adepts. Where once we could manifest our will, we now find the skein of thought difficult to traverse.

The dark mechanics and the bright cannot coexist, it seems. Our limitless body of possibilities has been corseted by science. The artificers explain our mysteries and debase the language of possibilities with facts and figures.

"To protect that which is most essential–our ignorance–the Thalass and I, and others who must remain nameless, have embarked on a dangerous course. This war is our doing, though it is but a means to an end: the restoration of divine dominion. The gods we worship, the very fabric of our thought, must be clear and distinct to have any meaning. The grayness of the eclectics, neither man nor machine, makes all things equal, all things permissible, in pursuit of true synthesis. To permit everything in the name of understanding is to knock down the walls that give us shape and form. We cannot brook the devaluation of humanity or the revelation of our sacred mysteries. We are in the end formed as much by our ignorance as our knowledge.

"To restore the old dialectic, we have been both the sponsors and the saboteurs of Urizen's return. Our factors have fed the eclectics with false intelligence, and we have betrayed our own to gain a future advantage.

"Though many may die because of this duplicity, their lives will save us from the Truth. Were I to wake to a world of certainty, where all secrets were revealed, where fear fled before omniscience, I would surely wish for death. Without fear and suffering, love has no meaning, and what is life without love? I hope you find in my cruel attentions a kind concern for the world and for you."

When Handel finished, Dahlia turned away, pressing her head against the stone wall by the door. The sour taste of anguish rose in her throat. "You said once that fervor and fever are reflecting fires. I think they are one and the same, and we have both been burned by them."

Handel rose and moved toward her. He placed his hand on Dahlia's shoulder. "You have always doubted your zeal because it is ugly, because you feel for those who fall before the sword. Though your conscience has kept us apart, I would have it no other way. I have been cruel that you might be kind."

Slowly, Dahlia turned and looked upon Handel and his fire-blasted skin, and raised her hand to his face. It felt smooth beneath her fingers, beardless, like a youth, but textured by scars. His lips were chapped, warmed by breath. Heat. It was all that remained between them: the fires of anger and of love.

"What am I to do with you?"

"Say good-bye," Handel said. "My knot in time is slipping."

"So soon?"

Handel nodded. "It has been a struggle to maintain my presence. I am too tired to remain."

Dahlia kissed him gently. It was a strange feeling, this counterfeit love. "Where is Skye, I wonder? In your clever words, wicked deeds, or frail flesh?"

"Where but in the mind's eye?" Showing none of the creases seen in someone more fair of face, Handel smiled. "The true Aver died the day he fell. See that he is commended. One day, perhaps, he will come again."

For a moment, Handel's form seemed to blur. He swayed and collapsed into Dahlia's arms. Dahlia knelt and laid him down. She could still feel his breath. The vacant look that had long been in Handel's dark eyes had returned.

Finally, he fixed his gaze on Dahlia. "I know you," he said.

"Handel?"

"I think you know me too."

Dahlia held his hand. "Yes, I do."

33

Gold to Rust

And I will show you something different from either
Your shadow at morning striding behind you
Or your shadow at evening rising to meet you;
I will show you fear in a handful of dust.

—The Burial of the Dead

The rain began to thin with the coming of the sun. Lost, Calx stood staring down a row of tents that seemed to extend to the horizon. In the distance, he could hear the eclectics smashing their way through the encampment, searching for the Aver.

A shaft of orange fire leapt skyward. A fulmin lance, he thought. Perhaps some of the Screen still lived.

Soldiers lay scattered about before him, some caught between dying and dead but most already there. The soft ground sucked them down, as if eager to reclaim flesh and bone. He walked warily among prone soldiers and their graceless contortions. The tips of lances planted upright in the ground sparkled in the morning sun, and for a moment it seemed that the stars had forgotten to retire.

The voice of a youth woke Calx from his despair.

"Who goes there?"

Calx turned toward the sound and saw a boy standing a short distance away. He wore a dirty white robe about his slight frame, over a silken tunic and trousers. His tangled mass of hair was the color of fresh-cut pine.

Falling to his knees, Calx said haltingly, "You are the Aver."

"Am I still?" The boy stared blankly at the breaking clouds. "What has become of Din?"

"Who?"

"My taster."

"I do not know, Aver."

The boy sighed.

"Aver, it's not safe here. The eclectics are coming."

"I am ready to die," the Aver said.

Calx grabbed the boy by the hand.

"What . . . what are you doing?" the Aver stammered.

"Saving you. Now be silent."

***

By the time the eclectics reached the encampment, the storm was passing and morning's light limned the dying. Water pooled in hoofprints, looking bronzed in mud and sun. Rain-saturated canvas slapped about in a breeze that drove the clouds away.

Rose feared they would search for hours. It was not the effort that bothered her, but lingering among the dying. The ruin of the Caballine Azure was horrible to behold, though they had hunted her like an animal.

Within minutes, the eclectics stumbled across a group of adepts checking for signs of life among the fallen caballines. It was a brief encounter, for Agar had his fulmin lance at the ready. He roasted them alive.

The adepts fell back screaming.

Irae smiled as they burned in suits of fire.

Rose understood. His suffering in the foundry was still fresh in both their minds.

When it became clear the eclectics would not meet much organized resistance, Irae ordered his companions to fan out in pairs to speed their search.

Rose accompanied Irae, suspecting that he wanted some time alone with her.

"Do you sense the Aver's presence?" Irae asked.

Rose shook her head. She could tell her answer was not what Irae wanted to hear, but what could she do? The Tongue was still, and offered no guidance. It hung from her arm, more weight than weapon.

It was then that a splinter of light lodged in her eyes. It had come from the east, a reflection.

She scanned the horizon and saw two figures on a horse, one smaller. She knew at once that one was the Aver.

She waved frantically at Irae to get his attention. There, she pointed, there he is.

Irae grasped Rose's shoulder. "Urizen is with us."

***

Cardinal Auric stood amid a cluster of tents with two other caballines, Tombac and Spar. All three looked ill, but none had succumbed to the poison. Their swords shone with the blood of adepts dead at their feet.

Casting his muddy cloak aside, Auric reloaded his fusil and adjusted his ceramic armor. "Aver or no, we must retreat. Our numbers dwindle."

"The adepts control the pickets," Spar said, pointing to a distant grove of trees where cavals and horses were tethered. "It will have to be on foot. Perhaps if we can reach the gorge."

"There are horses about," Tombac countered. "We just need to look."

Auric held up his hand. "Do you hear that?"

Flexing his sword arm, Tombac nodded. "Not horses."

Spar laughed nervously.

Auric looked at his men and offered a grim smile. "Do honor to Bright Halo, caballines."

"Caballines," a voice cried out. "Can you hear me?"

Auric pointed at a tent to the north and whispered to his men, "Ordinal Sepia."

The voice continued, "If any of the éclat are among you, we offer quarter. Speak now or die."

Auric aimed his fusil in the direction of the voice and fired. A sharp cry came from the far side of the tent, followed by the sound of confused footsteps.

As he dropped another ball in his fusil, five adepts emerged from behind the tent and formed a line. Ordinal Sepia stood among them, clutching his blood-soaked shoulder.

While Auric scrambled to reload, Tombac and Spar charged.

The adepts were prepared.

Stones and buckets and the boots of dead men leapt from the ground and flew at the two caballines. Stinging pebbles swarmed them, drawing blood. They pressed onward, desperate to reach the adepts, but the torrent of flying debris brought them to their knees and filled their screaming mouths until they could no longer breathe.

Auric trained his fusil at Ordinal Sepia and pulled the trigger. But the hammer did not ignite the damp charge. Cursing, he hurled the weapon to the ground and reached for his sword.

Twenty paces away, the five adepts grinned.

Sepia said, "We bear a message from Cardinal Skye."

***

Glancing over his shoulder at the dwindling encampment, Calx saw two riders in pursuit. Somehow, the eclectics had seen him. The rest were probably not far behind.

He returned his fusil to its holster behind his saddle, moving slowly so as not to startle the Aver. He had only three loads, so he would have to aim carefully. If it came to swords, he knew he would lose. With the boy sitting behind him, mounted combat would be disastrous.

"Skye Redan lies to the east, if I am not mistaken," he said. "You should be safe there."

The boy grinned oddly. "As you see fit, caballine."

"To the east then. Hang on tightly, Your Grace. We have a hard ride ahead of us."

"I was meant to die here, you know," the Aver added.

"Surely, you have better dreams than that."

Calx urged his borrowed horse onward.

34

Ascension

Love calls to war:
Sighs his alarms,
Lips his swords are,
The field his arms.

—Bridal Song

In the morning, Dahlia had the true Aver's shrouded body ex-humed from the garden and carried down to the great broadsword below Skye Redan for commendation on a proper funeral pyre.

The sun and the clouds could not decide which reigned that day. Patches of light danced across the countryside, followed by swaths of shade. The air still had a bite, but it smelled of spring.

Just east of the village for which it was named, the broadsword of Downskye stood atop a slight hill, through fields ready for planting. Like the rest of the blade monuments, it was tall as a ship's mainmast, without stain or rust. The grass around it was well tended in a diameter equal to its height. To the northeast, among the trees, stood Skye Redan.

Dahlia dismissed Handel and his men, that she might have some time alone to commend the Aver.

***

Flux awoke to the sound of a fusil firing, and tree bark splintered overhead. The horse lurched forward, but stopped under rein. The scent of the forest reminded him of happier days with Cardinal Skye. Skye Redan had to be nearby.

Calx fumbled with his fusil. "Irae. And Rose. There, through the trees. Stay low."

"The eclectic will miss you," Flux said emphatically. "There is a flaw in the weapon's barrel." He could see Irae's weapon in his mind, and it became as he described it.

Irae fired again.

The lead ball struck the ground, much farther off the mark than the previous shot. His curses carried through the winter-thinned forest.

Calx took aim.

"Higher," Flux suggested. "Head rather than chest. There. You have it."

Calx fired. The projectile took Irae squarely in the forehead, knocking him from his horse.

"Not bad for a swordsman," Calx remarked. "He should have used a fulmin."

"They want me alive. You should reload quickly."

Calx tossed his fusil away. "No, I will not harm her."

"Who is that with them?" Flux said.

"Rose. An acquaintance of mine."

"No, there is another. One of great power."

Looking back over his shoulder, Calx said, "Your eyes deceive you." He spurred his horse onward, urging the tired beast through the low branches faster than was prudent. But for a few scrapes, they traveled swiftly.

Soon, the great broadsword of Downskye appeared through the trees. To Flux, it was a vertical white line. Behind it, he saw the dark silhouette of Skye Redan against the horizon. They emerged from a sparse grove of oaks and headed across fields ripe with the tang of freshly turned soil. As they neared the towering blade, Flux heard the voice of a woman. He knew the voice well.

"That would be the Limnal Dahlia," he said.

"So it is." Smiling, Calx slowed his horse. "We meet again, Limnal."

"Caballine. Who rides with you?" Dahlia called out as Calx approached.

"The Aver is with me." Calx dismounted in the shadow of the great blade. He continued, almost breathless, "I found him amid the dead. We come from the plains, where the army of Sarcos lies betrayed. Limnal, the adepts ... they poisoned them all. Tajo, too, was their doing."

Dahlia sighed. "I know, caballine, I know." She walked over to the Aver and reached up. "Take my hand."

"Thank you." Flux slid to the ground, nearly losing his balance. "This is strange chance indeed."

"The more so because I am here commending the Aver to Stardome." Dahlia gestured at the body lying in a shroud at the base of the great blade.

"I do not understand." Calx approached the dead boy.

Dahlia knelt in front of Flux. "Your father was called Cuckold, was he not?"

Flux nodded. "His given name was Jet. The true Aver is dead then?"

"Aye. He died shortly after his fall."

"That cannot be," Flux insisted. "Cardinal Skye said..."

"The Cardinal lied," Dahlia replied.

Calx stared at the corpse and turned back toward Flux. "Who are you, then?"

"I suppose I am an actor." Flux could think of no better answer.

"? I risk my life to save you, and–"

Flux held a finger to his lips. "Listen. They come."

Dahlia turned to see a rider galloping across the fields. "Friend or foe?" she asked.

"Ordina Rose of Fin Redan," Calx answered, drawing his sword, "a newly minted eclectic." Turning to Flux, he asked, "Have you any more mind tricks, Aver, or whoever you are?"

Flux shook his head. "Her will is strong, and I am spent from deforming the other one's fusil."

Rose closed fast, her sword arm held out as if she carried something noxious. She clutched the reins in her left hand.

"What do you know of the Aver's Tongue?" Calx asked as he moved to interpose himself between the boy and Rose.

Dahlia gasped. "How did it come to join with her?"

"Ordina Rose!" Calx bellowed as Rose came within earshot. "You are deceived. The Aver is dead already."

A stone's throw away, Rose reined her horse to a halt. She stared down at Calx, a look of confusion upon her face.

"He speaks truly, Ordina," Dahlia said. "This boy is an impostor. A figment of Cardinal Skye's imagination."

Stand aside, Rose said in her language of signs, but no one complied. She then waved Calx away with her changed arm, but he lifted his own sword against her and she backed off.

Flux closed his eyes and listened attentively. To end his glorious performance as a fraud, like his father, would be worse than death. Quite suddenly, he realized that the beggar Skye had spoken of had been his father. In a strange way, he had known it all along. He was Skye's apology to the past. He was not merely playing the Aver; he had to become the Aver.

"They lie," Flux said firmly, reassuring himself more than anyone. "They deny me to save my life, but I am the Aver."

Rose dismounted and advanced, her red hair billowing like flames.

"Are you trying to get yourself killed?" Calx said, advancing between Rose and Flux.

"The boy knows not what he says, Ordina," Dahlia said, though she sounded uncertain. She stepped toward Flux and turned his vacant face toward hers. "What are you doing?"

Flux smiled and whispered, "I am the Aver."

"Why are you doing this? She will kill you."

Calx lashed out with a warning strike at Rose, but his feint did not fool her. She lunged forward, slapping his fingers with the flat of her blade. His sword fell to the ground.

With the tip of Rose's sword swaying snakelike before him, Calx retreated. "If you kill me, know that I wish you well," he said.

Without warning, Flux pulled away from Dahlia and threw himself at Rose. He could see the Aver's Tongue clearly through the haze of his vision.

Rose reached out to catch him, and he fell upon her blade.

All about, the air crackled. Jagged bolts of lightning stabbed down from the clouds, blackening the monumental sword. Motes of brilliant light coalesced into floating images and resolved into scenes from the sacred kinos, some richly colored, others black and white.

Rose started shaking. Perspiration beaded on her skin, glistening. Then the liquid sheen turned silver, as if she were sweating mercury.

Calx and Dahlia backed away.

Urizen had come.

Torrents of energy surged through Flux. He howled in agony as liquid silver flowed up Rose's arm and into his chest. For a moment he shared the god's thoughts. He saw the world as it was in the Dim Age. He saw the moment the machines awakened.

Light coursed through his glass veins. His reach was vast. He was aware of everything, like a spider sensing every strand in its web.

Like the spider Skye killed to demonstrate the bright mechanics, Flux felt the approach of death.

His veins swelled. He was burning from the inside, afire with Urizen's frustration.

Engrams not found, he and the god thought as one.

Link failure.

Pictures of bridges formed in his head.

He heard Skye's words in the maelstrom of his mind: "Understanding is the bridge you build to a point of view."

Urizen did not understand. How could the humans worship the wrong one? The Aver's Tongue was a bridge to nowhere. There would be no entrance. There were only walls.

End transmission.

With the emanations of the departing god, the great broadsword hummed like a swarm of bees.

Then it was still again.

"I had a dream," Flux gasped, "that I saved you." His hands reached up and grasped the sword in his chest that was Rose's arm.

The blade melted into nothingness, and Flux fell to his knees holding Rose by the hand.

His eyes closed.

***

"The boy is dead," Calx said, cradling Flux in his arms.

Dahlia gazed skyward. "Urizen too, it seems."

"What became of the Aver? The other one?" Calx asked.

Dahlia stared at the base of the broadsword. The body of the other boy was gone. Calx lay Flux on the ground where the other body had been and bowed his head. The two women stood beside him.

"I don't know what became of the other," Dahlia said in a daze. "Perhaps the false Aver's belief in himself denied the other existence. A talented adept knows few limits."

Rose touched Flux's face with her restored hand. Tears filled her eyes.

Calx offered his hand. "When I served Ordinal Fin," he said, "I used to watch you. I would stand outside in winter and never felt cold when you were in my sight. I was that much in love with you. When I heard you had been seen on the road to Tajo, I jumped at the chance to pursue you. I never intended to turn you in."

Rose reached out to him, and they embraced.

Shortly before sunset, with the villagers of Downsyke and the staff of Skye Redan in attendance, Dahlia commended the Aver's body to the flames. If anyone noticed the Aver's resemblance to one of the late Cardinal's favorite apprentices, no one said anything.

***

Months later, Dahlia awoke with a start. She had been dreaming. In her dream, she walked along a white road that was the great broadsword of Downskye. The road reflected the fire of the sun. Cardinal Skye walked with her, and there was someone else, wrapt in shadow.

"Who is the third who walks always beside you?" Skye asked.

For the first time, she knew the answer.

"There is no one but you and I," she said, for she had looked into the shadows of her doubt and seen herself.

Skye embraced her, then turned to go.

Someone knocked at her door. It was Pavo's Day again, and visiting celebrants filled the Pelage Deep. Perhaps the eclectics had agreed to Azo's terms for peace. No longer of one mind following the departure of their god, they had to be eager to end the hostilities.

The knocking grew more insistent.

"Limnal?"

Dahlia rose, still weary, and donned her night robe.

"Aye?" Dahlia opened the door and tried her best to conceal her irritation.

"All about the Pelage, people are dreaming," said the ebullient Mere. "I myself had a dream last night, and I have heard some among the picayune dreamed too."

"I dreamt as well," Dahlia said.

"What will become of us if the gods speak to everyone? What use will a celebrant be?"

"We will manage somehow," Dahlia said. "Perhaps we will reinvent ourselves."

REFERENCES

Epigraphs in the chapters listed below were borrowed from the following public domain texts:

Like Tears in Rain, Gold to Rust
T.S. Eliot, *The Waste Land*

Interrogation, Steel Tongue
William Blake, *The Book of Urizen*

Enmity
William Shakespeare, *Richard III*

Prison and Palace and Reverberation
Paraphrasing of the Bible, John 1:14

Ascension
George Chapman, *Bridal Song*